NO
RESERVE

Also available by Felix Francis

Books by Dick Francis and Felix Francis

Books by Dick Francis

FELIX FRANCIS

NO RESERVE

A DICK FRANCIS NOVEL

CROOKED LANE

NEW YORK

Published in the United States by Crooked Lane Books, an imprint of The Quick Brown Fox & Company LLC.

Crooked Lane Books and its logo are trademarks of The Quick Brown Fox & Company LLC.

Library of Congress Catalog-in-Publication data available upon request.

ISBN (hardcover): 978-1-63910-674-5
ISBN (paperback): 978-1-63910-677-6
ISBN (ebook): 978-1-63910-675-2

Design: © Blacksheep Design

Printed in the United States.

www.crookedlanebooks.com

Crooked Lane Books
34 West 27th St., 10th Floor
New York, NY 10001

First Edition: September 2023
Trade Paperback Edition: April 2024

10 9 8 7 6 5 4 3 2 1

With my love and thanks, as always,
to Debbie

"The unnamed Newmarket based bloodstock sales company depicted in this novel is fictional, but it is inspired by Tattersalls Ltd, the real Newmarket based bloodstock sales company, and I hereby acknowledge, with thanks, the help and encouragement I have received from all the staff at Tattersalls Ltd."

FOREWORD

Horse racing and gambling are intertwined, always have been, always will be. Right from the earliest recorded races at Smithfield, London, in the twelfth century, wagers have been placed on which horse was the fastest.

Racing as we know it today wouldn't exist without gambling, but the biggest gambles in racing are not placed with a bookmaker or in the betting shops; they occur in the sale rings, where vast sums are staked on untested, unridden, and as-yet-unnamed yearling colts, in the hope they will turn out to be world beaters and future sires of champions.

Sometimes it happens and sometimes it doesn't.

The American colt Justify was sold at the 2016 Keeneland September yearling sale for US$500,000. He raced just six times, all of them as a three-year-old. In just one hundred and eleven days, between 18 February and 9 June 2018, he won all of those six races, including the Kentucky Derby, the Preakness and the Belmont Stakes to become only the thirteenth horse in history to win the coveted American Triple Crown. His prize money on the track was an impressive US$3.8 million. But that figure is dwarfed by his potential future earnings as a stallion. Over a fifteen-year stud career, he is expected to amass fees in excess of US$150 million—making him worth at least six times his own weight in pure gold.

However, back in 1983, in the same Keeneland sale ring, Snaafi Dancer, a son of the great Northern Dancer, was bought by Sheikh Mohammed bin Rashid Al Maktoum for $10.3 million, a world-record price for a yearling at the time (well in excess of thirty million dollars in today's money). The horse never made it to a racetrack, as it was "embarrassingly slow," so he was sent straight to stud, where he was found to have fertility problems. In all, he sired just four foals, none of which ever won a race.

Now, that's what I call gambling!

1

"THE BID IS two million six hundred thousand guineas. I'm looking now for two million seven."

My voice boomed around the sale ring and outside through the public address speakers via the microphone clipped to my suit lapel.

"Two million six hundred thousand guineas I have."

I scanned the rows and rows of expectant faces, searching for a tiny movement of a hand, a slight nod of a head or even a brief raising of an eyebrow—anything that might indicate another bid.

"Two million six hundred thousand in the stairwell at the back. Two million six. Now looking for two million seven." I said, scanning the faces again from my lofty position on the auctioneer's rostrum. "I'll take two million six-fifty, if it helps."

There was slight hush in the sale ring, reserved only for those special occasions when everyone realised that very serious money was about to be paid for a very young, untried horse that might, just might, turn out to be a world beater on the track and then go on to sire generations of future champions, in the manner of the great Epsom Derby winner Galileo.

Could this bay colt circling around the sale ring in front of me turn out to be "the special one"? Maybe even a modern-day Northern Dancer? Or perhaps his son, Sadler's Wells, the most successful sire in the history of British and Irish Thoroughbred breeding, who fathered no fewer than seventy-three Group 1 race winners on the flat, as well as the winners of seven Champion Hurdles, a Cheltenham Gold Cup, and two American Grand Nationals over the jumps.

A man in the second row of seats across the ring from me removed his baseball cap and wiped his forehead in the early October heat. Was that a bid? I wondered. I stared in his direction, but he didn't catch my eye. He replaced his cap.

"The bid is two million six hundred thousand guineas at the very back." To avoid any confusion, I pointed at the bidder, barely visible in the right-hand stairwell at the top of the building. "Any more? The hammer is up. Last chance."

I was about to bring my gavel down on the rostrum when a large man, standing near the main horse-entrance door to my left, lifted his right hand, placed his index finger on his temple, and then removed it, almost as if in a salute.

"Two million seven hundred thousand guineas," I said. "Two million seven. Two million seven."

I glanced up at the stairwell.

I could only see the previous bidder's head and face, the rest of him hiding below the level of the stairs. And he appeared irritated, pursing his lips and frowning.

He nodded at me, hardly moving his face while keeping his eyes firmly on mine. Just the slightest of movements for such a large sum of money.

"Two million eight," I called. "The bid is now two million eight hundred thousand."

I knew these two remaining bidders well, all others having dropped out when the price passed two million.

The one at the back was a local top racehorse trainer in his sixties, called Brian Kitman, and the other was a bloodstock agent, aged about fifty, whose full name was Elliot Mitchell, although he was uniformly known simply as Mitch.

I also reckoned I knew who they were each bidding on behalf of, as would everyone else, or at least those seriously involved in the horse-racing industry rather than those just present for the excitement of watching horseflesh sell for so much.

One of Brian Kitman's owners was a brash Yorkshire businessman who had made a vast fortune by owning car dealerships across the country, and I strongly suspected that it might be his money that was behind Kitman's bids.

Elliot Mitchell, meanwhile, had a large number of high-profile clients for whom he bought horses, but I believed the only one with this sort of financial firepower was an Irish syndicate of wealthy individuals he had set up to challenge the buying power of the many Arab sheiks who were investing heavily in British and Irish bloodstock.

"Two million eight hundred thousand guineas," I called again. "Looking for two million nine."

I shifted my attention back to Mitchell near the main horse-entrance door, in the area known colloquially as "the gate."

I leaned down on the rostrum, facing in his direction.

"Come on now," I said to him. "Make it up."

He lifted a mobile phone to his left ear—*to receive instructions,* I presumed.

He lowered the phone and used his right hand to show me three fingers.

"The bid is now three million guineas," I called into the hushed silence. "Three million in the gate."

I glanced down at the animal in question, being led slowly round the ring, seemingly unconcerned by the huge sum riding on his rump. He was the full brother of the current leading two-year-old that had won all six of his races so far.

Not that being a sibling of a superstar necessarily meant that he would be a superstar too, but in racehorses it made it slightly more likely. In 2014, Noble Mission won the Champion Stakes at Ascot, the most valuable horserace in Britain, two years after victory in the same event by his far-more-famous, older full brother, Frankel.

"Three million guineas, I have," I said. "Looking now for three million two."

I looked up, but Brian Kitman had disappeared. I glanced across to the other stairwell, searching for him, but there was no sign. He had just gone down and away, as he always did when the price became too high.

"Three million guineas," I said again. "Are you all done? I'm selling this time round. The bid is three million. Last chance. Fair warning."

I theatrically lifted my gavel and had one more scan of the faces in front of me. Kitman had not reappeared, and no one else was moving, not even a twitch in case it was misconstrued as a bid. Indeed, the only sound was the clip-clop of the horse's hooves as it continued to be led around the ring.

After the horse had passed me one more time, I brought my gavel down onto the rostrum with a sharp crack.

"Sold to Elliot Mitchell."

A smattering of applause broke out from a group of onlookers at the top of the tiered seating who knew no better than to make unnecessary noise that might frighten the horse. Three-million-guinea sales were not unheard of, but they were rare. It was certainly a first for me, and I felt like applauding too. My maximum before this had been a mere six hundred thousand.

There was a pat on my back.

"Well done, Theo."

I turned to find the chairman of the sales company standing behind me—Peter Radway—my boss. He had been due to relieve me prior to this lot but he had been late arriving, so I had simply carried on.

"Thank you, sir."

"Have a rest now," he said. "I'll take over."

I stepped back from the rostrum. I reached up and tried to unclip the lapel microphone to give to him, but my hands were shaking.

"Adrenalin," Peter said with a smile. "It's okay—I'll do it."

He unclipped the microphone with ease and transferred it to his own jacket.

"Right then," Peter said confidently, standing tall at the rostrum. "Don't go away, anybody. Next up we have lot number one hundred sixty-seven, a fine filly by Star of Wessex out of a Galileo mare. Plenty of quality in the pedigree with this one, and a half-sister to a two-time winner as a two-year-old. Who will give me three hundred thousand for her?" He paused fractionally. "Two then? One?" He glanced down to his left. "Fifty?" He pointed at no one specific. "Thank you, sir. The bid is fifty thousand. Sixty. Seventy. Eighty at the back. Giving him a gap then, aren't you? A hundred thousand. Well done. One ten now. One twenty."

Locating those actually bidding was an art, and Peter was one of the best, assisted by several spotters placed at strategic points around the edges of the sale ring.

"The bid is one hundred and twenty thousand guineas. She's a steal at that price. One thirty, thank you. One forty now. One fifty. One sixty."

One of the spotters shouted and raised one hand while pointing with the other at a new bidder sitting in the seats to the right of the rostrum.

"One seventy." Peter turned. "One eighty now, in the gate."

He switched his attention back to the new bidder.

"Make it up."

He waited and the man fractionally raised his catalogue.

"Two hundred thousand," Peter said. "Thank you. Selling now."

"Selling now" was code that the bid price had reached the reserve set by the vendor, and all future bids would result in a sale.

"Two ten in the gate."

I decided to leave Peter to it. All day, I'd been drinking lots of water to keep my voice in good shape, and now I urgently needed a pee.

I made my way out of the back of the auctioneer's box, situated behind the rostrum, and then outside into the last of the afternoon sunshine.

"So what is a goddam guinea anyway?"

A large American lady in a smart designer pink coat and high-heeled black leather boots was asking a man wearing a blue puffer jacket and a baseball cap, who was standing with her.

"It's twenty-one shillings," the man answered.

The woman rolled her eyes. "And what, for Christ's sake, is a shilling?"

I inwardly smiled and paused a moment to listen. This could be fun.

"A shilling used to be what is now five pence," said the man. "There were twenty shillings to a pound—that was before our currency went decimal in the 1970s."

The woman stared at him. "You Brits are totally crazy. So a guinea is a pound plus five of your pennies?"

She made it sound as ridiculous as it was.

"That's right."

"Why don't you simply use just pounds, or even dollars like the rest of the world?"

"It's historical," said the man. "Horses have always been sold here at Newmarket Sales in guineas. It used to be that the vendor received all the pounds, and the auction company simply kept the extra shillings as their commission. But VAT has changed all that."

"What's VAT?"

"Value Added Tax. It's a bit like American sales tax, but it applies to goods and services, so it's charged on both the sale price and on the commission."

The woman rolled her eyes once more. "And what the hell is *value added* about commission? It's more like *value subtracted*."

I had to agree that she had a good point.

The two of them drifted away and out of my earshot.

What the man hadn't told her was that a guinea was called a guinea because the first British "guinea" coins had been made of gold mined in the Guinea region of West Africa. Their value had originally fluctuated with the price of gold until it was fixed by the British government at twenty-one shillings in 1717. The original gold coins have long since disappeared as legal tender, not least because their gold content would make them worth hundreds of times more than their face value, but the guinea as a monetary unit is still used, not only for buying horses but also for some medical and legal fees.

I rushed into the main office building and ran up the stairs to the small gents' restroom on the second-floor landing. By now, I was almost bursting.

The two urinals were occupied by others, so I dived into one of the two empty cubicles, struggling to unzip my fly before I wet myself.

As I thankfully relieved myself, I heard the two men who'd been at the urinals talking about the unusually warm weather.

"No doubt due to this wretched global warming," one of them said.

"I suppose it's better than an ice age," said the other with a laugh.

They were still chatting as they left, the sound of their voices disappearing as the outside door closed behind them.

I finished and did up my trousers. I was about to flush when I heard the door open again.

"Bloody hell, Mitch," said a voice, almost in a whisper. "I thought for a moment you were going to leave me in there at two million six."

"Shh! Someone will hear you," said a second voice that I took to be that of Elliot Mitchell—Mitch.

I felt rather than saw the cubicle door behind me open slightly and then swing shut again, me not having locked it in my haste.

"There's no one in here."

I wondered if I should cough or flush the toilet or do something to let them know of my presence, but instead I stood stock still, silently listening.

"But I told you beforehand that I'd go to three," Mitchell said with a laugh.

"I know you did, but you took your bloody time about it. And that young auctioneer nearly dropped his hammer early. I could see it in his eyes as he stared up at me."

So the other man was Brian Kitman, and he was right. I had almost dropped the hammer at two six, when he had been the high bidder.

"Beyond your limit, was it?" Mitchell said with amusement.

"A long way beyond. I was really sweating."

Mitchell laughed again. "We had somehow got out of step, so I had to jump by two hundred grand to get it to three million."

"I know," Kitman said. "And damn glad I was of it too. Nice touch, though, using your phone like that. I could just see you from the stairwell."

"To tell you the truth," Mitchell said, "I was worried the bloody thing would ring while I had it up to my ear. I'd forgotten to put it on silent." He laughed loudly once again.

I remained standing absolutely still, scarcely believing what I was hearing.

Agents or other persons conspiring together to bid up a horse to a predetermined maximum was a clear breach of rule seven of the Bloodstock Industry Code of Practice and could be considered as a criminal fraud against the person who had to pay the bill.

What should I do?

I went on being silent, hardly daring to breathe.

"Have you fixed the insurance?" Kitman asked.

"I certainly have," Mitchell replied. "I always do it as soon as the hammer falls on anything I buy, just in case something happens to the horse before I get the money back from my principal. I just send my broker a text with the lot number and the price. He does the rest."

"So you're sure it's covered for death from natural causes?"

"Positive. I checked. It's covered for every eventuality for the next thirty days."

I could hear as they washed their hands and then the loud noise of the hand dryer running. Finally, I heard the outside door open and then close.

I remained exactly where I was for quite some time, desperately trying to listen for any sound. Had they both gone? Or just one?

I heard the outer door open again, and someone came in, humming a tune.

Was it Mitchell or Kitman coming back?

I thought it unlikely, but I couldn't stay in here for the rest of the day. I was due back in the sale ring shortly.

I took a deep breath, flushed the toilet, and then stepped out of the cubicle.

The newcomer was Nigel Stanhope, another member of the team of auctioneers. In his mid-forties, Nigel was a work colleague rather than a friend. In fact, I didn't believe Nigel had any friends, certainly none at work.

"Oh, hello, Theo," he said, glancing at me over his shoulder as he stood at the urinal. "What are you doing hiding in a gents' cubicle?"

"I wasn't hiding—just going to the toilet like anyone else."

"Could have fooled me," he said. "I hear you just got bloody lucky."

"In what way?" I asked.

"That three million lot. Fell into your lap, I hear, and only because Peter was late arriving." He said it without amusement. He was clearly envious. But little did he really know how much that lot had actually fallen into my lap.

I wondered if I should I tell him about Kitman and Mitchell fixing the price.

I washed my hands and dried them in the hot air stream while I thought about it.

Both of them would be certain to deny saying any such things, and it would be just my word against theirs. And I hadn't even seen their faces, to be certain it was them.

I decided not to tell Nigel.

In truth, I'd be hard pressed to tell Nigel anything, even the time of day. Perhaps I'd have a quiet word with the chairman later, to ask for his advice.

"Are you on again today?" I asked, trying to waste a little time so that Nigel and I would leave the gents' together, just in case Kitman or Mitchell were waiting outside.

"No. I'm done. How about you?"

"I'm doing a stint as a spotter in ten minutes. I'm covering for Alex Cooper. He's had to go to the dentist," I replied.

"Nothing trivial, I hope."

I smiled wryly.

There was a considerable degree of ill-disguised animosity between Nigel Stanhope and Alex Cooper. Indeed, there was a degree of animosity between Nigel Stanhope and almost everyone else, but he seemed to have it in for Alex in particular.

I reckoned that Nigel was jealous of Alex simply because he came from a rich family—at least much richer than his—but then again, Alex was equally jealous of Nigel for being an auctioneer on sale days while he, Alex, only acted as a spotter. But Alex was still only twenty-four. *Give him time,* I thought.

"One of his fillings has come out."

"So it won't be fatal, then?"

"No."

"That's a pity."

"Come on Nigel, be reasonable. Alex is a nice boy."

"Well, you would say that, wouldn't you, as you live with him."

"I rent a room in his flat."

"That's not what I've heard. Share a bed do you?"

"No, we don't. Who told you that?"

"It's common knowledge amongst the staff."

"Well, it's not true."

I realised that Nigel was provoking me on purpose, as he regularly tried to do at some stage to all his work colleagues, and I was beginning to wish that I'd left the gents' straight away and taken my chances outside with Kitman and Mitchell.

"Sleeping with another man is nothing to be ashamed of," Nigel said, washing his hands, both physically and metaphorically. "Not these days."

"I wouldn't be ashamed of it," I said. "It's just not the case."

"If you say so." He said it in a manner that indicated he didn't believe me.

"I do bloody say so."

Nigel guffawed loudly, as if he knew better.

I'd had enough of his nonsense, so I turned on my heel and went for the door.

If Kitman and Mitchell had been waiting for me outside, I'd have probably walked straight into them, but the landing was empty, so I went down the stairs, two at a time, and out into the fresh air.

How could I have allowed Nigel Stanhope to annoy me so easily? No doubt, he would be laughing now, chalking up another little victory over one of those he sadly saw as his adversaries rather than his colleagues.

I wondered why Peter Radway didn't get rid of him, but I knew the answer—Nigel Stanhope was a very good auctioneer, able to squeeze more out of the bidders than anyone else, often even more than the chairman himself. And higher prices paid at auction for the horses meant more commission coming the way of the sales company. All those extra shillings from the guineas, with or without the VAT.

I walked down to the lower paddock, trying to compose myself before going back into the sale ring.

Did Nigel really think that I was gay, or was he just making mischief?

Perhaps I should have been more open in my overtures to the opposite sex, but I'd always been somewhat reticent when it came to girls, something I put down to having been educated at an all-boys private boarding school, followed by a male-dominated college at Oxford.

Strange, really, I thought, because I'd always been somewhat forthright in every other aspect of my life, often getting myself into trouble at school for answering back to the masters.

But with girls, it had mostly been a closed book.

Not that I hadn't had the occasional sexual experience while at university, and afterwards in Australia, but they had been clumsy, awkward, embarrassing encounters rather than truly loving relationships.

When I had arrived here to work, I had again been somewhat reserved in that department, not wanting to acquire a dubious reputation for chasing girls in the office, especially Janis Thompson in Accounts, who I fancied rotten and even dreamt about.

So far, I had been too self-conscious to ask her out on a date, but I resolved to make some headway by asking her to join me for a drink one evening after work.

2

I FINALLY CALMED DOWN from my abrasive encounter with Nigel
Stanhope. In hindsight, I realised I should have just laughed
at him rather than getting angry, which was the response he had
clearly been seeking.

I did my stint covering for Alex as a spotter in the sale ring,
standing behind the auctioneer in the box.

My job was to scan the rows of faces, making sure that no
bids were missed, and to assist in identifying the winning bidder.
However, on this occasion, as a result of my encounter with Nigel
in the gents', my mind was wandering so much that I would have
probably missed someone waving a bloody great red flag, let alone
a slight raising of a finger or a sales catalogue.

Fortunately, it didn't seem to matter, as there were no shouts
of complaint from any missed bidder, and the final ten lots of the
first day sold without incident, two of them to Elliot Mitchell.

I decided I should go and speak to Peter Radway about the
conversation I had overheard, but he was in a meeting with some
of his fellow directors. His secretary told me that, as soon as the
meeting was over, he would be rushing off to host a private drinks
reception at the National Horseracing Museum in the town, before
having an early night.

I wondered if I should tell anyone else, but decided it could wait until the following morning. And the more I thought about it, the more improbable the whole thing sounded.

Why would anyone bid up a horse to a predetermined higher amount when they could have bought it for less? It didn't make any sense.

Who would benefit?

The vendor would obviously gain, as they would receive more for their horse than would otherwise be the case—and it was specifically not against the code of conduct for the vendor, or a representative of the vendor, to bid on their own horse to try and raise the price, but they ran the risk of being left as the high bidder at the end of the auction, and so not having sold the horse at all, while still needing to pay the auctioneer's commission.

Had either Kitman or Mitchell been bidding on the vendor's behalf? It certainly hadn't sounded like it. And even if they had, it was still against the rules to have a high-bid limit agreed beforehand by separate bidders.

The auction company, of course, would benefit from a higher hammer price, securing more from their five per cent commission. And, if a bloodstock agent was used to make the purchase, as was almost exclusively the case and was certainly true in this instance, then the agent's five per cent commission on top would be greater too, charged to the unfortunate purchaser who had also paid over the odds for a horse without even realising it. It was surely a criminal fraud.

Five per cent of three million was one hundred and fifty thousand.

Not a bad little earner for Elliot Mitchell, but the horse, as a full brother to the current champion two-year-old, had been previously forecast to make a million at least, maybe a million and a half, and possibly even close to two, so forcing an extra million onto the hammer price meant the agent's commission had increased by only about fifty thousand.

At first sight, that might seem like a large amount of money, but Elliot Mitchell was one of the most widely used and successful bloodstock agents around, buying large numbers of horses in France and Ireland, as well as in the UK, for tens of millions of pounds each year, so why would he put his whole future earnings at risk for an illicit gain of just fifty thousand guineas?

But there again, he hadn't been expecting to be overheard admitting it, and an extra fifty grand in commission was nothing to be sniffed at.

I thought back over the day.

The first day of the Newmarket October yearling sales was always an exciting time. Here the cream of the yearling crop were paraded and sold for eye-watering sums of money. Some would turn out to be champions, and others would be a major disappointment, but which was which?

No one would really find out until they started racing the following summer as two-year-olds, and their real worth wouldn't show for another year after that when some would run in, and maybe win, the great Classic races such as the Epsom Derby, the Oaks and the St Leger, writing their names forever into the history of Thoroughbred horse racing.

In all, over the next two weeks, more than fifteen hundred yearlings would go under the hammer, for a combined sum approaching two hundred million guineas, in what were known as the Book 1, Book 2, Book 3 and Book 4 sales. It was in the first three days—at the Book 1 sale—that the very best of the best would appear, those sired by former Classic winners or champions of the past.

All the lots will have been here at the sales complex for at least the last four days, housed in one of the more than eight hundred separate stables on the site, available for inspection by prospective buyers and bloodstock agents, and particularly by their vets.

It is where the term *vetting* originates from, to mean the checking of a candidate's suitability for a job, or for a specific security clearance.

During vetting, a horse's conformation is studied and measured. It is made to walk, to ensure it isn't pigeon-toed or splayfooted and that its rear legs follow the fore in a perfect line. And a series of thirty-two X-rays of its leg joints, submitted digitally to the company repository facility, are closely examined for abnormalities such as errant cartilage growths or bone chips due to osteochondritis dissecans, or OCD, a development disease of all young, fast-growing animals, which can affect between five and twenty-five per cent of Thoroughbred foals, to a lesser or greater extent.

For bones to enlarge as a horse grows rapidly in its first year of life, cartilage must first be laid down at the growth plates at the ends of the bones. This cartilage matrix is then used as a scaffold for bone production—a process known as ossification—with the cartilage effectively turning into new bone.

OCD lesions can arise due to an imbalance, when fast cartilage growth outpaces ossification. With the ossification unable to keep up, deeper layers of the cartilage can die, and its attachments then break down, forming cartilage flaps and bone chips in the joints. The degree of severity of the abnormalities can have major significance on the ability of the horse to race in the future.

Small lesions in the fetlock are commonly seen. These can usually be easily managed, and they do not stop a runner from winning. But larger damage, especially in the femoral joints may lead to chronic joint inflammation and lameness. For these, even with surgery on the damaged tissue, the prognosis for withstanding training and racing can be poor.

All the yearlings up for auction in the Book 1 sale would be most unlikely to have anything more than minor problems, but it is only those whose conformation and X-rays are perfect in every way that make the big money, provided, of course, that they also have the right parents, grandparents, and great-grandparents.

* * *

This was my third year as an auctioneer at the Newmarket October yearling sales, and so far, with the exception of having to work alongside Nigel Stanhope, I was greatly enjoying myself. But did I want this to be my career for the rest of my life?

I would be thirty-four on Christmas Eve and felt that I was still young enough to do something else if I wanted.

Aged twenty-two, after graduating from Oxford with a master's degree in engineering science, I had decided to see more of the world. So I had crammed all my meagre belongings into a rucksack and had set off with an ambitious plan to circumnavigate the globe in the six months before I was due to join a civil engineering firm in Derby that specialised in building bridges, specifically railway bridges for the new high-speed train lines.

In early July, I had flown from London to New Delhi and spent three weeks trekking in the Himalayas, including a six-night stay in a remote monastery built into the side of a mountain in the Ladakh region of northern India. There, I had risen at four each morning to share fruit, nuts and seeds with the monks before spending the rest of the day meditating, fasting, and studying the teachings of Buddha.

Perhaps I should have remembered those teachings earlier today.

Buddhism states that anger is one of the three great poisons— the others being greed and ignorance—and that anger is a hindrance to realisation, a necessary step towards achieving the final goal of true enlightenment. It also states that anger is not something that infects you from the outside—it is not people and things that make you angry—but something that comes from within.

Buddha had obviously never met Nigel Stanhope.

After India, I had travelled down through Myanmar, Thailand, and Malaysia to Singapore, from where I had caught a flight to Cairns in Australia, and it was here that my plans came unstuck.

Like many backpackers, I was greatly attracted to the laid-back surfing lifestyle on the Australian east coast beaches. So, instead of the planned journey across the Pacific to South America and beyond, I worked my way slowly south from Cairns via the Whitsunday Islands and the Sunshine Coast, past Brisbane and the Gold Coast, finally ending up in Byron Bay in northern New South Wales.

However, by then, my hard-saved cash was running out fast, and I desperately needed a job to earn enough to eat and also to buy a ticket home.

I offered to scrub floors or wash dishes in the local restaurants, but so many others had made the same offer ahead of me, and there was no work of any kind to be found locally.

Then one of my temporary roommates at the backpackers' hostel in Byron, an Australian called Brett, said he would call his father, who ran a business in Sydney.

"Doing what?" I had asked.

"Selling horses."

Brett said he was sure to offer me a job.

So I had used my last hundred Australian dollars to buy a ticket for the overnight bus journey from Byron Bay to Sydney, and it had changed my life.

Having been taken on only as a handyman to steam-clean the stables, I was quickly promoted to utilise my engineering design expertise in the refurbishment of the sale ring, which included the building of a new roof.

When my six months' travel time were up in December, the thought of leaving the warmth of an Australian summer to return to a cold, dark English winter, and then to end up knee-deep in mud on a railway bridge construction site somewhere in the Midlands, filled me with horror. So I wrote to the civil engineering firm in Derby, explaining that I was sorry, but I wouldn't, after all, be taking up their kind offer of employment, and stayed put in Sydney, sponsored by Brett's father's company to obtain a work visa from the Australian Government.

At their next yearling sale, held in February in the southern hemisphere, the upgraded sale ring was hailed as a major triumph, and I was invited to help with the running of the rest of the business.

A year later I sold my first horse from the auctioneer's rostrum.

Five years after that, my mother called to say that my dad had been diagnosed with an inoperable brain tumour, so, as their only offspring, I reluctantly packed everything back into my rucksack and headed home.

Brett's father had been very sorry to see me go and had offered to give me a glowing reference as an auctioneer if I ever needed it, something I had relied on a year later, after my father's protracted decline and eventual death, to land this job in Newmarket.

But was it what I wanted going forward?

I felt a little guilty that all those years spent studying structures, mechanics, material dynamics, energy systems, and computational design, with the associated project work and endless engineering process evaluation, were all going to waste, to say nothing of the university fees that my parents had scrimped and saved to help provide.

But life is surely about enjoying one's job, and I was certainly doing that—at least I had been until Nigel Stanhope had thrown his spanner into the works.

*   *   *

At the end of the day, I went out of the sales complex through the pedestrian gate next to the sales cafeteria building, and walked back to Alex Cooper's flat.

Alex and I had joined the company at almost the same time, me as an auctioneer and he as an executive assistant and trainee, fresh out of Aston University.

We had met up on my very first day, and it had been a fortuitous meeting.

I had planned to stay in a local Airbnb for a few nights, while I found somewhere to rent, but Alex said he had a spare room, so why didn't I stay with him instead? We had both intended the arrangement to be temporary—only until I found my own place—but reasonably priced flats in Newmarket had proved far more difficult to find than I'd been expecting. Hence, Alex and I had made the temporary arrangement permanent, with a proper tenancy agreement and me paying him rent for my room to help with his mortgage payments.

He was already home from the dentist when I arrived back at twenty past seven, and he was lying on the sofa feeling very sorry for himself.

"My whole face is numb," he said indistinctly. "Bloody dentist drilled on both sides."

It was quite difficult for me to understand Alex at the best of times, him having a very strong West Midlands accent, but with a face full of novocaine, his words were almost impossible to discern.

"Do you want anything to eat?" I asked him.

"No," he mumbled.

"You must have something."

"Not until this bloody stuff wears off." He indicated towards his mouth.

"Bad, was it?"

"Awful. It wasn't just the one filling. He drilled out two others and replaced them."

I tried not to laugh, or even to smile. Why was it, I thought, that other people's medical misfortunes could be so funny? Just as long as they weren't terminal.

"I could make you a nice soft omelette if you like. We've got plenty of eggs."

"What are you having?" he asked.

"Probably that. There's some cheese and ham in the fridge. I'll put those in it."

"Okay," he said. "That would be nice."

It struck me that anyone witnessing this domestic interchange may have believed that we were, indeed, a loving couple.

"I had a confrontation with Nigel Stanhope today," I said.

"Hard luck. What did he want?"

"Just to annoy me. At least, I think so. He told me it was common knowledge amongst the staff that we shared a bed."

Alex stared up at me from the sofa and smiled.

"Well," he said. "I'm game if you are."

CHAPTER

3

I HAD A VERY restless night, tossing and turning for hours, unable to sleep.

And not because I had taken Alex up on his offer—I hadn't— but simply because he had made it in the first place.

Had I been sending out the wrong vibes?

And had Alex been creating a certain aura that I had failed to detect when everyone else around me had, including Nigel Stanhope?

I lay awake, as the window turned from dark to light with the coming of the dawn, thinking back to the previous evening.

Initially, I had laughed at his response, thinking he was joking, but it had quickly become apparent that he was being deadly serious.

What had once been a happy mutual business relationship between landlord and tenant had suddenly become something different altogether. Would there be any going back to the former arrangement, I wondered, or was it time for me to find alternative accommodation?

The thought of that distressed me.

This flat was within easy walking distance of my work, and of the shops and restaurants of Newmarket High Street, and just renting a bedroom was cheaper than a whole flat.

Alex and I had seemed to get along well, too well perhaps, and I hadn't felt that the situation had cramped my style with potential girlfriends, not ever having had the opportunity while I'd been living here of bringing a girl home to my bed anyway.

I decided to get up just after six, to go and have my breakfast in the sales cafeteria rather than sit through another awkward meal with Alex, as had happened last night.

The morning was bright and cold after another cloudless night, with a high-pressure system centred over Scandinavia firmly in charge of the British weather. Highly pressurised was also how I felt at the moment, with my mind racing with what to do about my living circumstances, as well as the question of the overheard conversation.

Even at this early hour, the cafeteria was busy.

As in all things equine, a day at the sales started well before dawn, with multiple horseboxes arriving to bring the yearlings to be auctioned the following week while collecting those lots sold late yesterday. Generally, horses had to be removed from their stables within two hours of the hammer falling, except that those sold in the last few hours of the day could remain overnight as long as they were off the premises by nine o'clock the following morning.

I took a plastic tray from the pile and moved along the buffet, collecting scrambled eggs and bacon, plus a large mug of strong black coffee, deciding that I needed something to keep me awake after such a disturbed night.

"Morning, Mr Jennings," said the cashier at the till. "You're up early."

"Couldn't sleep, Doris," I replied, flashing my company ID card at her so she could charge the bill to my account.

I looked around for an empty table, but they were all occupied, so I carried my tray over to one on the far side, next to the window, where there was a free seat.

"Do you mind if we share?" I asked the man already sitting at the table.

"Go ahead," he replied.

I sat down and started eating.

"Have you heard the big news of the day?" the man asked.

"What big news?" I replied.

"One of the yearlings has been found dead in its box."

"One that was sold or unsold?" I asked, loading my fork again with scrambled egg.

"Sold," the man said. "It's that colt that made three million yesterday."

The fork had been on its way to my mouth, but it never made it, stopping short while I stared at the man.

"Are you sure?"

"Quite sure. I was there when they found it not half an hour ago. Dead as a doornail, it was. Heart attack, I reckon, by the look of it."

I stood up. "I've got to go."

I left my half-eaten breakfast on the table, grabbed my coffee, and made my way towards the door. All I could hear in my head was the last part of the exchange I'd overheard between Kitman and Mitchell yesterday in the gents'.

"Have you fixed the insurance?" Kitman had asked.

"I certainly have," Mitchell had replied. *"I always do it as soon as the hammer falls on anything I buy, just in case something happens to the horse before I get the money back from my principal. I just send my broker a text with the lot number and the price. He does the rest."*

"So you're sure it's covered for death by natural causes?"

"Positive. I checked. It's covered for every eventuality for the next thirty days."

And now the horse was dead.

* * *

I went over to the sales offices and found Peter Radway, the company chairman, already in his office, and he was wearing his overcoat.

"Excuse me, Mr Radway," I said, standing in the open doorway. "I urgently need to talk to you."

"Sorry, Theo, I'm too busy to talk right now. I've been called in early by security. It seems there's a crisis in one of the lower stable blocks, and I have to get down there immediately."

He came over towards the door, but I stood my ground and refused to budge.

"It's because of that crisis that I need to talk to you," I said.

He stopped and looked straight at me.

"This had better be good," he said.

"I think you should arrange for a full post-mortem to be carried out immediately, before the body is taken off site and disposed of."

He stared at me. "Why?"

Was I overstepping my authority as the most junior of the auctioneers? "I just do," I said. "I'll tell you why later, when you've got more time."

I stepped to one side to allow him to pass, but he didn't move.

"I think you had better tell me right now."

I took a deep breath and jumped in.

"I have good reason to believe that the hammer price on that colt was artificially inflated by collusive bidding up. I also happen to know that the horse was insured as soon as the hammer fell. And now it's dead. I just feel that it might be prudent for us to make sure that the death was due to natural causes, and not intentional."

"That's quite an accusation you're making, Theo. Do you have any evidence?"

"Only a conversation I overheard yesterday afternoon. I did try to come and speak to you about it last night, but you were not available."

"And who was this conversation between?"

"Brian Kitman and Elliot Mitchell. They were the only two left bidding on the colt after it had passed two million. Mitchell finally secured it at three."

The chairman nodded and audibly drew breath in through his teeth. "Where did this conversation take place?"

"In the gents' along the corridor here. Not long after the sale. I was in one of the cubicles when they came in together, talking."

"Are they aware that you overheard them?"

"No, I don't think so."

He thought for a moment.

"Right," he said finally. "I'll go and get things sorted with the horse. You wait here for me to get back, and then we'll make a plan of what we should do about it."

"Can't I come with you?"

"No. I think you should remain here. Sit down at my desk and write down exactly what you heard before you forget it."

"I won't forget it," I said confidently. "And I'd much rather see the horse for myself. We need to have the post-mortem carried out here while we as a company still retain some measure of control. Once the horse is removed, even to the local equine hospital, we'll have no authority any longer to demand it."

He shrugged his shoulders. "Okay," he said. "You're right, and I suppose you can come with me if you really want to."

I did really want to.

I also wanted to check if Elliot Mitchell was hovering about, concealed somewhere close by, or maybe Brian Kitman would be hiding in the shadows, as he had been during the auction the previous afternoon.

*   *   *

There was absolutely no doubt that the yearling was dead, and it had been so for some time.

A small crowd of ghoulish onlookers stood in the stable doorway, and Peter Radway had to ask them to move aside so he could enter. I followed him in.

A galloping Thoroughbred racehorse is such a stylish animal, graceful and elegant, its four fine legs working in unison, like rapidly pulsating pistons, to allow it to cover the ground swiftly in a seemingly effortless fashion, whilst its proud noble head remains steady, focussed only on the way forward.

So the sight of such a highly tuned racing machine lying there, inert, flat out on the straw; its mouth open and its tongue hanging out, its normally large bright eyes now dull, sunken, and unseeing was unsettling, to put it mildly.

It was almost enough to make me cry.

And if I'd believed that Elliot Mitchell might have been hiding somewhere out of sight, I was much mistaken. He was right at the centre of proceedings, stood on the far side of the dead horse, and he wasn't happy.

"How the hell could this have happened?" he demanded loudly of no one in particular.

"How could what have happened, exactly?" I asked.

"That the bloody horse is dead," Mitchell almost shouted back at me. "I paid three million guineas for this yesterday." He indicated towards the carcass at his feet. "And now it's fucking worthless." He threw his hands up towards the roof in despair.

Not totally worthless, I thought.

"Wasn't the horse insured?" I asked.

Mitchell looked across at me with disdain.

"What are you implying?"

"Nothing," I lied. "I just wondered if it was insured."

"It was insured against being stolen or being injured," Mitchell said. "I'm not sure if was covered for keeling over from a heart attack."

That was not what he'd told Brian Kitman in the gents' yesterday. He'd clearly stated that it was covered for every eventuality, including natural causes.

"So you think the horse had a heart attack?" Peter Radway asked him.

"That's what it looks like to me."

"Well," Peter said, "the post-mortem examination will tell us for sure."

"Post-mortem?"

Was it just my suspicious mind, or did Elliot Mitchell sound slightly worried by the mention of a post-mortem examination?

"Yes. I called the local equine hospital on my way down here. They are sending a vet over straight away to carry it out here."

"Is that really necessary?" Mitchell asked. "I am the owner of the horse. Surely it is for me to decide if there is to be a post-mortem."

"I'm sorry, Mr Mitchell," Peter responded with authority. "The death occurred on my premises, and hence a post-mortem is absolutely necessary. As a sales company, we must be satisfied that there is nothing that we have done, or have failed to do, that contributed in any way to the death of such a valuable horse whilst stabled on our site. We will cover the cost."

Mitchell just stared at him. There was no arguing with that.

At that point the vet from the equine hospital arrived, carrying a large black case.

"Oh dear. Oh dear. Oh dear," he muttered quietly while pacing round and round the corpse. "Oh dear. Oh dear."

"I'm Peter Radway," the chairman said. "Chairman of the sales company. It was me who called you."

"Yes, indeed," said the vet. He stopped his pacing and faced Peter. "Hello. I'm Andrew Ingleby. I'm the equine necropsy specialist."

"Necropsy?" Peter asked, shaking the offered hand.

"Study of the dead," the vet said, clearly having had to answer the same question many times before. "From ancient Greek—*nekros*, meaning 'dead body,' and *opsis*, meaning 'sight.'"

He laid his case down on the floor, opened it, and began to unpack his equipment, laying it out on the ground. There were several different-sized knives, a sharpening steel, a large hacksaw, and what looked to me like a pair of tree loppers with eighteen-inch handles. He saw me staring at them.

"For cutting through the ribs," he said matter-of-factly while pulling on a pair of plastic gloves, an apron, and some protective goggles. Next, he took a rectal thermometer from his case and inserted it into the horse's rear end.

"Did anyone see this animal fall?" he asked, looking around at Peter, Mitchell, and me, and also those still standing in the doorway. No one answered.

The vet lifted the horse's left foreleg and tried to bend it before tapping on the animal's abdomen with his knuckles. Then he removed the thermometer and looked at it. "This horse has been dead for some time, maybe six hours or more. It's impossible to be exact about when it died, or even close, especially after such a cold night. Is there a heater in this stable?"

He looked up and around.

"No," Peter said. "None of our boxes have heaters."

"But he was wearing a rug," Elliot Mitchell said, pointing at a pile of blue material now crumpled up in the far corner. "I pulled it off when I came in and found him."

"And what time was that?" asked the vet.

"Six o'clock. He was due to be moved to my holding yard in the town."

The vet inspected the horse's mouth. "Was he fed last night?"

"He had a bowl of feed around seven and also some hay."

The vet nodded. "I now need to do an internal examination of the organs." He lifted his largest knife and sharpened it expertly on the steel. "It's better for you if I'm left alone for that. It can get quite messy. It should take me about an hour, maybe ninety minutes."

"Right," Peter said, moving gratefully towards the door. "I'll get security to ensure you're not disturbed."

"Thank you. And it might be best to move the other horses in this stable block to somewhere else. There will be bacterial gases already forming in the abdomen, and they might be distressed by the smell."

Peter wrinkled his nose. "I'll sort it. And please come to my office when you've finished."

We moved outside and shut the stable door.

The crowd of onlookers had grown considerably, and I could see some of them were journalists, their notebooks and pens at the ready.

This was going to be a big story.

"I had better go and inform the insurers," said Elliot Mitchell, "before they hear about it on the news."

Yes, I thought, *you had,* and I reckoned they weren't going to be very happy about it.

4

"So what exactly did you hear them say?"

The chairman and I were back in his office, having moved the other horses and sorted out security for the vet.

I'd always had a good memory for what people said, and I recounted the whole overheard conversation, word for word, from start to finish.

"And you are sure it was Kitman and Mitchell?"

"I didn't actually see their faces, but who else could it have been?"

"And there were no other witnesses?"

"I don't think so. But Nigel Stanhope came into the gents' just after they left. He may have seen them leaving together."

The chairman went out, and I could hear him calling for Nigel, but without success. He came back in.

"Nigel isn't in yet. I think I'll wait to speak to him and also to get the vet's report on the horse before we do anything. I would not be at all happy making such an accusation against two of our most respected clients without there being something else to back up what you are saying."

"Don't you believe me?" I asked him.

"It's not that I don't believe you, Theo. It's only that, as things stand, it would just be your single voice against the two of theirs, and they would be sure to deny any such conversation ever took place. Or they would say you misheard or misunderstood what they were saying, and that they have done nothing wrong."

I could see the logic in what he was telling me, but it didn't change the fact that I had indeed heard what I'd heard, and Mitchell and Kitman were both guilty of collusive bidding up, if nothing else.

"So what do we do?" I asked.

"We simply carry on as normal. But if the post-mortem shows that the horse was deliberately killed, then we will go straight to the police."

"And if it doesn't?"

"Let's wait and see."

"What about CCTV?" I asked.

"What about it?"

"Is the door of that box covered by a camera? If so, it would have shown if anyone went in there after the horse was fed last night."

"I'll check with security. In the meantime, I suggest you do as I said before. Go and write down all you can remember of the conversation, in case we need it later."

I went out of the chairman's office and walked down the corridor to my own, a much smaller affair, which I shared with Nigel Stanhope.

Auctioneering was only one part of my job.

In all, there were about thirty-five days a year of actual sales in the Newmarket sale ring. For the rest of the time, as part of the Bloodstock Sales Team, I would visit and liaise with stud farms, breeders, bloodstock agents, and racehorse trainers, to help put together the lists of horses that would be coming up for sale by our company in the future.

The current October yearling sale was the undoubted highlight of the sales year in Newmarket, but there were also other yearling sales in September and November, as well as separate foals' and mares' sales in December, and various horses-in-training sales at other times. In all, some six thousand lots would go under the hammer here in an average year.

In total, about twelve thousand Thoroughbred foals are born each year in Britain and Ireland, and a substantial proportion of them would be offered for sale in our ring as foals or yearlings, with others appearing later as mares or horses already in training. Indeed, it was common for the same horse to pass through our sale ring several times during its lifetime. And we weren't the only sales company vying for the business.

It was my job, along with colleagues in the bloodstock team, to try and ensure that the cream of the crop was sold here, to help maintain the reputation of Newmarket as the preeminent bloodstock sale in Europe.

I sat down at my desk, opened my laptop computer, and began to type a verbatim record of what I'd overheard the previous afternoon.

I'd almost finished when Nigel Stanhope arrived.

"The chairman's looking for you," I said, without warmth.

"Why?"

"He wants to speak to you about our meeting in the gents' last night."

"Been telling tales about me, have you?"

"No, I have not. It's about the dead horse."

"What dead horse?"

"That yearling I sold for three million yesterday afternoon was found dead in its box this morning."

"Bloody hell. That's expensive dog meat. But what's it got to do with me and my trip to the gents'?"

I decided that it was for the chairman to tell him, if he wanted to, not me.

"I've no idea."

At that point the chairman put his head through the doorway.

"Ah, Nigel," he said, "you're here. Do you have a moment? I understand from Theo that you met in the gents' along the corridor yesterday afternoon. Is that right?"

"Yes," Nigel replied warily. "What about it?"

"Did you see anyone else? In particular, did you see anyone leaving the gents' just before you went in?"

Nigel shook his head. "I wasn't really looking. Why?"

"Nigel, please think," the chairman insisted. "It's very important that you remember back. Was there anyone coming out of the gents' just before you went in? Or maybe there was someone in the corridor or on the stairs who might have just left?"

Nigel shook his head again. "I'm sorry but I don't remember anyone. What's this all about anyway? Has Theo been making up stories again?"

The chairman looked at him. "What do you mean by *again*?"

"Theo is always making things up. He's tried to tell us that he'd lived as a monk in a Buddhist monastery. Complete load of old hogwash, if you ask me. And yesterday he even denied that he's sleeping with Alex Cooper, when we all know it's true."

The chairman turned to me with concern. "Is it true, Theo?"

"As it happens, it is not true," I replied, "but I'm not sure that who I am sleeping with is any of your business. Nigel is the one that makes things up, not me. And I never said I'd lived as a Buddhist monk. All I said was that I once stayed for a week in a Buddhist monastery in northern India, which I did."

But I could see, from the chairman's facial expression, that doubt was beginning to crystalize in his mind.

"Thank you, Nigel," he said. "Theo, please come with me."

I followed him along the corridor to his office, with a feeling of dread in my stomach. We went in and he closed the door.

"Now listen, Theo," he said, turning to me sternly, "I'll give you a last chance. If you tell me now that you have made up the story of the overheard conversation, then nothing more will be said."

I looked the chairman straight in the eye. "I did not make it up," I said earnestly. "Every word I told you earlier was totally true. I swear it. Nigel is just up to his usual mean tricks. You know what he's like."

I felt like a naughty schoolboy in the headmaster's study, try-ing to convince him that I wasn't guilty of what I'd been accused.

At that point there was a loud knock on the door.

"Come in," Peter Radway called, sounding clearly irritated by the interruption.

Andrew Ingleby, the vet, opened the door and stuck his head in. "Now a good time?" he asked.

"Yes, fine, Andrew, of course. Come on in. Thank you, Theo, that will be all."

Taking my job, if not my life, into my hands, I stood my ground.

"I would much prefer to stay and hear what Andrew has to say."

"Not much actually," the vet responded before the chairman had a chance to throw me out. "The cause of death is still inconclu-sive. I've taken some samples for further testing, but I couldn't find anything initially that clearly indicates a specific cause of death."

"So it wasn't a heart attack then?" I said.

"Unlikely. Horses don't have heart attacks in the same way as humans do, especially not young horses like this. For you and me, what we call a heart attack is actually a myocardial infarction, when a coronary artery becomes blocked, usually due to build-up of fat or cholesterol that results in a blood clot, which then causes the blockage. That in turn starves the heart muscle itself of blood and oxygen.

"That doesn't happen in horses because there's no fat or cho-lesterol in their diet, so sudden cardiac death is more often associ-ated with a rupture of the aortic arch or an electrical malfunction causing arrhythmia or an arterial fibrillation. Each of those can result in the heart just stopping.

"On examining the heart, I found no evidence of an aortic rupture—or of anything else, for that matter. But arrhythmia wouldn't leave any physical signs on the heart anyway; it would just suddenly stop pumping, causing sudden collapse and death."

"What causes arrhythmia?" I asked.

"All sorts of things can cause it. In particular, a sudden rush of adrenalin into the bloodstream can be responsible."

"Maybe caused by an injection?" I asked. "Such as with an EpiPen?"

My roommate during my first year at Oxford had carried an EpiPen with him everywhere because he was strongly allergic to peanuts. He had even taught me how to use it to inject him in the event he was unable to do it for himself. But in his case, a shot of adrenalin could be a life-saver rather than a life-taker.

"Most unlikely," the vet replied. "EpiPens are designed for humans, and a horse is many times the mass of a human. You would have to use multiple pens to have the same effect. Also, an injection of adrenalin causes the hairs around the injection site to stand up on end, and I found no such indications on the horse, even though, I suppose, those might have disappeared in the hours since death. The adrenalin is far more likely to have been caused by strenuous exercise. Was the horse wind tested after sale?"

"Almost certainly," said the chairman. "They all are."

Wind testing was when a horse was lunged round and round in a tight circle at speed while a vet listened for spurious respiratory tract noise, indicating a turbulent airflow through the larynx and pharynx, something that might compromise future racing prospects. An auctioned horse has to pass the wind test otherwise the sale is declared void, and the animal is returned to the vendor.

"At what time was the test?"

"The horse was sold about half past five," I said. "I was the auctioneer, and it was the last lot I sold. The wind test would have been done pretty soon after that, almost certainly by six, six thirty at the latest."

"And then it was fed at seven. High adrenalin in the system and then food on top. It's a potentially dangerous combination."

He pursed his lips and shook his head, perhaps at the folly of feeding a horse so soon after exercise.

"But couldn't the colt have been suffocated?" I asked, trying my best to throw some suspicion back into the discussion. "I heard once of a horse that died because someone put Ping-Pong balls in its nostrils."

"I suppose it's technically possible," Andrew said. "Unlike humans and most other animals, horses can't breathe through their mouths because their nasal passages are not connected to their oral cavity. On the plus side, it means that horses can never choke to death on their food."

He thought silently for a moment.

"However, I think asphyxia is unlikely. A horse that was suffocating to death would probably lash out with its legs, most likely injuring itself, and there were no signs of that having happened. But the samples I have taken will tell us for sure. Asphyxia most often produces bursts of the tiny capillaries in the whites of the eyes, resulting in little red dots called petechiae. It can also cause small ruptures of the alveoli, the little air sacs in the lungs. I've collected samples from the eyes and also from the lungs. There don't appear to be any petechiae or ruptures present, but I'll need to examine them under a microscope to be certain."

"So you're saying that nothing has actually showed up in the post-mortem," the chairman said. "And everything else is just mere speculation."

The vet nodded. "That is correct."

"In fact, we are none the wiser as to why the horse died."

"Indeed, we are not," said the vet. "As I said, I've found nothing so far to indicate that the horse didn't die from natural causes, but a closer examination of my samples, including a toxicology report on them, will show us if death was due to asphyxia or to any drug involvement, even an excess of adrenalin, natural or otherwise."

"And how long will that take?"

"My preliminary report will be available in a day or two, but full results can take several weeks."

"Several weeks?" The chairman clearly wasn't happy. "Why so long?"

"Because there is much to be done. I have taken a large number of other samples in addition to those from the eyes and the lungs—tissue from the brain, heart, stomach, liver, and so on, as well as blood from several different places around the body. If the preliminary results show that drugs are present in any of them, then more sophisticated tests are needed to determine the concentration and whether the cause is natural or induced. I assure you, the lab will work as fast as they can, but it takes time to get it right."

"And what do we do in the meantime?" the chairman asked.

"In what way?"

"Do we need to keep the body?"

"Oh no." The vet laughed. "No need for that. I have all the samples I require. If they don't show anything positive, then the death will be recorded as by natural causes, or possibly as unexplained, and that will be the end of it. There are no formal inquests for dead horses." He laughed again. "And there's no inheritance to sort out, unlike with us humans."

"So what do we do with it?"

"What do you usually do with dead horses?"

"We don't *usually* have dead horses," the chairman said indignantly. "This is the first I have known since I arrived here ten years ago."

"Really?" said the vet. "In my job I see little else."

How depressing, I thought.

"So are there any special procedures to follow to get rid of a dead horse?" asked the chairman.

"Most people just call the local hunt," said the vet. "They'll send a man with a truck. The carcass then gets fed to the hounds."

As Nigel had said, the horse was now just extremely expensive dog meat.

"Hadn't we better consult Elliot Mitchell before we organise anything?" I said. "After all, he is technically still the owner of the animal, alive or dead, or maybe his insurance company is now, and we should ask them."

"If it's all right with you, I'll leave all those details for you to sort out," said Andrew Ingleby, stepping towards the door. "The sooner I get the samples back to the lab, the sooner we'll have the results."

"Yes, of course," said the chairman. "Thank you for coming out so quickly."

Andrew left the office and closed the door, leaving the chairman and me alone.

"So now what?" I asked.

"I'd better have a chat with Elliot Mitchell about what he wants done with the remains."

"I meant about the conversation I heard?"

"There is nothing we *can* do. Even if it happened, neither you nor I can prove it."

"It did happen," I said.

"I only have your word for that."

"Isn't that enough?"

"Sorry, Theo, but no, it's not enough. It's not enough for me, and it certainly wouldn't be enough for the Bloodstock Industry Ethics Committee, which is the body that enforces the code of conduct. It will be for the best if we just continue on as normal, as if that conversation never took place, even if it did. Be satisfied that you have done the right thing in reporting what you believe you heard to me, and I have investigated it."

"But you haven't investigated it," I replied, trying hard not raise my voice. "You haven't spoken to Mitchell or Kitman to ask them what they were talking about. And surely, you should at least report something to the Ethics Committee."

"I certainly can't do that," he said. "Mitchell and Kitman would both claim that I was making an unsubstantiated accusation against them, which was damaging to both their reputations and livelihoods. They would almost certainly seek financial redress against me through the courts."

"You cannot sue someone for telling the truth," I said pointedly.

"But is it actually the truth? Did you really hear what you thought you heard? Could you have been mistaken? Or could you have misunderstood what they were talking about? I am sure that is what they will claim."

I could see that I was getting nowhere fast.

"So you are saying that we do nothing at all," I said in resignation. "And what about if Mitchell and Kitman do it again later today—or maybe tomorrow or on some other day?"

"We would still need more proof. Simply your word against theirs is not enough."

It was enough for me, I thought.

And I'd be watching them.

CHAPTER

5

THE SECOND DAY of the Book 1 yearling sale started at eleven o'clock sharp, but I wasn't due to be acting as the auctioneer until after twelve thirty, so I spent the morning trying unsuccessfully to work off my frustrations.

It was bad enough having heard someone admit so blatantly that they had broken the rules, but then not being believed by my boss about it was somehow worse. It was as if he was questioning my integrity more than those who had actually done wrong.

I went back to my office, but Nigel was in there at his desk, gloating, and I couldn't stand the hostile atmosphere, so I went for a walk outside, down towards the lower yard where the dead horse still lay on the straw.

The earlier crowd of ghoulish onlookers had long since dissipated as there had been nothing more for them to see, the stable door having been firmly bolted against their inquisitive gazes. Even now, it was still solidly shut, and it was also closely guarded by a man from the sales security team.

I flashed my company ID card at him, opened the door, and went in.

There was a slight unpleasant smell remaining in the stable, but it was not as bad as I had expected. The vet had tried his best to make things look normal again after his butchery, shoving everything gory back inside and roughly stitching his large incisions together with twine. That is if the sight of a prostrate, dead Thoroughbred racehorse could ever be described as normal.

If Andrew Ingleby had found nothing to suggest that the horse had died of anything but natural causes, there was no chance that I would, but still I felt that I had to look.

I searched around the edges of the box and in the straw, but of course there were no incriminating syringes or empty bottle of poisons to be found, nor any stash of discarded and discharged EpiPens. There was also no feed remaining in the manger, indicating that at least the horse had enjoyed its last supper before keeling over.

I unfolded the rug that Elliot Mitchell had removed, which was still piled up in the corner farthest from the door, but there was nothing suspicious to be found amongst the folds of blue fabric either—just "Property of Six Barn Farm" stitched in small haphazard red letters along the edge in one corner.

I stared down one last time at the horse.

"What *did* happen to you?" I asked it.

Unsurprisingly, it didn't answer, and I felt a little foolish.

At that point the stable door opened very slightly.

"There's a man out here," said the security guard through the gap. "Says he's come to collect the dead horse."

"Okay," I replied. "Let him in."

The door opened wide, showing me a man in denim jeans, red-checked shirt, quilted grey gilet and tweed cap.

"Hello, I'm Kevin," said the man jovially. He looked down at the dead horse. "I assume that this is the carcass for collection?"

"Where are you from?" I asked.

"Fallen Stock Collection Service at Mildenhall Foxhound Kennels," he replied. Then he guffawed loudly. "Not that we hound foxes anymore, of course. Not since the bloody law changed. The name has just stuck because that is what the dogs are—foxhounds—it's the name of their breed."

I nodded. *It must be confusing,* I thought—especially for the dogs, not being able to do what they'd been bred for. I wondered what we would call racehorses if the law banned racing. Just *horses,* I suppose. I laughed inwardly at my little joke. Laughing out loud didn't seem appropriate in this place right now, even though that clearly hadn't bothered Kevin.

"Who called you?" I asked.

"Someone called Mitch," he said. "He gave me this box number. He asked me to take the horse away and get rid of it. Are you Mitch?"

"No," I said, "but this is the right place."

"Yes. I'll get on then."

Kevin disappeared and presently came back driving a small flatbed lorry, which he reversed towards the door. He left the engine running but stepped down from the cab and went to the control unit behind. As he pushed the yellow-topped levers, the bed of the truck slid backwards, and then down at an angle, until the rear end of it was touching the ground just outside the stable door, forming a ramp.

Kevin then walked up the ramp and came back down, pulling a cable out from a winch. He went into the stable and secured the cable round the body behind the front legs.

He looked across at me as I just stood there watching him.

"Can you just check for me that the head or the front legs don't snag on the doorway?"

I nodded, not really relishing the thought of being involved in this exercise in any way.

Kevin went back to the control unit, and after the winch had taken up the slack in the cable, the poor dead animal began to slide across the floor.

Thankfully, neither the head nor front legs snagged on the doorway, and slowly, inexorably, the horse's corpse was dragged completely out of the stable and up onto the ramp, just as if it had been a broken-down car being collected from the side of the road.

But for this particular means of conveyance, there would be no repair and redemption in a local garage.

I briefly checked the straw underneath where the horse had been lying, but as before, there was nothing untoward to be found there.

Meanwhile, Kevin walked up onto the ramp and covered the horse with a large blue tarpaulin, tucking it under the legs before strapping everything in position with several wide webbing belts so that, in the end, all anyone could see was a blue-covered mound that could have been anything.

"Stops people gawking," Kevin said, laughing again.

"So what do you do with it now?" I asked.

"The useful meat gets fed to the hounds. The rest, like its hide, hooves, head, bones, lungs, guts, and stuff, will all be incinerated."

I rather wished I hadn't asked.

Kevin pushed his yellow control levers once again, and the ramp was drawn up and returned to its former position as a flatbed on the truck, now with its sorry load fastened on top.

"Right, then," he said. "I'll be off. There are hungry hounds to be fed."

He was whistling happily as he climbed back up into his cab. Then he drove away, leaving me standing there feeling somewhat forlorn.

My first, and quite possibly only ever, three-million-guinea sale would never provide me with any pride in its running and winning. And its offspring would never pass through the sale ring as yearlings, with me being able to say to people: "I once sold that one's sire for three million."

Instead, any useful meat from it would be quickly consumed by Kevin's hungry hounds at Mildenhall, and the remainder burnt as mere rubbish. No record of it would remain in the stud book, nor anywhere else, and it had lived its short life and died without even having been given a name.

Not that I would ever forget it.

*   *   *

I arrived at the auctioneers' box in the sale ring in good time to start my twelve thirty shift at the rostrum.

In all, there were five of us in the auctioneer team for this particular Book 1 sale, rotating in approximately thirty-minute shifts, from the start of proceedings in the ring at eleven o'clock sharp, to the finish around seven in the evening, at a rate of approximately twenty-one or twenty-two lots per hour, one hundred and eighty lots per day, for each of the three days of the sale.

As was the case in this sale, I was taking over from Nigel Stanhope, who purposefully dropped the clip-on microphone as he went to give it to me. As I leaned down to the floor to pick it up, he pushed his groin into my face.

"While you're down there," he said, laughing crudely.

"You're disgusting," I said, picking up the microphone.

"You're the disgusting one, Theo."

With difficulty, I ignored him and stepped up to the rostrum, clipping the microphone to my own tie.

"Next up, ladies and gentlemen," I said, "we have lot one hundred and ninety-nine. A fine bay colt by the highly successful Australian stallion, Opera House Star, out of a Camelot mare. Half-brother to three winners at two years old, and with plenty of black type in his extended pedigree."

Black bold type was used in the printed catalogue to indicate a first-three finish in a Group or Listed race on the flat or a Graded race over the jumps, those races of the highest quality.

I watched as the colt was walked round and round the ring, right in front of me. "Isn't he a fine-looking fellow? Come on then, who'll open it up? Someone offer me two hundred thousand guineas for him."

No one moved. I hadn't expected anything else. It was a little game we all played with each new lot in the ring. "One hundred thousand then?" Still nothing. "Fifty? Forty? Thirty thousand—thank you, sir," I said, pointing towards the gate, even though no one there had actually raised a hand, but I wasn't prepared to go any lower. The little game was over, and the bidding had to now start in earnest. Everyone knew that this colt was worth at least a hundred grand, perhaps nearer a hundred and fifty.

I checked the computer tablet in front of me. The vendor had set a reserve of a hundred and forty thousand. Rather too high, I thought, for this particular colt, but unless someone bid that amount or greater, the colt would remain unsold, and he would be returned to the vendor, who then might try and do a private sale on the side, away from the ring.

"Thirty thousand guineas, I'm bid," I said. "Thirty thousand."

One of the spotters on the far side shouted and raised his right arm high while pointing with his left. A genuine bid at last.

"Forty thousand now."

I scanned the faces in front of me, but there was no movement.

"Forty thousand," I repeated. "Come on now, we all know he's worth much more than this."

As often happens, the serious bidders were holding back initially, hoping to see how many others were in the market and who they were.

"Forty thousand."

A short man in a cap, standing against the rail on the far left, was looking worried. I recognised him as the owner of the local stud farm where the colt had been bred. He eagerly waved his catalogue at me.

"Fifty thousand," I called.

Some others now dived in at this point, and the bid price rose rapidly through a hundred thousand and onwards.

"One hundred and twenty, I have," I said. "Looking now for a hundred and thirty."

Elliot Mitchell was standing in the gate, and he raised a finger, touching his temple briefly with it before pulling it away.

"One hundred and thirty now bid."

I glanced up at the stairwell at the far back right, and there was Brian Kitman, standing in his usual place, such that I could just see his head above the tiered seating.

Another of the spotters across the ring suddenly shouted and pointed at a new bidder.

"One hundred and forty," I called. The reserve had been met. "Selling now."

Mitchell raised his finger to his temple again.

"One fifty."

I looked across at the other bidder, but he shook his head. He'd clearly been hoping that a single bid might secure the colt, or maybe he'd also been bidding on behalf of the vendor to ensure it made its reserve.

But now Kitman, high above, waved his catalogue at me.

"One hundred and sixty."

The spotter standing behind me touched me on the shoulder and pointed at Mitchell, who again had his finger to his temple.

"One seventy."

I looked up at Kitman, and he nodded back at me.

"One hundred and eighty," I said. "Now looking for two hundred thousand."

Mitchell saluted at me once more.

"Thank you. The bid is now two hundred thousand guineas."

I looked up at Kitman and he again nodded.

"Two hundred and twenty thousand. At the back." I pointed up at Kitman on the stairwell.

Again the spotter behind me tapped me on the shoulder.

"Mitch is bidding again," he whispered in my ear.

Mitchell and Kitman were the only two bidders left in this auction, everyone else having dropped out at a hundred and forty thousand.

Were they at it again?

By all measures, this colt was now selling for far more than it had been expected to fetch. Had Kitman and Mitchell decided that this auction should go on up to half a million, or even more? And would the horse then be dead in the morning?

"Two hundred and twenty thousand I have," I said, ignoring the spotter. "The bid is at the back. Are you all finished?"

The spotter behind me spoke again urgently into my ear, much louder this time. "I told you that Mitch has bid again."

Again I ignored him.

"The bid is two hundred and twenty thousand guineas at the back. Are you all finished?" I raised my gavel theatrically.

At this point, Mitchell gave up just using his usual one-finger-salute bidding mechanism. Instead, he bellowed loudly across the ring. "I bid two hundred and forty thousand guineas."

That was difficult to ignore, but I still didn't turn to him. I went on watching Kitman, but I now had no option but to take this new bid.

"Two hundred and forty thousand guineas." I repeated what Mitchell had shouted at me and gently lowered my gavel. "The bid is now in the gate."

There was obvious clear relief in Kitman's body language, even though I could hardly see anything of his body other than his head, and that only fleetingly, as he turned and went rapidly down the stairs, out of my sight, and right out of the sale ring.

Only now did I switch my attention to Mitchell.

"Two hundred and forty thousand guineas is the bid," I called, staring hard at him. "Any more from anyone else? I'll sell this time round."

Mitchell glanced up, from me towards where Kitman had been standing.

I wondered if he had been expecting another bid from him, maybe many more bids, to drive the sale price even higher. But Kitman had long gone.

"Fair warning," I called loudly. "The hammer is up."

There was no sudden new bid, so I rapped my gavel down sharply on the rostrum.

"Sold to Elliot Mitchell for two hundred and forty thousand guineas."

He didn't look particularly pleased with his purchase. Perhaps the sale price had been too low for him, but he could hardly bid against himself to raise it further.

His five per cent commission on two hundred and forty thousand guineas was over twelve and a half grand in pounds.

Not a bad return for three minutes' work.

But Mitchell had clearly wanted more, much more.

6

"WHAT THE BLOODY hell do you think you were doing?"

I was back in the chairman's office, standing across the desk from where Peter Radway was sitting in his high-backed black leather executive chair, and this time, I really was in trouble.

"Mitchell and Kitman were trying it on again," I replied. "So I initially ignored Mitchell's bid. The auctioneer reserves the right, without giving any reason, to ignore any or all bids. It says so in our terms of business, which are reproduced in all our sales catalogues."

"But that is only if we consider that a bid is frivolous or from someone who we haven't agreed terms of credit with."

"I believe that Mitchell and Kitman *were* making frivolous bids, or at the very least they were colluding to bid the price up, something that is strictly against the industry code of conduct."

"But you alone cannot make that decision. And you have no proof of collusion. I thought we had been through all of that this morning."

"I was trying to get proof. Kitman was really sweating when it looked like I was going to leave him in as the high bidder. His relief when I finally allowed Mitchell's bid was unmistakeable. And he clearly gave up at that point and left before Mitchell was ready. I could see Mitchell looking up to where Kitman had been. He had been expecting another bid from him, maybe many more bids, and that's collusion."

"But you didn't get any proof that we could present to the Ethics Committee, and now I've had an official complaint from Elliot Mitchell about your handling of the auction of that lot. You must remember, Theo, he is one of our most important clients. We cannot afford for him to stop buying horses from us and go elsewhere."

"He already goes elsewhere," I said. "I've seen him at other companies' sales, both here in the UK and in Ireland, and also in France at Deauville. He buys from all over, even at Keeneland in Kentucky. He's not being loyal to us, so we should have no loyalty towards him. He's not the one doing us a favour by buying horses here. Rather, we are the ones doing him the favour by putting the very best horses available up for him to buy."

"We still can't afford to lose his business. Nor that of Brian Kitman either."

I felt like saying we would be better off without them both, but I'd probably said too much already. Maybe it was time for me to be contrite before I talked myself out of my job.

"I'm sorry," I said. "It won't happen again."

But I was too late.

"Damn right it won't happen again," Peter said, looking up at me. "I'm removing you from the auctioneer roster for the rest of this sale. I will make a decision about your future here next week." He then looked down at some papers on his desk. "That will be all."

I didn't move. Instead, I stared down at him until he looked up at me again.

"So I'm in danger of losing my job just for trying to protect the good name of this company?"

"Our good name? You, young man, have just brought this company into disrepute by refusing a perfectly valid bid from a well-respected bloodstock agent in an auction that was streamed live on the internet worldwide, so don't lecture me about protecting our good name."

If I'm already up to my neck in hot water, I thought, *I might as well go in the whole way.*

"Mitchell may be well-respected by some, but I believe that he is breaking the rules, and we, as a company, are being complicit in doing nothing about it."

"But as I keep telling you, we have no proof that he breaks the rules."

"Maybe not, but at least you should question him about it, even if it's to stop him doing it again."

I was getting quite emotional. I couldn't help it.

"Theodore Jennings," the chairman said sharply, "calm yourself down. The rest of the team will cover your shifts. Come and see me again at eight thirty tomorrow morning, when you've had time to reflect on your actions and your words. Now, go home."

He pointed towards the door of his office, and short of annoying him even more, I had to go.

It all sounded rather terminal to me as far as my employment was concerned.

Only yesterday I had been wondering if this job was what I wanted to do for the rest of my working life, and now it looked as if that decision wouldn't be mine to make. And all because I'd overheard a conversation in the gents'. I now wished I had made my presence known to Mitchell and Kitman as soon as they had walked in. But I hadn't, and it was too late to change things now.

And I was also angry. Angry that it was me who was the one in trouble, when I'd done nothing wrong.

It also irked me beyond measure that Elliot Mitchell had had the audacity to make an official complaint against me, when I was quite certain it was he who was manipulating the system for his own ends, even if I didn't yet have the evidence I needed to put before the Bloodstock Industry Ethics Committee.

I went out of the chairman's office and walked along the corridor to mine, staring at the floor in despondency.

So what did I do now?

"Go home," the chairman had said, but going back to Alex's flat didn't seem very attractive at the moment, not after my troubled night.

"Hello, Theo," said a voice, bringing me back from my trance. I looked up at the person walking toward me.

"Oh, hello, Janis."

Janis Thompson from the Accounts Department. Her of my dreams.

"Are you all right?" she asked with a concerned look on her face.

"Yes, fine, thank you," I said. "I'm just thinking."

She smiled. "Well done yesterday. Three million guineas! We've all been talking about it in Accounts."

"But didn't you hear? That was the colt that died in the night."

"Oh no! How awful." She looked genuinely upset. "I'd heard that a horse had died, but I didn't realise it was that one. I'm so sorry."

"Yeah," I said with resignation. "So am I."

"I'd better go and tell the other girls."

She started to go.

"Janis," I said. She turned back to face me. "Perhaps we could . . . No, it doesn't matter."

"What doesn't matter?"

"I just wondered if . . . No, never mind."

"You just wondered what?" Janis said, standing her ground.

I took a deep breath.

"I just wondered if you would like to come out for a drink with me sometime."

She smiled at me again, broader this time. "When had you in mind?"

Perhaps I wouldn't have a job here tomorrow.

"How about tonight?" I said quickly, before I lost my nerve. "After work?"

I thought she was about to say no, she couldn't, as she was already seeing her boyfriend or watching television, or some other made-up excuse, but she didn't.

She smiled at me again, and this time it reached all the way up to her eyes, which caused my heart to go flip-flop. "Tonight would be lovely. I usually finish at five, but I'm here until six today. Where shall we meet?"

"Do you have a favourite place in town?" I asked.

"Me and the other girls often go to The Yard for a white wine after work, but I'd rather go somewhere else, if that's all right with you."

"Perfectly all right," I replied.

I would much rather go elsewhere too. The Yard may have been the nearest pub to the sale ring, and I'd been in there a few times, but I didn't really relish having the rest of the sales team in there with us, watching our every move, while the jukebox played at full volume in the corner.

"Perhaps somewhere quieter," I said.

"I know it's a bit of a way away, and it is quite expensive, but I absolutely love the Roxana Bar at the Bedford Lodge Hotel."

"Then that'll be where we shall go. I'll meet you there at six thirty."

"Don't you have to stay here on site until the end of the sale?"

"Not today," I said.

"Okay," she said, smiling. "I'll see you there at six thirty."

I watched as she walked away from me along the corridor, back to Accounts, turning once to wave.

Wow! I thought. *I've really managed it at last.*

"What are you smiling at?" Nigel Stanhope demanded as I walked into our office. "I hear you're deep in the shit."

He was clearly enjoying that, rubbing his hands together in glee.

"Nigel, why are you such a bastard?" I asked.

"Comes naturally, I suppose," he replied with a laugh.

But I knew he was only a bastard to those he saw as a threat from below. To the senior auctioneers and board members, those he believed might have a say in his promotion up the greasy pole towards a directorship, he was all sweetness and light, becoming almost Uriah Heepish in his grovelling and toadying.

"What a naughty boy, you are," he said, almost giggling with joy. "Fancy ignoring a bid from our most valued client."

"I didn't ignore it," I replied. "I just took my time to accept it."

"I heard that Mitch had to shout his bid out across the ring to get your attention, even though you'd already been told twice that he was bidding."

"How do you know about it, anyway?"

Nigel had left the sale ring as soon as I'd taken over from him at the auctioneer's rostrum, after he'd dropped the microphone to the floor.

"The spotters told me, dear boy. Those that are after your job. And now one of them might get it." He laughed again. "Fancy your lover being one of those that grassed you up."

"He's not my lover," I said, but it was clear he didn't believe me.

My joy at having finally plucked up the courage to ask Janis out had quickly evaporated. What if she also thought I was sleeping with Alex?

I decided that even being at home in Alex's flat was preferable to staying here with Nigel sniping away at me with such enthusiasm, so I packed my work laptop into its carrying case and left.

"If you can't stand the heat," Nigel called after me.

I could hear him laughing loudly as I marched along the corridor, past the gents' that had been the undoing of my job, down the stairs, and outside into the fresh air.

Maybe Nigel was right, and this kitchen was too hot for me. Was it time for me to get out of this horse-selling business and start building railway bridges? Perhaps that would be the best thing for me in the long run.

At least, I wouldn't then have to share an office with Nigel Stanhope, or a flat with a man who wanted to take me to bed.

* * *

I arrived early at the Bedford Lodge Hotel and managed to secure a table for two in the corner of the Roxana Bar, ordering myself a gin and tonic from the waiter.

As expected, the hotel was busy, as all local accommodation would be during the Book 1 sale.

But not as busy as it would be the following week, mind, when some days of the sale would coincide with the Future Champions Festival at the Rowley Mile Racecourse just down the road. Finding a hotel bed for the night in Newmarket then, or even a restaurant table for dinner, was nigh on impossible unless you had booked it almost a year in advance.

Half past six came and went, and there was no sign of Janis.

Had she had second thoughts about coming?

I berated myself for not having asked her for her phone number, or at least having given her mine.

I looked again at the time on my phone. Twenty to seven.

"Would you like another?" asked the waiter, indicating towards my empty glass.

"Perhaps in a minute. I'm waiting for someone."

"I can't let you keep this table unless you're drinking," said the waiter. "I have others waiting."

"In that case," I said, "I'll have another gin and tonic. Thank you."

He didn't look very happy, but presently he returned with my new drink.

Another look at my phone. Ten to seven.

What had I been thinking of? Of course she wouldn't be coming. Her work colleagues had probably laughed at her when she told them. "Don't you know that Theo is gay?" they would have said. "And he's about to lose his job anyway, so don't waste your time."

It had not been my best day, that was for sure.

I took another swig of my expensive gin and tonic. *Maybe I'll get drunk*, I thought, *but not at these hotel prices.* Perhaps I'd buy a bottle of cheap gin from a supermarket on my way home. Except that presenting myself at the chairman's office in the morning with bloodshot eyes and a hangover probably wasn't the best plan for getting a decent reference—that is, if he would give me one anyway.

But Janis did come, at five to seven, and she was out of breath.

7

"I AM SO SORRY," Janis gasped, sitting down opposite me. "I was afraid you'd have already left. I've run all the way up through the town."

I smiled at her.

"I got asked to do an extra job just as I was about to leave. It took longer than I thought. I'm so sorry."

"It's fine," I said. "You're here now, and that's what matters. What would you like to drink?"

"What are you having?"

"Gin and tonic. I'm afraid this is my second."

"A gin and tonic would be lovely."

I waved at the waiter, who took the order as Janis removed her black coat. Under it, she wore the sales company uniform of white shirt, red and blue neck scarf printed all over with the company logo, and a blue jacket with matching skirt.

"I'm sorry," I said. "I should have given you time to go home and change."

"It's all right. I rather like this outfit anyway. And it would have taken too long. I live in Soham."

"Oh."

"That's everybody's reaction these days. When I was a young child, no one had ever heard of Soham, but now everyone has."

Soham was a small market town about eight miles north of Newmarket, and it had been the scene of one of the most notorious child murders in British history, when ten-year-olds Holly Wells and Jessica Chapman were killed by a man called Ian Huntley, the caretaker at a local secondary school.

"I was at the same primary school as them," Janis said sombrely. "They were two years above me. It was awful. And it still is, some twenty years later. The damn television companies keep making graphic programmes about it all, documentaries and dramas, so we who live there never get a chance to forget."

"You could always move."

"I want to, but it's so expensive to get a flat of my own. I still live with my parents. My dad is a science teacher at Ely College, and my mum works in the admin office of the local community hospital here in Newmarket. Soham is midway between the two, so it's very handy for them."

The waiter arrived with her drink.

"Cheers," I said, lifting mine.

"Cheers," she echoed, doing the same with hers. "How about you? Where are you from?"

"I was born in Oxford. My dad was also a science teacher— A-level physics. I went as a pupil to the school where my dad worked, just south of the city, and then to university in Oxford as well, I'm afraid. Very parochial."

"So why Newmarket now?"

"The job," I said.

"And where do you live?"

"I rent a room in Alex Cooper's flat, in a block called Beaumont Court, just off the High Street."

I watched her as I said it, searching for a reaction.

"Oh yes," she said. "I heard."

"What *exactly* did you hear?"

She blushed, and that gave me my answer.

"What Nigel Stanhope says doesn't happen to be true," I said. "I just rent a room. Nigel is always spreading lies about me. As he does about everyone."

"Why does he do that?"

"Why?" I laughed. "Because he's a bastard."

She laughed back at me. "He's also a bastard to all of us in Accounts. In fact, he bullies us. And he makes unwelcome sexual remarks to all the girls. He thinks that he can lord it over us because he's an auctioneer, and that makes him somehow superior to us. *Bastard* is absolutely right."

She laughed again and looked at me. I stared deeply into her eyes, and after a couple of long seconds, she turned away, as if slightly embarrassed.

"Tell me more about you," I said.

"What do you want to know?"

What I really wanted to know was *did she have a boyfriend?*, but I couldn't ask that—not straight out.

"Is this your first job?" I asked instead.

"It's my first proper job," she said. "After school, I worked in Newmarket Tesco as a checkout girl for year while I did my basic bookkeeping course. Then the sales company took me on, and now they pay for my training. It's great."

"So are you a chartered accountant?"

"Oh no," she said with a laugh. "Not yet anyway. But I'm working my way towards it slowly. I have currently what is known as a Level Three Diploma in Accounting, and I'm studying for my Level Four. I do one day a fortnight at an accounting college in Cambridge. How about you? How did you train to be an auctioneer?"

"I didn't train at all," I replied. "I just sort of fell into it while I was in Australia. I actually studied to be an engineer."

"That sounds exciting."

"Not really. It's mostly just maths."

She laughed. "So is accounting."

"Fancy another?" I asked.

"I shouldn't."

"Because you're driving?"

"No. I don't drive." She paused. "I did start to learn several years ago but never got round to taking my test."

"So how do you get to work?"

"Mum brings me in every day on her way to her job. After work, at five o'clock, I usually walk through the town to the hospital, and she drives me home again." She smiled. "But I called to tell her I was working late today and also meeting someone for a drink, so I'd get a taxi home." She looked at her watch and then smiled at me. "Go on then—one more drink won't matter."

I ordered us two more gin and tonics plus a packet of peanuts.

"So you're not driving either," she said when they arrived. "Not after three drinks."

"No. My car is safely parked down near Alex's flat. I walked here."

"What sort of car do you have?"

"An Audi A3."

"Nice."

I didn't tell her the car had been four years old when I'd bought it, and that had been three years ago now, or that the interior passenger door handle didn't work.

"How do you manage without a car?" I asked.

"Easily. I get lifts from Mum and Dad, and for a while I had a boyfriend who owned a car. He'd always take me where I wanted to go."

"Had?" I said tentatively.

"His name was Darryl. We broke up about six months ago. I think he got fed up with my mum grilling him all the time. She didn't approve of him. But in fact, I don't think she would approve of any boyfriend I might have. She doesn't really trust men. Not after what Ian Huntley did to those girls. Even my dad gets the third degree sometimes when he's late home. Darryl now says he wants us to get back together, but I'm not interested. I found out afterwards that he was cheating on me with one of my friends, even when we were together."

"Silly boy," I said.

She smiled and looked down at her drink.

"Do you fancy staying for dinner?" I asked.

"I can't," she said. "I told my mum I'd be home by eight." She looked again at her watch. "I thought I had plenty of time, but I was so late leaving work."

"You could always call your mum and say you were going to be later."

"She wouldn't like that. She didn't really like it that I was not going home with her in the first place. Kept asking who I was meeting."

"But, surely, you're old enough to make up your own mind."

"You don't understand," she said. "It's not that easy. Mum is very nervous about me not being home when I say I'll be. It all stems from those damn murders. Those poor girls were missing for almost two weeks before their bodies were found. It felt like forever. You can't imagine how dreadful it was for us all, not knowing what had happened to them for so long. It affected Mum badly at the time, and she hasn't really recovered since. And she's not alone. There are plenty of mothers like her in Soham, treating their grown-up daughters as if they are the little children they were way back then. I suppose they still have a fear of losing them."

"I'm sorry," I said.

Twenty years ago, Holly Wells and Jessica Chapman had been aged ten, and if Janis had been two years below them at school, that made her about twenty-eight now. Old enough, I would have thought, to stay out for dinner if she wanted to.

"Even now, Mum will be perched on the back of the sofa in the front room, looking out through the window, waiting for me to get home. If I'm late, she starts to panic. Even if I call her to say I'm staying out longer, it would make little difference."

"I'm sorry," I said again.

"Yeah, me too. I would have loved to have had dinner with you."

"Perhaps we could do it next week," I said, smiling at her. "You could tell your mum beforehand."

That's if I still had a job by next week, or even by tomorrow.

* * *

Janis left the Bedford Lodge in a taxi at ten to eight for the eight-mile journey to Soham, which meant she was going to be late arriving home, with all the associated angst that would cause her mother. She had wanted to leave earlier, but she said something just as she was about to go that made my ears prick up.

"Next time, I'll try not to be late," she said with a smile as she put on her coat, and we walked out together to her waiting taxi. "Just before I left work to come here, I was asked to complete the purchase payment for that three-million-guinea colt—you know, the one that died."

"Who asked you?"

"Mr Pollard. He was very insistent that it be done immediately."

Mr Pollard was the sales company's finance director.

"Couldn't it have waited until tomorrow?"

"I think he is worried that, as the horse has died, we won't get the payment or our commission unless we move fast. Or at least we will have to wait months for it, until any insurance claim is sorted."

"So what did you do, exactly?" I'd asked earnestly.

"I applied for payment from the direct debit we hold on Elliot Mitchell's bloodstock trading account at his bank. It's the thing we always do when he buys one, but we normally wait a while, up to thirty days, but Mr Pollard wanted it completed today. Then I sent an email to Mitchell, telling him what we'd done, with copies to Mr Pollard and the bank, detailing the purchase price, our commission, and all the VAT amounts. The usual stuff."

"And did you receive the money?"

"I don't know yet. The bank was shut by then, so I was unable to get confirmation that the payment had gone through. It often takes them at least twenty-four hours to process it anyway."

"Then what happens?"

"Provided everything has been received into our account, I will make the necessary payment to the vendor thirty days after the date of the sale."

"Who was the vendor of that colt?"

"I don't know, but it will be in the catalogue. I never even bother to look up the vendor until after we have received the purchaser's money." Once again, she glanced at her watch. "Look, I'm sorry, but I really must go now."

"Of course. Thank you so much for coming."

She climbed into the taxi and had been driven away into the night.

I hadn't given her a goodbye kiss or anything—not even a peck on the cheek. It didn't seem quite right, so I ended up standing on the hotel driveway with a mixture of pleasure and disappointment—pleasure that I had finally asked Janis out for a drink and that she had turned up, but disappointment that nothing concrete had come from it, although she had indicated that there might be a next time.

But I still hadn't asked her for her phone number.

* * *

I picked up a takeaway pizza on my way back from the Bedford Lodge and opted against the bottle of cheap gin, buying a can of Diet Coke instead.

I ate the pizza alone in the kitchen of the flat.

To be honest, I was quite relieved that Alex was out when I got home, and he was still not back when I went to my bed soon after ten.

The Book 1 sale was always the high point of the sales year, when everything was magnified—not just everyone's anticipation and the sale prices, but male testosterone levels too, and in all species. It was often said that if you couldn't get laid during the Book 1 sale, you couldn't get laid at all.

Not that I thought I had much chance of getting laid at the moment, not unless I was willing to accept Alex's advances.

I had another bad night, sleeping only in snatches and waking often, but it was not because I was worried about my flatmate making another pass at me. Rather, I tossed and turned, wondering what I should say to the chairman in the morning. Did I stick to my guns and insist that he launch an investigation into what I'd heard, or did I acquiesce to his demands to forget it, and get on with life as if it had never happened?

And would it make any difference anyway? Had he already decided that my time was up? And for what?

For telling the truth.

In the end, I decided that if my job were indeed terminated, then I would fight back. I had spent some of my enforced afternoon at home, looking up employment law on a government website. It stated that your dismissal could be unfair if your employer did not have a good reason for dismissing you. It also said that your dismissal was very likely to be unfair if you were fired for exposing wrongdoing in your workplace.

I wasn't sure if the wrongdoing had to be done by one's employer rather than by others, but I decided that, nevertheless, I would certainly make a loud noise about it if I were sacked.

* * *

I rose early on Thursday morning, again before Alex was awake, and walked into work at seven o'clock on the last day of the Book 1 sale, and maybe the last day of my present employment.

I collected a coffee at the sales cafeteria and went up to my office. I didn't feel like any breakfast; I was far too nervous to eat.

How was it, I wondered, that American prisons always reported that the condemned man had enjoyed a specially chosen meal just prior to being put to death by lethal injection, or how NASA astronauts had the traditional steak and eggs breakfast before being strapped into their capsule perched atop a glorified firework? The very thought of eating anything in such circumstances would make my stomach turn.

I sat down at my desk and tried to concentrate on my emails, but without success. So, while I waited for the hands of the clock on the office wall to crawl their way round the dial to eight thirty, I looked up the answer to the question I had asked Janis the previous evening.

According to the sales catalogue, the three-million-guinea colt had been consigned for sale by an entity called Starsign Bloodstock. But this didn't necessarily mean that Starsign Bloodstock was the vendor. It was quite usual for the consignor to be an agent acting on behalf of the vendor.

I googled Starsign Bloodstock on the internet, but there were no hits, and there were also no returns from my search of the *Thoroughbred Business Guide*, the bloodstock industry's directory. Intrigued, I searched for Starsign on the Companies House website. There were plenty of companies with Starsign in their names, but none of them were bloodstock agents. So Starsign Bloodstock was not a UK-incorporated company, and it didn't have its own web presence, but it could very easily just be an individual or a partnership. All you needed to set yourself up as a bloodstock agent was a bank account and some clients—no qualifications were required.

Perhaps I would ask Janis later if she had discovered who the vendor was, in order to pay them.

At a quarter past eight, Nigel Stanhope walked into the office.

"I thought you'd been fired," he said bluntly.

Did he know something I didn't?

"What gave you that idea?" I asked.

"Because you didn't turn up yesterday to take over from me. Peter had to ask us to do extra-long stints to cover for you." He made it sound like it was entirely my fault that he'd had to do more work.

"Well, I'm not fired," I said. *But I might be soon,* I thought.

"So where were you?" Nigel demanded.

"I wasn't feeling very well."

"You were feeling well enough to go out drinking."

How did he know that?

Surely Janis wouldn't have told him.

"I have my spies, you know," Nigel said with a knowing smirk, tapping his nose with his right index finger. "Not much goes on in Newmarket that I don't get to hear about. And now you're off to see the boss for a caning. Got an extra couple of pairs of pants on, have you?"

He was clearly enjoying himself at my expense, but the last thing I needed was to have a row with Nigel just before I went in to see the chairman, so I stood up from my desk and walked out. I went down the corridor to the gents' restroom, the very scene, it seemed, of all my troubles.

This time, thankfully, the place was empty.

I looked into the mirror above the washbasin.

"Come on," I told my reflection. "You know you are a good auctioneer, so don't get browbeaten out of doing it. Stand up for yourself."

In a way, I quite surprised myself by saying it.

So, deep down, did I really want to keep this job after all?

Yes, maybe I did.

8

"So what have you to say for yourself?" Peter Radway asked. At least he had asked me to sit down in the chair across the desk from him, rather than to remain standing, as I had been yesterday lunchtime.

"I admit that I was wrong to initially ignore the bid from Elliot Mitchell. I had made an assumption that he and Brian Kitman were again colluding to bid up the price of the colt, in contravention of the Bloodstock Industry Code of Conduct. I still believe that to have been the case, but I realise now that I handled things badly. I should have stopped the auction and immediately reported my concerns to you or another member of the board. For that, and for that alone, I apologise to you."

I leaned back in the chair and waited for him to respond.

Had I said the right thing?

Had I been sufficiently contrite, or had I gone too far by reiterating that I still believed Mitchell and Kitman were colluding together to increase prices?

The chairman sat and looked at me, with his elbows on the desk and his hands clasped together under his chin, as if he was thinking.

"Thank you for your apology to me," he said finally. "But I think you also need to apologise to Elliot Mitchell."

"That I will not do," I replied curtly. "I was well within my rights, as the auctioneer, to ignore any or all bids, so I have nothing to apologise to him for."

It was Mitchell, I thought, who should be apologising to *me*, for making an official complaint in the first place.

"And what if I make that a condition of you remaining here?"

"Then I will claim constructive and unfair dismissal and take you to an employment tribunal."

I could tell that the chairman was rather taken aback by my response. To be honest, so was I. I hadn't really expected to be so forthright.

"I don't think there is any need for that sort of talk."

"No, I would hope not," I agreed. But I had left him in no doubt as to the alternative of reinstating me as an auctioneer. I was not going to meekly resign and walk away.

"So what now?" I asked. "Am I back on duty for today?"

I could tell that he wasn't very happy. I imagine that he thought he would be in control of this conversation, and I had just stolen the initiative.

"Er, well . . . I suppose that might be for the best."

"Good," I said, standing up. "So we return to the original roster. I will be at the rostrum at twelve thirty to take over from Nigel Stanhope."

I turned to leave.

But mentioning Nigel had reminded me of something else I had read on the government's employment law website:

Constructive dismissal is when you are forced to leave your job against your will because of your employer's conduct.

The reasons you leave your job must be serious, for example:

- *they do not pay you or suddenly demote you for no reason;*

- *they force you to accept unreasonable changes to how you work—for example, tell you to work night shifts when your contract is only for daywork;*
- *they let other employees harass or bully you.*

I turned back to face the chairman.

"There is also one other thing," I said. "Could you please tell Nigel to stop harassing and bullying me and the other staff, especially the female staff in Accounts? He makes unwelcome sexual remarks towards them, and he's also homophobic towards some of the male staff, making lewd comments and gestures. We are all fed up with it, and we shouldn't have to put up with such behaviour in the workplace."

The chairman looked up at me in surprise.

"Surely you need to take that up with Nigel."

"No, we don't. I've been reading the law, and I'm afraid that it is actually *your* responsibility, as our employer, to prevent harassment and bullying of your staff by any other employee. So please talk to him."

I could tell that he didn't like being told what to do, and especially by me, the most junior member of the auctioneer team. Perhaps I had gone too far. Maybe it was time for me to leave his office. But I was only halfway to his door when I remembered something else.

I turned back again.

"Peter, have you ever heard of an entity called Starsign Bloodstock?"

He shook his head. "What about them?"

"They were the consignor of the three-million-guinea colt, but I can't find any details about them anywhere, or the vendor they represented. That colt was the only one in the whole sale consigned by them, but they still must be registered with us."

"Which member of the Bloodstock Sales Team dealt with them?"

"I've no idea. It wasn't me."

There were eleven members of the Bloodstock Sales Team in total, three of whom, including Nigel Stanhope and me, also acted as auctioneers on sale days.

"Leave it to me," the chairman said. "I will look them up on the registration system and let you know."

"Thank you."

Again I turned to go, and again I turned back to him.

"Did security say anything about the CCTV? Is the box where the colt died covered?"

"Sadly not," said the chairman. "It should be, but it appears that the cable to all the lower yards was cut when a new water pipe was being laid last month, and it hasn't been repaired yet."

How convenient, I thought.

This time I made it all the way out of his door and back along the corridor to my own office. It was empty. I sat down at my desk and blew out my cheeks. That had gone so much better than I had feared. In fact, I was quite proud of myself.

"Still here, then?" Nigel said, coming in through the door with a coffee.

"Yes," I replied. "And I intend staying here too."

He mumbled something under his breath, which I didn't fully catch.

"What was that?" I asked.

"I said, not if I can help it."

"And what the hell do you mean by that?" I asked indignantly.

"What I say. You arrived here, still wet behind the ears, and were made an auctioneer from day one. How old were you? Twenty-two, twenty-three?"

So he *was* jealous and saw me as a threat, as if I didn't already know that.

"I was thirty."

"I had to work here for eight years before I was asked to conduct my first auction. By then, I was almost forty."

"That's not my fault," I said. "And I was an auctioneer for five years in Australia before I came here."

"Australia! What do the bloody Australians know about racehorses?"

"As much as us, possibly more. There are six times as many racecourses in Australia than there are here. And you must have heard of the Melbourne Cup."

"It's a bloody handicap."

So he had heard of it.

"So? The Grand National is also a handicap. As are the Chester Cup, the Ebor, and about a third of all the races run at Royal Ascot. And the Melbourne Cup happens to be the richest handicap in the world. Over four million goes to the winner."

Nigel waved a dismissive hand at me. There was clearly no point in arguing with him when he was in this mood.

"Have you ever heard of Starsign Bloodstock?" I asked, changing the subject.

"What have they got to do with Australia?"

"Nothing. Have you heard of them?"

He shook his head. "Nope."

I reckoned he wouldn't have told me even if he had.

It must be such hard work, I thought, being so unpleasant and unhelpful all the time.

What Nigel needed, I decided, was a hefty dose of Buddhism. Not that there was any chance of giving him some. You cannot thrust Buddhism down anyone's throat. Unlike in Christianity or Islam, there are no Buddhist missionaries offering eternal paradise for those that instantly convert, while threatening excruciating pain and horror in an everlasting hell for those who don't.

In contrast, Buddhism is the most peaceful of religions, but it has to come from within yourself rather than being forced upon you. It fosters a belief that the continuous circle of life and death can only be broken by meditation, spirituality, and physical labour, conducted with good and kindly behaviour, on the path to eventual nirvana—the final quenching of the activities of the worldly mind and all its related suffering.

Nigel Stanhope wouldn't recognise good and kindly behaviour if he tripped over it. He was far more a fire-and-brimstone sort of character, with the emphasis on the fire, at least in my case.

The chairman put his head round the door.

"Ah, Nigel," he said, "could I have a word?"

"What about?" Nigel asked.

"In my office, if you don't mind," replied the chairman, not answering the question. Peter's head then withdrew from the doorway.

Nigel looked at me. I shrugged my shoulders at him, as if I didn't know what it was about, although I thought I probably did. He went out through the door, and I wondered if it was his turn to wear some extra pairs of pants.

I decided that I didn't really want to be in our office when Nigel got back, as I imagined he would be very angry, and as I was now feeling more hungry than nervous, I went down to the cafeteria to get some breakfast.

As always during the Book 1 sale, the place was buzzing, with small groups sitting together at the tables, their heads bowed close in conversation so that others couldn't overhear what they are saying.

The action in the sale ring itself may not begin until eleven o'clock on these three sale days, but prospective purchasers, their vets and agents will have been up since long before dawn, nervously checking and rechecking on any yearlings they still have in mind to bid for. They will also have been assessing who else has shown an interest in the same animal, trying to gauge whether they have any prospect of success against them in the upcoming auction.

Indeed, many months of planning will have gone into this sale, ever since the first publication of the catalogue. Bloodstock agents will have heavily scrutinised every page, targeting only those lots where they think they may have a chance of coming out as the top bidder and within their clients' respective budgets.

Now, tactics for the auction itself were being finalised: Which of us will actually do the bidding, and when; what is our expected limit; and are we ever prepared to break that limit in the hope that one final bid might secure our top choice?

I collected a toasted bacon sandwich from the cafeteria buffet, together with a coffee, and took it outside to one of the tables set up on the grass. I sat down and began to eat.

"Hello, Theo," said a soft voice from over my left shoulder.

I turned round to find one of my fellow Bloodstock Sales Team members sitting at the next table.

"Hi, Liam," I said. "I'm sorry, I didn't see you there. Shall I join you?"

"Be my guest."

I stood up and took my tray over to his table.

Liam Barton, a genial Irishman from Donegal, aged about fifty, was a former regular auctioneer, but now worked for us almost exclusively in Ireland, spending his time sweet-talking the Irish breeders and stud farms into sending their equine offspring over to us for sale in Newmarket rather than to rival companies in their homeland.

Almost half the yearlings sold in the Book 1 sale each year are bred in Ireland, and roughly the same number are from Great Britain, with just a sprinkling from America, France, and Germany, and the very occasional one from Australia or the United Arab Emirates.

"Well done on Tuesday with that three-million colt," Liam said. "Rather overpriced, though, if you ask me. It was a bloody shame he snuffed it so quickly, as we'll never find out how good he could have been. Do we know the cause of death?"

"Not yet. We're waiting for the post-mortem report. Was it one of yours? It came over from Ireland."

He shook his head. "What was its breeding?"

"By Foxtrot Mike out of a mare called Lucky Lass. The dam sire was by Camelot, so there was some value there."

"But not three million guineas of value," Liam said sarcastically.

I had looked up Foxtrot Mike. He was a ten-year-old Irish stallion, which had been standing at Holycross Stud, a small setup just outside Thurles in County Tipperary, for the past six years. He himself had a reasonable pedigree, with Northern Dancer as one of his great-grandsires, but he was not particularly well fancied as a stallion, having sired no progeny of note during his first few seasons.

Lucky Lass had never been much hailed before as a brood mare either, but together they had produced one really spectacular offspring, notably Lucky Mike, the leading European two-year-old of the current year. And Lucky Mike had been sold last November as a yearling, before his exceptional racing talents had been apparent, for just eight thousand euros at a rival company's sale just outside Dublin.

A real example of lightning striking where it was totally unexpected.

But would it have struck again with his full brother?

We would never know.

"It was consigned for sale by something called Starsign Bloodstock," I said. "Have you ever heard of it?"

He shook his head.

"Nor have I, but Starsign must be registered with us to act as a consignor. Peter is looking them up for me."

"Why the interest?" Liam asked.

"I don't know really. I just feel that the whole sale of that colt was rather strange, and then it ends up being found dead the following morning."

Did I tell him about the collusive bidding-up conversation? After all, he had just said that he thought the colt had sold for more than it was worth. But I had promised the chairman that I would do nothing further on that score, not unless the post-mortem results showed something suspicious.

"How well do you know Elliot Mitchell?" I asked him instead.

"Pretty well, I suppose. We cross paths all the time. But he always gives the impression that he is somehow in competition with me."

"For what?"

"Influence with the breeders mostly. All too often, if I make a suggestion to a breeder, they will reply, *'But Elliot says this, or Elliot says that,'* which is invariably the opposite. For example, if I suggest to a breeder that their yearling should be nominated for sale with us and is a good prospect for Book One, he will have told them it is likely going into Book Two or Book Three, or even into Book Four, and that they might want to consider a different company. And sometimes vice versa."

"Does that annoy you?" I asked.

"Not really. We're both just doing our jobs. And we're both after the same thing—the highest possible price for the horse at the sale."

Which yearling went into which book was not determined by the vendors or by their bloodstock agents. As one of the five yearling inspectors in the bloodstock team, I would go out to breeders and look at over a thousand yearlings every year between May and July, and my decision on which book they went into was based on the animal's pedigree, its conformation, and the number of other yearlings of a similar or higher calibre in that year's crop.

The Book 1 sale was by far the most prestigious, when all of the big-money purchasers would be present, but it was limited to five hundred and forty lots in total, one hundred and eighty per day for three days.

"So, overall, do you think Elliot Mitchell is pretty honest?" I asked Liam.

He laughed. "He's as honest as any other bloodstock agent, but that's not saying much." He laughed again. "I was one of them myself once, remember, before I joined here. Make no mistake: everyone in this game is in it for themselves—agents and breeders alike, but especially the agents. Mind you, we as a sales company are no better. We all want the prices sky-high."

As long as someone else is paying, I thought.

But who would actually be paying for the three-million-guinea yearling?

And paying it to whom?

CHAPTER

9

I TOOK OVER FROM Nigel Stanhope at the auctioneer's rostrum just after twelve thirty, as planned, and he was unexpectedly good-natured towards me, helping to pass the microphone from his tie to mine. He even smiled at me.

I didn't smile back.

"Next up, we have lot four nine six," I said. "A fine bay filly by Cadogan Hall out of a Galileo mare, consigned by Blewbury Blood-stock. Foaled on February tenth, she's a half-sister to a Group Two winner, and there's plenty of black type in this one's pedigree. Who'll bid me what to start? Two hundred thousand guineas?" I looked around, but nothing. "One hundred, then?" Still nothing. "Fifty, then? Forty? Thirty?" I said as we played the usual game.

Elliot Mitchell was standing, as always, in the gate. I looked at him, but he was not even facing my way. Instead, he appeared to be deep in conversation with someone next to him wearing a blue gilet and a red baseball cap. He seemed disinterested in this particular lot, but many potential buyers try to appear disinterested initially.

"Come on now," I said. "We all know she's worth more than thirty thousand. Who will start me?"

A man leaning on the rails opposite waved his catalogue.

"Thirty thousand. Thank you, sir. Thirty thousand I have. Forty anywhere?"

Alex Cooper was doing a stint as a spotter on the far side of the ring from me, and he shouted, raised his right hand, and pointed with his left at a man in the third row of seats.

"Forty thousand," I said. I looked back at the first bidder, and he nodded. "Fifty." A new bidder, standing next to Elliot Mitchell in the gate, raised a hand. "Sixty thousand."

The man on the rail lifted his catalogue again.

"Seventy thousand." I said. "Eighty now," as the man in the seats rebid.

I switched my eyes back again to the first bidder, the man leaning on the rail. He shook his head. Surely he hadn't expected to acquire such a fine filly for that money, but maybe he'd been bidding on behalf of the vendor, just to get things going.

Still Elliot Mitchell didn't make a move. Maybe he really wasn't interested. But the man next to him still was.

"Ninety now, in the gate."

I scanned the faces in front of me, and a movement up at the back caught my eye. Brian Kitman was in his usual place at the top of the right-hand stairwell, and he had just raised a hand above his head.

"New bidder at the back," I said. "One hundred thousand guineas bid."

The man in the gate lifted his hand in response. "One ten. One twenty now, in the seats."

I looked up to the high stairwell. Kitman nodded at me.

"One thirty."

The man in the seats again raised his hand.

"One forty. Selling now."

We had reached the vendor's reserve.

"She's a lovely-looking filly," I said. "A half-sister to a Group winner, remember. One fifty now, in the gate."

I switched my attention in turn between the three bidders as we went through one more cycle of them all bidding again.

"The bid is one hundred and eighty thousand guineas in the gate. Will anyone make it up to two hundred?"

Elliot Mitchell had turned round to watch the proceedings but seemed content to let the others fight it out.

Brian Kitman in the stairwell raised two fingers in my direction.

"Two hundred thousand now, at the back."

I looked across at the man in the seats, who was sitting very still.

"Decision time, sir."

He briefly shook his head.

"Okay. Thanks for your help." I switched my attention to the man in the gate. He didn't immediately bid.

"Two hundred thousand at the back," I repeated pointing up at Kitman so there was no mistake. Still the man in the gate made no move. "Two hundred thousand. Looking now for two twenty." Still no movement. "I'll take two ten, if it helps."

The man in the gate nodded.

"Two hundred and ten thousand guineas," I said slowly. "The bid is now in the gate."

I looked up at Brian Kitman. He mouthed, "Two twenty."

"Two hundred and twenty thousand guineas now, at the back."

The bidder in the gate shook his head and turned away, pushing past Elliot Mitchell as he left the building.

I looked at Mitchell, who stared back at me. Was he going to bid? Were he and Kitman up to their tricks again? There was no movement of Mitchell's hand or head, not even a raising of his eyebrow.

"The bid is two hundred and twenty thousand guineas at the back," I said. "Are you all done?" I looked once more at the man in the seats, but he again shook his head. "Two hundred and twenty thousand, then. Selling this time round."

I scanned all the faces one more time. Nothing.

"Last chance," I said. "Two hundred and twenty thousand guineas. The hammer is up."

Still nothing from Elliot Mitchell.

I raised my gavel and brought it smartly down onto the rostrum with a loud crack. "Sold for two hundred and twenty thousand guineas. Brian Kitman. Thank you, and the very best of luck with her."

It was a fair price for a filly with that breeding, and for all my concerns, there was no reason to think that anything about that auction was amiss.

I watched as the animal in question was led out from the sale ring through the large exit door. As one high-class yearling departed to my right, the next arrived from my left, like a continuous conveyor belt of young equine talent with the potential to be world beaters—at least that's what the purchasers were praying for.

"Next up is lot four nine seven," I announced through the public address system. "A chestnut colt by High Fidelity."

And so it went on, lot after lot, with nothing seemingly suspicious happening throughout my stint, until I was relieved by the chairman soon after one o'clock—lunchtime, and I was hungry again.

I went out of the sale-ring building and along to the self-service restaurant. I collected some breaded scampi with chips from the buffet, together with a bottle of sparkling water, and sat down at an empty table.

"Can I join you?" asked a voice over my left shoulder.

It was Alex.

"I thought you were spotting."

"I'm on my break," he replied. He sat down opposite me, with just a packet of cheese and chutney sandwiches on his tray.

"I'm really sorry about the other night," he said quickly. "I don't know what came over me."

"It was rather a shock," I said. "I didn't realise."

"No." He paused. "Neither did I really. Not until then. I mean . . . I've always been rather confused in that regard. I knew I was not attracted to girls much, if at all, but . . ."

He tailed off.

We were surrounded on all sides by tables of others eating and drinking, some noisily toasting their success at buying or selling. It was hardly a place for such a private conversation.

"Look," I said, "it's very noisy in here. Would you rather go somewhere else to talk?"

"I thought you might prefer having other people around you—for added security."

I smiled at him. "I don't think I need protecting from *you*, Alex. Let me finish this"—I indicated towards my lunch—"and we'll go somewhere quieter."

But he opened his pack of sandwiches. "I haven't got much time." He looked at his phone. "I need to get back soon."

"I'll be as quick as I can," I said, popping two more scampi into my already full mouth.

Alex lifted one of his cheese and chutney sandwiches towards his mouth, but it never got there.

"I think, overall, it's a relief," he said, clearly wanting to go on now rather than to wait. Perhaps it was best, once he'd started, to continue. "At last I've admitted to myself that I must be gay. Before, I've just kept shoving the question away, but I suppose that deep down I've always suspected. I just haven't been prepared to admit it, even to myself, let alone anyone else. And now that I have, it's somehow liberating." He smiled. "I don't know what my mother will say, mind. I'm an only child, and she keeps going on and on about one day having grandchildren. She's desperate for them."

He sighed and put the uneaten sandwich back down on his tray.

"So?" I said. "Elton John has kids."

He looked at me and smiled. "So he has." He picked up his sandwich again and took a bite from it. "So you're not angry with me?"

"Angry? No. Of course not."

"I was afraid you were. You seemed to be avoiding me yesterday."

"It was not on purpose. I just got up early because I couldn't sleep. And it was you who was out all last evening. I was home by eight thirty."

"I was hiding."

"From whom?" I asked.

"Myself, mostly. I walked all the way to the White Horse at Exning for a few drinks on my own. I couldn't bear being with anyone I knew. I wanted time to think."

Exning was a small village just to the north of Newmarket, which had now almost been swallowed up by the seemingly inexorable red-brick advance of the town outwards into the surrounding countryside.

"What time did you get back?"

"Around midnight."

I hadn't heard him come in. It must have been during one of my short sleeping stretches, as opposed to the long waking ones.

He suddenly glanced at his phone. "Sorry, I've got to go."

"Will you be at home this evening?" I asked as he stood up. "We could continue talking then, if you like. I should be back well before eight."

He looked down at me and smiled broadly. "That would be great. Thanks. I'll make some supper."

"But don't get the wrong idea," I said with a laugh.

"No," he replied. "I won't. I promise."

I watched as he rushed out of the restaurant door, back to his post as a spotter in the sale ring.

How, I wondered, did someone get to be twenty-four years old and still be confused by his sexuality? I'd been pretty certain of mine by the time I was about fourteen, and that was in spite of attending an all-male boarding school.

Maybe I'd just been lucky.

But who really knows what's going on in other people's heads? Alex was a good kid, and if I could help him by talking or listening, then so much the better.

Perhaps I wouldn't have to look for alternative accommodation after all.

* * *

I did two more stints at the auctioneer's rostrum before the end of the day.

There must have been something of the showman in me, because I relished being in control of an auction, having the whole sales process in my hands, cajoling buyers into making just one more bid, perhaps against their better judgement, to secure a purchase. It was exciting, and I absolutely loved it, never really wanting to hand over to the next auctioneer when my time was up.

As the chairman took over from me at six fifteen for the last few lots of the sale, he paused briefly.

"Theo," he said, just before he attached the microphone to his tie, "come up to my office at the end of the sale. I've received the interim report from the vet on the colt that died."

Before I had time to reply, he clipped on the microphone and stepped up to the rostrum.

"Right, ladies and gentlemen, next up is lot five hundred twenty-eight, and have we saved one of the best to nearly last. A colt by Frankel, no less. A real treat for you all."

I smiled. Peter was a real pro, and he could have easily sold coals to Newcastle, and at a profit.

I hung around the auctioneer's box while Peter coaxed the price of the Frankel colt up to eight hundred and fifty thousand guineas, and then he ran through the remaining lots in double-quick time.

"Thank you, ladies and gentlemen," Peter said after his gavel had fallen for the last sale. "That concludes the October Yearling Book One sale. The Book Two sale will begin on Monday morning at ten o'clock."

By this stage there were very few people left in the sales building anyway, but those that were now made their way outside, back to their cars, homes or hotels. The excitement was over for this week but would recommence in four days' time.

I followed Peter out of the sales building, across into the management centre, up the stairs, and along the corridor to his office. He sat down at his desk and held up a single sheet of paper.

"Andrew Ingleby emailed his preliminary post-mortem report over to me earlier this afternoon. I asked my secretary to print it out."

I waited while Peter read through the report. He then laid the paper down on the desk.

"There are no indications of any abnormal or unusual drugs present in the blood samples he took. And there were no signs of asphyxia in the whites of the eyes or in the lungs. He has sent the organs for further analysis, but he doesn't expect anything will show up in those as there was absolutely no trace of anything in the blood. He is therefore of the opinion that the death is unexplained and was most likely a result of a sudden, catastrophic, and fatal cardiac arrhythmia. Natural causes."

"Was there any excess adrenalin present?" I asked.

He looked again at the paper.

"Apparently not. All that was detected was the sedative acepromazine, and in a very low dosage, insufficient to have caused death."

I knew that acepromazine, or ACP, was commonly used to sedate yearlings prior to sale. Young horses can be highly strung creatures, especially the colts, and they can be very difficult to handle both during vetting and in the sale ring. So ACP is often administered in the form of an oral gel called Sedalin. It calms them down and makes them more manageable. Any forms of sedative are banned for horses in races but are allowable at the sales.

"So there was nothing suspicious found?" I asked.

"No."

"So what happens now?"

"What do you mean?"

"What is our next step?" I asked.

"We don't have a next step. That's it. Finished."

I thought of requesting a second opinion from a different vet, but with the horse's body now having been either consumed by the hounds or burned, there would be nothing left for a second vet to look at anyway.

"It appears," Peter went on, "that it was just an unfortunate but naturally occurring death."

Did I really believe that?

"So we go on as if nothing has happened."

"That's right," the chairman agreed.

"Okay, but I would like it officially recorded by you, as the chairman of this company, that I have made a statement to the effect that I believe Elliot Mitchell and Brian Kitman are together guilty of collusive bidding in respect to the sale of that colt. Even if it goes nowhere else, and nothing more is done about it."

He nodded. "I acknowledge that."

"I would like it in writing, please."

I think he was astounded by my determination in the matter, but he recovered quickly.

"I will get my secretary to type it up in the morning," he said, standing up and retrieving his overcoat from the hook in the corner. "I have to go home now. I'm attending a black-tie dinner in the Jockey Club Rooms this evening at eight o'clock, and I need time to change."

I needed to get home fairly soon too, I thought, to continue my promised discussion with Alex.

Sadly, however, I didn't make it.

10

I WALKED ALONG FROM the chairman's office to Accounts, hoping that Janis might still be at her desk. She wasn't, but Geoff Pollard, the financial director, was still at his.

"Hi, Geoff," I said. "How are things?"

"Never better," he said, looking up at me with a smile. "That was the best Book One sale we've ever had. I've been adding up the final figures. Can you believe that over the last three days, we have sold more than a hundred and twenty million guineas worth of horse?" He laughed. "Recession? What recession? The buyers have gone crazy. In all, sixteen yearlings in this sale were sold for over a million guineas, with that one that you sold at the top, at three."

"I hope none of the other fifteen died."

He looked at me. "Yes, that was a real shame."

"Did we get the money?"

"What money?"

"The three million guineas from Elliot Mitchell? Janis Thompson mentioned that you'd asked her to apply for it through the direct debit on his trading account."

He appeared slightly irritated that one of his staff had been discussing accounting matters with someone outside of his team, and I mentally kicked myself for mentioning Janis by name, but he told me the answer, nevertheless.

"The bank refused our direct debit demand because of a lack of funds in the account. Elliot, meanwhile, has requested the usual thirty-day grace period so that he could have discussions with his principal, and also with the insurance company."

"Who was his principal for that sale?" I asked. "Was it his Irish syndicate?"

"I've no idea," Geoff replied. "You know that Elliot never reveals his principals. He's renowned for it. That's why we always process everything through his own trading account, rather than invoicing the principals direct."

"How about the vendor?" I asked.

"What about them?"

"Who are they? According to the sales catalogue, the yearling was consigned by an entity called Starsign Bloodstock, but I can't find out anything about them or who they represent."

He shook his head. "We only deal with the vendor once the sale money is in our account."

It was the same answer that Janis had given me.

Geoff looked up at the clock on the wall of his office.

"Look, I'm sorry, Theo—I must go home now. We have friends over for supper tonight, and my wife will be having kittens that I'm not already there to help her."

He stood up, grabbed his jacket from the back of his chair, collected his laptop computer from his desk, and hurried away.

Meanwhile, I went back to my office to have a final check of my emails.

About ten or fifteen minutes later, as I walked out of the complex, I noticed how quiet the place seemed, with an end-of-term feel about it. The bar, normally busy until long after the end of the sale day, was almost deserted, and the fine-dining restaurant had closed early for the night.

It was only four days until we would be back here again for the start of Book 2, and the yearlings for that sale had already started arriving at the stable yards, ready to be vetted over the weekend, but tonight everyone, it seemed, was taking the opportunity to take the evening off to recharge their batteries, and give their livers a rest from the alcohol intake.

The nights were beginning to draw in fast as October progressed, and there was no light left in the western sky as I went out through the pedestrian gate next to the cafeteria and onto Queensberry Road, turning left towards home. It was only a few weeks now until the clocks would be going back an hour, and then the feel of impending winter would really set in.

I hated the long, dark evenings, when the sun would set well before four o'clock in the afternoon, and it would be pitch-black by a quarter past. Each year, I would count down the days until the shortest one. There were only seven weeks between the clocks going back and the days starting to get longer again. Surely, I thought, anyone can survive seven weeks?

I followed Queensberry Road round to the right and then turned left into the access drive behind Beaumont Court, where there were several blocks of garages, all built at right angles to the drive itself.

I thought about what I should say to Alex.

What was right? The last thing I wanted was to inadvertently say something inappropriate that might upset him.

I decided that the best thing was simply to listen and try to be supportive.

A pair of car headlights came on at the far end of the driveway. Perhaps one of the other residents of the block was going out for dinner. The car's engine started.

I held my phone in my hand and started looking at some of the latest posts on Instagram—a video of boys riding bikes while standing with one leg on the saddle and the other on the handlebars; and another of a dog wearing goggles, being carried on a motorbike. So engrossed was I in this futile waste of time that I didn't immediately spot that the car headlights were coming straight towards me, and very quickly.

I waved at the driver, but it made no difference. Perhaps he or she couldn't see my dark navy suit against the black background. I moved rapidly to one side, close to the wall at the end of a garage block, but the headlights followed me. Only then did I begin to realise that they were heading my way on purpose, and the car was getting ever faster. I was already up against the wall to the right, and I had nowhere else to go.

At the last second, when the lights were only a couple of yards away, I jumped upwards as high as I could to avoid either being run over completely, or rolled against the wall.

The headlights flashed by underneath my feet but there was no way I could jump high enough to escape being hit altogether. My feet struck the windscreen, causing me to somersault right over the roof of the car, landing heavily on the ground behind it.

I landed badly on my left leg, twisting my ankle. I screamed in agony.

The car braked suddenly to a halt, its tyres skidding and screeching on the loose tarmac surface. The reversing lights immediately came on, and I was under no illusion that the driver was coming back to check that I was all right. Quite the opposite, in fact. I was sure he was coming back to have another go at finishing me off.

I tried to stand up and run, but my left leg didn't seem to be working. Looking down, I could see that my ankle seemed to be totally out of shape, with my left foot pointing strangely sideways. *Dislocated,* I thought, and it didn't fill me with much confidence for my future as the star striker of the sales company's five-a-side soccer team.

But no matter what damage had already been done, remaining here in the middle of the driveway was not an option. I would be a sitting duck to be run over with far worse consequences, not just to my left foot but all over my body, and with no chance of jumping out of the way for a second time.

I quickly looked around.

There were three vans parked in a line on the opposite side of the drive from the garages, next to the wooden fence.

Gritting my teeth against the pain, I rolled over and over sideways on the ground towards them as the car started to gather speed backwards. I reached the line of parked vans and simply went on rolling, right underneath the middle one of them, just as the car flashed past, missing me by only inches.

Again the car screeched to a halt, but this time, the engine stopped, the door opened, and the driver got out.

I could hear the crunch of his footsteps as he moved closer to my hiding place. I thrust the knuckles of my right hand into my mouth, to stop me screaming from the excruciating pain that was sweeping up all over me from my foot.

From my position lying on my back, I twisted my head to try and see the driver's approach.

As he did so, all I could see from under the van were his shoes—plain, black, unremarkable shoes. But they came towards me, inch by little inch, lit by the car's still-on headlights, as the man searched for me.

Did I cry out for help, giving away my position, or did I stay still and as silent as possible in the hope of avoiding detection?

I opted for the silent, still approach, and on a number of counts.

First, no one was likely to hear my cries of help anyway. With the main road just on the far side of Beaumont Court, the flats all had double-glazed windows, not only to keep them warm in the winter but also to keep the noise out, and even if someone did hear me, they would surely be unlikely to come outside in the dark for fear of coming face to face with danger themselves.

Second, there was always a chance that he wouldn't find me, albeit a small chance. And third, even if he did find me, what could he do about it if I stayed where I was, under the van?

He could hardly run me over under here.

Then I wondered if he had some other sort of weapon with him as well, such as a gun or a knife, and that thought frightened me even further. But if he did, why not just wait in the shadows and shoot or stab me at point-blank range as I walked past him? Much more certain than trying to run me over. But it wouldn't have then looked like an accident. But this wasn't going to look like an accident now anyway, whatever he did.

All these thoughts went round and round in my head, and still the plain, black, unremarkable shoes got ever closer, until the man wearing them was almost standing alongside the van I was under.

I held my breath.

Where was my phone? Could I use it to call for help?

I felt for it in my pockets, but to no avail. Then I remembered that I'd been looking at it just before the car hit me.

Where did it go?

Did it matter?

All I knew was that I didn't have it with me any longer.

A phone, a phone, my kingdom for a phone.

A car turned into the end of the driveway from Queensberry Road, lighting up the scene with yet more headlights.

The black shoes immediately turned round so that the face of the man would not be lit up by the new lights, and then the shoes retreated rapidly back to his own car. I heard the door slam and the engine start, and I moved my position slightly to try and read the car's registration as it drove away, but the number plate was not visible, as if it had been covered by something.

I laid my head back on the cold ground and considered my options.

Staying here much longer was definitely not one of them.

It may only be the beginning of October, but the high-pressure system meant that the sky was clear of clouds. "Clouds act like the blankets on your bed," my late father used to say to me when I was a child. "They keep the warmth in during the night." With no clouds to stop it, the heat gained from the sun during the day simply radiated back out into space at night. The hardest frosts always occur when the sky is clear and, while I didn't exactly expect a frost tonight, it was already becoming too cold to be lying on the ground outside, especially with a badly dislocated ankle, which in turn might be disrupting the blood supply to my foot.

I thought about the alternatives.

Would Alex wonder why I hadn't arrived home for our promised talk, and come out looking for me, or would he just conclude that I didn't want to talk after all and had decided to spend the evening, and maybe the whole night, elsewhere?

Almost certainly the latter.

So, if I couldn't stay under here all night, no one was coming to look for me, and I had no phone to call for help, then I had no alternative but to move myself.

I rolled onto my side, and a wave of pain swept over me, leaving me gasping for breath. *How,* I thought, *am I ever going to be able to get out from under this van, let alone make my way home, or to anywhere else I could get help?*

I suddenly heard more footsteps approaching—crunch, crunch, crunch on the loose tarmac surface.

Oh God. Was the man coming back?

I twisted my head to see, and waited as whoever it was got ever closer.

More shoes came into sight—white shoes, small white shoes. I could just make them out in the moonlight.

I breathed a huge sigh of relief, but then I feared that Black Shoes might have an accomplice in white.

The white shoes came quickly closer as the person moved alongside the van in a manner that suggested the wearer was simply walking past rather than actively searching.

I had to take a chance.

"Please help me," I called out.

The white shoes did not stop.

"Help!" I cried out louder. "Help me!" Louder still.

This time the white shoes wavered, stopped, but then moved on again.

"Please!" I screamed. "Please help me."

The shoes stopped again.

"Where are you?" asked a female voice in some alarm.

"Under the van," I shouted back. "And I've hurt my leg. Please call an ambulance."

I had a dread that she was about to run away from this strange voice from an invisible source.

"Who are you?" she asked.

"Theo Jennings. I live at number twelve. A car hit me, and I've ended up under here with a dislocated ankle. Please don't go away." I was pleading.

The white shoes turned one way and then the other, as if she was looking for reinforcements. Then a light came on, and the woman leaned down and shone it under the van, followed by her face appearing into my sight.

"Hello," I said, quite calmly, even though I didn't feel it. "Please get help. Call nine-one-one. I need an ambulance. And also the police."

The light was from the torch on her phone, and she now used the same device to make the call.

I almost cried with relief.

CHAPTER

11

THE POLICE AND the ambulance arrived together, both with their blue lights flashing and sirens blaring, bringing a crowd of the block's residents outside to see what was going on.

One of the paramedics crawled under the van with a torch.

"My left ankle is the problem," I said.

He inspected it in the torchlight.

"Does it hurt?" he asked, looking at my sideways-facing foot.

Is the Pope Catholic?

"Yes, it does hurt," I replied. "A lot."

"Can you move?"

"No."

He didn't ask how I came to be under the van in the first place. In fact I wasn't sure how I had managed it. I suppose that the human instinct to survive is so great that the rush of adrenalin it produces shuts out pain, at least for a while, until the adrenalin wears off—as it had by now.

In the end the paramedic placed a blanket on the ground next to me, then rolled me onto it so that he and his colleague could pull me out into the open. Only then did they give me some pain relief in the form of a nitrous oxide and air mixture to breathe in through a plastic mouthpiece.

Nitrous oxide—laughing gas. Don't make me laugh!

It didn't seem to make any difference to the pain.

They also fitted me with a neck collar—no need for that I said to them in vain; it was my ankle that hurt, not my neck. Finally, they strapped me onto a scoop stretcher and lifted me into the ambulance.

A uniformed policeman had hovered nearby throughout, and he now came into the ambulance with me.

"Can you tell me what happened?" he asked.

"I was hit by a car," I replied. "And it was on purpose."

"Are you sure?"

"Positive."

At this point, one of the paramedics told the policeman to leave. When the policeman objected, he was told in no uncertain terms that if he wanted to speak to me further, he would have to do it at the hospital. There were tests that had to be run, the paramedic explained, and the patient needed to be calm and untroubled for them.

Calm and *untroubled*, however, were not the terms that would instantly spring to my mind to describe how I was feeling.

Despite breathing the nitrous oxide mixture for several minutes, my ankle and foot still hurt like hell, and I was also worried that Black Shoes might come back to finish off what he'd started. I was quite certain that he hadn't just packed up and gone meekly home, and I would have much preferred the policeman to have remained with me as my bodyguard.

The paramedic took my temperature, pulse, and breathing rate—all normal. Next he measured my blood/oxygen level—ninety-eight per cent; and finally, he took my blood pressure, which was through the roof at 205/130.

"It's the pain," he assured me, nodding. "Pain always puts blood pressure up."

I wondered why that was, but I'd take his word for it.

"Can't you give me something stronger than this?" I asked, holding up the plastic mouthpiece.

He inserted a cannula into the back of my left hand and pumped in some morphine.

Bliss.

I closed my eyes and drifted away.

* * *

The ambulance took me to the Emergency Room at Adden-brooke's Hospital in Cambridge, where an orthopaedic surgeon tut-tutted over my sideways foot for about ten minutes before grabbing it with both hands and snapping the ankle back into its proper place.

Those ten minutes were meant to give the ketamine, which he had injected through the cannula in my left hand, time to work. But I still felt it all right when he grabbed my foot. And how.

I heard the noise too—a great clunking sound as the ankle slipped back into position, perceived by my brain more via the bones in my body than actually through my ears.

"There," said the surgeon with a smile. "That looks better."

It felt better too, much better. It had been like clicking a light switch, turning off the pain. What joy!

"We'll put that ankle in a plaster cast for now and then get a CT scan to ensure everything's back in the right place. Provided the scan's clear, you can go home."

"How long will the plaster be on for?" I asked.

"Depends on what the scan shows. The X-ray didn't show any obvious fractures, but something might have been hiding, or you may have a tear in a ligament or a tendon. They don't show up on X-rays. If the scan shows you're clear, then the plaster can come off, but it might be best to keep it on for tonight, and maybe over the weekend. In fact, the longer the better. It will give your stretched ligaments a chance to recover. We don't want that ankle dislocating again, now do we?" He laughed.

No, I thought, *we certainly do not.*

"But if there is a fracture or a tear, the plaster will be on for six weeks. That's assuming you don't need immediate surgery to repair it."

The surgeon left the cubicle and was soon replaced by a nurse with the plaster trolley.

"I thought plaster of Paris was a thing of the past," I said, as the nurse pulled a sleeve stocking over my leg up to my knee.

"Still the best thing for this job," she said as she wrapped wet plaster-impregnated bandages round my leg on top of the stocking. "It moulds very easily, so you get a good tight fit."

"There," she said, stepping back and admiring her handiwork. "That will set quickly now. Try and keep it as still as you can."

After I had been lying there totally still for about twenty minutes, a porter arrived to take me for the CT scan, pushing the bed along the corridor to the radiography department.

Afterwards, the same porter wheeled the bed, with me on it, back to the ER, where the uniformed policeman from earlier was waiting for me.

He introduced himself as PC Langford before pulling forward a plastic chair to sit on beside the bed.

"Is it broken?" he asked, indicating towards my plastered left leg.

"I hope not," I replied. "Nothing showed up on an X-ray. My ankle was dislocated. The doctor put it back in place, and I've just had a scan to confirm it's now in the correct position."

He nodded while removing a notebook and pen from the pocket of his yellow high-visibility jacket. He made a note, then looked at me.

"Now then, sir," he said formally, "can you please tell me exactly what happened this evening that resulted in you ending up under that van?"

I went through the whole incident from start to finish, missing nothing.

"And are you sure that the person in the black shoes wasn't just coming back to check you were all right after hitting you accidentally?"

"He tried to reverse over me. There's no doubt about it."

"Could he have just not seen that you were lying on the ground behind his car?"

I stared at the officer. "I'm telling you, the man was trying to kill me."

His expression clearly indicated that he thought I was being overly dramatic, which I wasn't.

"Now, why would anyone want to kill you?" he asked, his voice full of cynicism and disbelief.

It was a very good question, and it was the one that I had been mulling over in my own mind for the past hour.

Who was on my short list?

Elliot Mitchell was clearly there, but murder was a huge step up from a little bit of collusive bidding, or even committing an insurance fraud. Brian Kitman was in the same category.

Did I mention them to PC Langford?

The only other candidate I could think of was Nigel Stanhope, but had I really upset him enough for him to try and kill me? I remembered the smile on his face when I took over from him at the rostrum. Was he smiling because he was already planning to get rid of me permanently?

"I have been having a little trouble at work," I said, "but I can't see how it would have led to this."

"What sort of trouble?" the policeman asked.

"I made a complaint to my boss about another employee earlier today."

"What is the name of the person you complained about?" he asked.

"Nigel Stanhope," I said. "He's a fellow auctioneer at the horse sales."

He wrote it down.

"And what did your complaint involve?"

"I told my boss to tell Nigel to stop bullying me and other colleagues, and to stop making unwelcome sexual comments towards some of the female staff."

PC Langford wrote it all down in his notebook.

"And where does this Mr Stanhope live?"

"Somewhere in or around Newmarket. I don't know exactly, but you could find out from the sales company."

"I'll get it off the electoral register when I get back to the station," the policeman said, looking across at me. "Do you know if he owns a car?"

I shook my head. "I've no idea."

"Never mind. I'll find out from the DVLA website once I have his address."

The policeman made some more notes. He also took down all my own details—full name, postal and email addresses, date of birth, inside leg measurement—okay, not the last one, but he was pretty thorough, nevertheless.

"Phone number?" he asked.

I gave my number to him. "But I've lost the phone. I was looking at it when the car hit me, and I must have let it go. I certainly didn't have it with me under the van."

"Maybe it's still where you dropped it, or someone may have picked it up. I'll check if it's been handed in."

He made yet another entry in his notebook.

"It's in a black fold-over leather phone case," I said. "Together with about twenty pounds in cash."

He wrote that down.

"Credit or debit cards?"

"No," I said. "Well, yes, there's a digital version of my debit card on my phone."

The actual card was stored somewhere in my bedroom. I'd have to find it. I didn't use the actual card much at all anymore. I had always used my phone to pay for everything, even getting cash from the local supermarket.

At this point, the orthopaedic surgeon returned to the cubicle and asked the policeman to leave.

"I'll follow this all up, sir," PC Langford said to me, snapping shut his notebook as he stood up to depart. "I'll be in touch with you sometime tomorrow or, more likely, on Monday."

Weekends, I thought, with dismay.

If you tried to murder someone on a Friday evening, you would likely have at least sixty hours to get away and cover your tracks before anyone comes looking for you.

"Right, Mr Jennings," the surgeon said after PC Langford had departed. "That ankle of yours looks absolutely fine on the scan." He smiled at me. "It's back in the right position, and you have no fractures and, as far as I can see, no tears in the ligaments or the tendons either. You're a very lucky man."

I wasn't sure that I fully agreed with him. I didn't think that having someone out there trying to murder me was particularly lucky. But I suppose I was lucky that he had done no permanent damage to my foot in the attempt.

"So can you take this plaster off now?" I asked, lifting it up off the bed.

"It might be best to keep it on for a few days. You may not have torn anything, but the ligaments will have certainly been stretched. The plaster will provide some stability while they recover."

"Can't you give me one of those plastic support boots instead?"

He thought about it. "I suppose we could. And it would save you having to come back here next week to have the plaster removed."

"Great."

The same nurse who had applied the plaster was summoned to remove it. She didn't seem to mind that it had only been forty-five minutes since she had put it on. "It's not even fully hard yet," she said to me, smiling. "So it will come off really easily."

She attacked the plaster with a large cutting tool that reminded me of the tree-lopping shears Andrew Ingleby had used to slice through the ribs of the dead three-million-guinea yearling.

The thought of that made me shiver, right down to my plastered toes.

"Are you all right?" asked the nurse with concern.

"Yes, I'm fine," I replied.

But was I really fine?

It was just beginning to dawn on me that someone had actually tried to kill me. Even if PC Langford had his reservations, I was certain of it. Perhaps if I had indeed died or had been lying here with injuries far more grievous than simply a reduced dislocated ankle with no tears or fractures, the policeman might have taken things more seriously. He hadn't even brought in a special detective to investigate what I firmly believed was attempted murder.

The cutting tool made short work of the plaster, which was soon lying on the floor in several pieces.

"There," said the nurse, washing the final remnants of the white plaster off my leg. "That was easy. I'll go and fetch the boot."

She went off, leaving me alone inside the blue-curtained space, and I suddenly felt very vulnerable.

What if Black Shoes had hung around at the Beaumont Court garages, mingling with the other local onlookers to see what happened when the police and ambulance arrived? Perhaps he had then followed the ambulance to the hospital, and he was, even now, waiting outside for me to leave; or, worse still, he was hiding somewhere inside, close by, hoping to get another opportunity to bump me off.

The blue curtains suddenly parted, and I almost jumped off the bed in fright, but it was only the nurse coming back in with the plastic support boot, together with more of the sleeve stocking.

"You will still need to be careful," she said as she fitted the stocking and then tightened the boot round my calf and foot with the five Velcro straps. "You should keep it rested and elevated as much as possible to start with, to prevent swelling, and absolutely no running or jumping for at least two weeks."

"I promise not to run or jump," I replied, smiling at her.

"Now let's see if that ankle will take your weight."

I eased myself down from the bed to the floor. My ankle still felt sore, but it was more of a dull ache than anything acute, and the pain did not get noticeably worse when I stood on it.

"It may hurt occasionally," said the nurse, "especially if you've been walking on it a lot. You can take paracetamol for any pain and use an ice pack, if necessary, to reduce swelling."

"So I can remove the boot?"

She laughed. "You have to remove it to wash and also to sleep if it makes you more comfortable. When you put it on again, make sure the straps are tight, but not so tight they restrict the blood flow to your foot. Always check that you can feel your toes."

I tried walking around the bed, and it felt all right.

"Okay," said the nurse. "You can go home now."

"How? I have no money, no bank card, and no trousers."

"No trousers?"

"One of your colleagues was overzealous with a pair of surgical scissors when I first arrived. It was my best suit too."

I had worn it especially for my earlier morning meeting with the chairman.

Wow, that felt like a long time ago.

12

I N THE END, I went home by taxi, paid for in advance by a donation from the hospital's charitable travel fund.

"It's really designed for those who can't afford the continuous
trips back and forth to hospital for cancer treatment," explained
the guardian of the fund's purse.

"I promise I'll pay it back," I said.

Just as soon as I find my bank card, I thought.

Hence, I climbed into the taxi, just outside the hospital main
entrance, wearing a white shirt and my suit jacket—with my tie in a
pocket, a pair of light blue nursing scrubs trousers, one slightly scraped
polished black shoe on my right foot, and a grey plastic ankle support
boot on my left. In my hands I carried an NHS white plastic bag containing my other slightly scraped polished shoe, a single black sock,
and the remains of my suit trousers, in the hope that the Newmarket
invisible menders could salvage something from the wreckage.

The driver took the Babraham Road out of Cambridge
towards the A11, and I reckoned he must have thought I was a
prime candidate for the nearby Fulbourn Psychiatric Hospital
when I asked him to drive twice round the roundabout near the
city Park and Ride.

"It will add money on the meter," he complained, "and I've not
been paid for that."

"I want to check that I'm not being followed," I explained.

"Followed? Are you some sort of spy or something?"

"Something," I agreed.

"Bloody hell!" he said, looking over his left shoulder at me. "You're not a bloody Russki are you? Like them others?"

"What others?"

"The other Cambridge spies. You know, Burgess and Maclean and that other one, Phil someone."

"Kim Philby," I said, "but that was decades ago, and no, I'm not Russian nor a spy. I just want to check that I'm not being followed."

So he drove twice round the roundabout while I looked out through the back window to see if any other cars followed us round. They didn't.

I then made him do it again at the big roundabout just southwest of Newmarket, the one with the large rearing stallion sculpture at its centre, near the July Racecourse, but again there was no one behind us doing the same thing.

Satisfied that we were not being followed, I gave the driver directions to the garage area behind Beaumont Court, asking him to stop short of where I'd been hit, but to leave his headlights on so I could search for my phone.

"I can't stop for long, mind," he said. "I've not been paid for waiting time, and I've got another job soon, in Cambridge."

But he did stop long enough for me to have a good look around. I even bent down and tried to peer under the van where I'd previously hidden, but there was no sign of my phone or its case.

Dammit.

Next I asked the driver if he would move forward and round the corner so that the whole route to the building's front door was lit up by his headlights.

Predictably, he moaned again about the time it would take, and he wasn't being paid to wait.

"I would be most grateful," I said in my most ingratiating manner. "I really don't want to fall down the four steps in the dark with this bad leg. I'd probably end up back at the hospital."

Reluctantly, the driver did as I had asked, and I could see in the light from his headlamps that there was no one hiding, waiting to leap out at me.

I made it safely down the four steps, without incident, to the front door of the flats, turned and waved my thanks to the driver, and then let myself in. It was almost eleven o'clock, and I was three hours later arriving home than I had expected.

Alex was still up, and he was in the sitting room, watching the television.

"What the hell happened to you?" he asked without turning round as I went in. There was more than a touch of irritation in his voice. "I made supper. I had mine but yours will be totally ruined by now."

"I'm sorry," I said. "I couldn't help it. I've been in the ER at Addenbrooke's Hospital, having my ankle put back together after being hit by a car on the way home."

He jumped up and was full of apology.

"Why didn't you call me? I'd have come to collect you."

"I lost my phone."

"You could have borrowed one."

I laughed. "What makes you think I know your number off by heart?" I said. "Whenever I call you, I just touch 'Alex' in my contacts list."

"Did you lose it in the accident?"

"Yes," I said. "But it wasn't an accident."

He stared at me. "What do you mean?"

I described how the car had tried to run me over on purpose, and his eyes got bigger and bigger as I went on.

"Have you told the police?" he asked.

"I certainly have, but I don't think they really believed me."

I wondered if it was just me that people in authority didn't believe. First, the chairman doubted that I had really overheard the conversation in the gents', and now the police were sceptical that someone had tried to murder me.

"But why would anyone want to kill you?" Alex asked, echoing the doubts of PC Langford.

"Maybe I know something that someone doesn't want me to tell."

"What's that?" Alex asked.

What, indeed?

*   *   *

I had another restless night, and not just because of the ongoing ache in my ankle, which paracetamol had failed to entirely subdue.

On several occasions I woke in a cold sweat after dreaming that Black Shoes had broken into the flat and was standing over me with a pair of lopping shears, ready to slice through my ribs. Each time, I lay there in the dark, my heart pounding, listening for the slightest unusual noise, but all was normal.

As I tried to get back to sleep, I wondered about what I should do in the morning.

The easiest thing would be just for me to call in sick and stay in bed all day, with my left foot rested and elevated, just as the nurse had advised. But how would that help? If there was one thing that was becoming clear to me, and only one thing, it was that no one else other than me was going to find out anything, at least not before I lay dead somewhere on a roadside. Only then would the police take the risk to me seriously, and that would be too late, certainly as far as I was concerned.

So I would not lock myself away and hide. I couldn't do it forever, so I wouldn't even start.

I resolved to get up in the morning, go to work, and find out what the hell was going on.

*   *   *

"Please don't mention anything to anyone about what occurred last night," I said to Alex over a cereal-and-toast breakfast in his kitchen.

"Why on earth not?" he replied.

"I'd just rather not let anyone else know."

I wasn't really sure why. Perhaps I felt that if whoever was responsible saw me walking around as if nothing had happened, it would somehow be to my advantage and might even give me a clue as to who they were.

"But won't someone wonder why you're wearing that bloody great boot?" Alex asked.

"I'm not going to wear it," I said.

My ankle felt a lot better, and I had taken the boot off to sleep. I'd even been to have a pee in the night without wearing it, and I hadn't really noticed.

"You remember last year when I twisted my other ankle playing five-a-side soccer?"

He nodded.

"I bought an elasticated ankle support back then. I'm wearing that under my sock and I hope it will be enough."

"You're crazy," Alex said.

"Not as crazy as the person who tried to kill me."

I did, however, ask Alex to walk with me to work rather than going on my own. It wasn't so much that I thought I might need help walking or that my assailant might be so crazy to try again in broad daylight; it was simply to provide another pair of eyes in the search for my phone.

My ankle felt fine as Alex and I left the flat and negotiated the four steps up to the garage area.

"This is where it happened," I said to Alex as I stood on the exact spot where the car had hit me. "I was holding my phone at the time."

We searched everywhere, even pulling up some of the copious weeds that were growing in the narrow gaps between the tarmac and the red-brick end walls of the garage blocks, but there was no sign of the phone or its black leather carrying case.

"Can you get down and have a good look under that van for me?" I asked, pointing at the middle three of the builder's vans that were still parked in a line on the opposite side of the driveway. "I don't think my ankle's up to it."

"Is that where you ended up?"

"Sure is."

Together, we searched all around and under all three vans, and also over the wooden fence beyond them, but there was no sign of the phone. Alex even used a discarded pallet as a stepladder to look on the roof of the garages in case I had inadvertently thrown it up there as I was struck, but with no success.

"It's not here," he said finally.

"Bugger."

We simply don't realise how much our phones become an extension of our being until we lose them. They are not just the means to communicate by making calls or sending texts; they contain a record of our whole lives—photos of memorable moments, numbers of our contacts, our notes, our diaries, and our calendars. They guide us when we're lost and play calming music when we're agitated. They are the guardians of our sports and train tickets, can order us taxis, and even act as contactless bank cards. They show us the time and the weather, the cricket scores and racing results, and they even record how many steps we take each day, to say nothing of their role as our primary portals to the magic of email and the wonders of the internet.

My parents had given me a gold watch for my eighteenth birthday present, but I'd almost never worn it. My phone had always been my timekeeper, sounding alarms to wake me and providing me with reminders for my job.

Twice during the previous night, I had instinctively reached out for it, to tell the time, and twice I hadn't found it, only then remembering.

"I'll get a replacement later from the phone shop in the town."

And with luck, I thought, most of the missing information would be retrievable to my new phone from the iCloud, wherever that might be floating. But it was all a bore, and not least because my current long winning streak at my favourite word game would be lost.

"Maybe it was picked up and handed in," Alex said.

"Where to?" I asked. "Newmarket Police Station closed years ago. No one would bother to take my phone all the way to Bury St Edmunds. It's half an hour away by car."

"You never know," he said, trying to be optimistic. "It may turn up."

"Or it may have been taken by whoever tried to run me over."

"What good would it do him? You must have a security lock on it."

"Only the usual four-digit one or my thumbprint. And there are plenty of computer programs you can download from the internet to unlock phones."

"But doesn't everything stored get wiped?"

"Not always. The police certainly have a way of opening phones without losing what's on them. That's how they know where suspects have been and who they've been talking to."

I tried to think if my phone contained anything that I wouldn't want my would-be assassin to see. Only the digital version of my debit card that was in the phone's "wallet." At least I'd eventually found its physical twin brother, tucked into the front pocket of my suitcase.

Maybe I should contact my bank to ask them to cancel the digital version, but that might also cancel the physical card as well, and then I'd have nothing left with which to pay for anything.

"So what do we do now?" Alex asked.

"We go in to work as if nothing had happened," I replied. "Remember to say nothing to anyone."

"If that's what you really want," he said in a rather disappointed tone.

He clearly felt that I was depriving him of a piece of juicy gossip to share with his mates amongst the executive assistants.

"Please, Alex," I insisted. "It is what I want, and it may be very important. If anyone asks, feign ignorance, and then tell me about it as soon as possible. Someone may have seen the police and ambulance lights, but even so, they are unlikely to know that it was me who needed them."

"Okay," he said with resignation.

Alex and I walked together down Queensbury Road and went into the sales complex via the pedestrian gate. So far, so good, as far as my ankle—and everything else—was concerned.

"We still need to have our chat," I said to Alex as we went in. "We'll do it over the weekend."

He sighed. "I can't. I have to go home tomorrow. To Stourbridge home. It's Dad's sixtieth birthday on Sunday, and my mum has arranged a bloody great lunch party for all their awful friends. She wants me there to help."

"What does your father do?" I asked.

"He's a lawyer. A solicitor. In Stourbridge." He threw his hands up. "God, I don't want to go back there."

"But it will make a nice change from Newmarket."

He gave me a sideways look, almost of panic.

"What do I say to them about me being gay?"

"Don't say anything," I said adamantly. "Only tell them when you're ready. You need to work things out in your own head first."

"But Mum will keep on asking me if I've found a girlfriend yet."

"Just say, no, you haven't. You don't have to tell her anything else."

He shook his head. "You don't realise what she's like."

I inwardly smiled at the irony. Janis's mother didn't want her to have a boyfriend at all, while Alex's mother was desperate for him to have a girlfriend—any girlfriend—in order to give her grandchildren.

How about my own mother?

I think she had given up hope of me ever producing any heirs to the family debts, but I certainly hadn't. I longed to have a long-term, loving relationship and maybe even to eventually become a father.

Such thoughts made my mind wander to Janis. If Alex were away tomorrow night, I would have the flat to myself. What chance would there be of enticing her into my bed?

"See you later," Alex said as he peeled away towards the sales admin section.

I watched him go. Could I trust him to stay silent about last night?

Probably not, but I had no other option.

13

WITH IT BEING a day off between the Book 1 and Book 2 sales, the whole place felt less busy than it had been over the past three days.

However, with over fifteen hundred more yearlings due to be auctioned in the coming week, about half of which were already standing in the stables, ready to be vetted by potential purchasers or their agents, there were plenty of people still about. Hence, the cafeteria was doing brisk breakfast business, with small groups at each of the tables, huddled close together in deliberation.

I bypassed them all and went through the main building and up the stairs to my shared office.

Nigel Stanhope was there ahead of me.

"Morning, Nigel," I said cheerfully as I went in. "You're here early."

"No rest for the wicked," he said without looking up from what he was working on. "Thanks to you, I have to write my lines: *I must not bully my colleagues, I must not bully my colleagues, I must not bully my colleagues.*"

I could tell he was angry with me, but for now, he had a grip on his emotions.

I looked down at his feet beneath the desk.

He was wearing black shoes. Highly polished black shoes with black laces neatly tied in a bow. Not the same black shoes as I'd seen last night, but that didn't mean anything.

I sat down at my desk and opened my computer.

The auctioneer roster for next week's sales had been sent out in advance, so each of us knew for which lots we would be on the rostrum.

The printed catalogue provides potential buyers with a huge range of information concerning a horse's pedigree, going back at least three generations, and details of the racing performance of antecedents and siblings. And while we had to be ready to sell any horse at any time, it helped to have prepared a few things to say as the animal made its way into the ring. It was also necessary to have some idea of the expected purchase price, and any vendor reserve, in order to know where to start the bidding.

I opened my file for the Book 2 sale and started to make some notes about the horses I would be selling.

"I had a visit from a policeman at seven o'clock this morning," Nigel said, interrupting my thoughts. "He wanted to inspect my car."

"What for?" I asked, trying hard to control my racing heart.

I took it all back about the police not really believing me, or caring.

"He seemed to think that it might have been involved in a hit-and-run incident yesterday evening."

"And was it?" I asked, keeping my voice as level as possible.

"No, of course not," he replied indignantly. "I drove straight home from work and remained there all evening."

"What did the policeman look for?" I asked.

"Damage to the front, apparently, and particularly to the windscreen."

"And was there any?"

"He found a small crack in the windscreen, but I told him it was the result of a stone hitting it, and it's been there for ages. I've been meaning to get it fixed for weeks."

Did I believe him?

Did the policeman believe him?

"Was anyone hurt?" I asked.

"The policeman didn't say. He just took some photographs and then went away."

"How strange."

We went back to our own silent deliberations of the upcoming Book 2 sale.

If Nigel had been the person responsible for trying to run me over, why would he have mentioned the policeman's visit? Or had he been fishing for a reaction?

I found it difficult to concentrate on extended pedigrees, sibling racing form, and potential auction starting prices when someone out there was trying to kill me.

After a mostly unproductive forty-five minutes or so, when the clock on the office wall had crawled round to half past nine, I stood up and walked down the corridor to Accounts. As I had hoped, Janis was at her desk, together with four other young women, all busy typing furiously into their computers.

"Hi, Janis," I said as I put my head round the door. "Do you have a moment?"

She stood up, looked at the others, and then came out into the corridor.

"A couple of things," I said. "Firstly, would you like to come to the races with me tomorrow afternoon?"

"Newmarket races?"

"Yes," I said. "And we could go for dinner afterwards." If I could find a table anywhere, I thought. "Or maybe we could get a takeaway."

"At your flat?" she asked.

"Yes. If you'd like."

"How about your flatmate?"

"He's away for the night. He's going home for his dad's sixtieth birthday party. You could stay over if you wanted to."

I couldn't believe how forward I was being, and I don't think Janis could either.

"You seem to have it all planned out nicely," she said with a laugh.

"Only if you say yes."

"Okay. Yes to the races, and yes to an early dinner, but no to a takeaway or to a sleepover. Not yet."

Not yet sounded promising. And it would do for now.

"Lovely," I said. "The first race is at half past one. If I pick you up from Soham at midday, we could have a bite of lunch at the course before racing."

"That sounds great," she replied, smiling. "I'll fix it with Mum."

She gave me her home address and her telephone number, not that I had a phone to call it on.

"I'm afraid you need to be ready to be heavily scrutinized when you arrive," she said.

"What happens if I fail her inspection?"

"I won't be coming with you to the races."

I laughed, but I could see in her face that she wasn't joking.

"Now, what was the other thing?" she asked.

"I was wondering if you could check the records to see if an entity called Starsign Bloodstock has ever consigned yearlings for sale here before this sale, or if they have an account with us."

"I can't. I got told off this morning. Mr Pollard said that I had a legal responsibility to keep details of our clients' financial arrangements confidential, and I shouldn't have been disclosing them to a third party."

"I'm hardly a third party," I said. "I work for the same organisation."

"He told me that I should only be discussing account information with him or with other members of my team, and only then if it was absolutely necessary. He said that it is his job, as the company finance director, to report such matters to the board or to anyone else who needs them, and not mine."

"I'm so sorry," I said. "That was entirely my fault. I should never have mentioned your name to him. Don't worry, then, about Starsign. I'll ask Mr Pollard about it myself."

"I must get back," Janis said. "My manager wants us to have all the Book One accounts finished by the end of today, ready for the big rush next week."

Whereas there had been five hundred and forty lots over the three days of Book 1, almost three times that number would be offered for sale in the coming week, with each of the days starting earlier and finishing later. Big rush, indeed. Horses would be arriving and leaving from the horsebox loading area at all times of the day and night.

"Okay," I said, smiling at her. "I'll see you tomorrow at noon. And I promise to be on my best behaviour."

"You'd better be." She laughed and then disappeared back into her office.

I stood there in the corridor, joyful at the thought of spending all the following afternoon plus half the evening in Janis's company.

"What are you smiling at?" said a gentle Irish voice that brought me back from my daydreaming. Liam Barton, our man from County Donegal, was walking towards me.

"Oh, hi, Liam. I'm just happy, that's all."

"Lucky you. Wish I was."

"What's the problem?" I asked.

"Nothing for you to worry your little head about," he replied with a wry smile. "My personal business."

He went past me and down the corridor.

I didn't fancy going back to spending more time in an office with Nigel Stanhope, so I went down the stairs and outside into the fresh air.

The high pressure over Scandinavia had finally started drifting eastwards towards Siberia, allowing frontal systems from the Atlantic to encroach over the UK. The forecast for Newmarket, as shown earlier on my computer, was for increasing clouds during the afternoon and rain overnight. But for now, the sun was still shining as I wandered down the service road towards the lower stable yards.

My ankle felt a bit sore but was holding up all right, with the elasticated support under my sock doing its job.

A car swept around the far corner at speed towards me.

Oh God, I thought, *not again,* but the car slowed before reaching me, and turned into the car park. My heart rate slowly returned to normal. Surely, I was safe here in the sales complex, in broad daylight with so many other people about?

Nevertheless, I turned off the service road and went through the white-painted gate into the horsebox area with its multiple loading and unloading ramps. There were four horseboxes currently parked there, each of them unloading yearlings ready for the sale.

Two of my colleagues from the sales company were also in attendance, their clipboards and electronic tablets at the ready, booking in each new arrival. They first checked the animal's details against its passport, before giving the groom a lot-numbered metal badge to attach to the horse's head collar. A pair of round white stickers, with the lot number printed boldly on them in black, were then applied firmly to each side of the animal's hind quarters before it was taken away to its designated stable ready for inspection and vetting.

With such a large number of young horses arriving and leaving in rapid succession, many of them looking almost identical, it was inevitable that there would occasionally be mix-ups. Even with the numbered stickers and the head-collar badges, there had been several occasions when one horse had been sold as another, the error only coming to light months or even years later, when the horse arrived at the track to race, only for its microchip number not to match the official record.

I started to walk past the horseboxes.

I felt totally lost without a phone in my hand and had decided that I would nip out to one of the phone shops in the High Street and buy myself a cheap pay-as-you-go replacement, which would do for now. At least I would then be able to call Janis in the morning if I couldn't find her parents' house.

As I rounded the back of the last horsebox in the line, towards the exit onto The Avenue, I walked slap bang into Elliot Mitchell and Brian Kitman, who were deep in conversation.

They suddenly stopped talking, and both of them stared at me. I stared back.

In the night, I had resolved to find out what the hell was going on, and now seemed like as good a time as any to start.

"So are you two busy hatching your next little scheme?" I said.

"And what do you mean by that?" Elliot asked rather pompously. Kitman, meanwhile, remained silent.

"I think we both know what I mean."

"I am sure I don't," Elliot replied, all innocently. "We were simply discussing a list of potential purchases for some of Brian's owners."

Brian nodded, as if in agreement.

"And were you also deciding which of them to bid up to ridiculous levels?" I asked.

"I don't like your tone, young man," Brian Kitman said, finally finding his tongue.

"And I don't like being taken for a fool," I replied. "Bid them up, insure them, and then collect a hefty payment when they die." I paused and looked at them closely—not a black shoe between them.

"How did you do that exactly?"

"Do what?" Elliot said.

"Kill the horse without leaving a trace for the vet to find."

Kitman looked somewhat anxious, but Mitchell remained stony-faced, even smiling slightly in his eyes, as if he was rather proud of what he had managed to do.

"I have absolutely no idea what you're talking about," Elliot said calmly. "And if you repeat that accusation to anyone else, I will sue you for slander."

"I would only be slandering you if I said something that was untrue, and we all know it isn't. You can't sue me for telling the truth, however much you might not like to hear it."

Kitman's anxiety deepened, lines furrowing his brow and beads of sweat appearing in his hairline.

"Come on, Brian," Elliot said, taking him firmly by the arm and steering him away. "We've heard enough of this nonsense."

I almost laughed as they walked away.

If I'd had the slightest doubt beforehand that the two of them were both up to their necks in sharp practice, Kitman's reaction had just proved it.

He was clearly the weaker of the two.

I reckoned that if I could just twist their little chain a little bit more, Kitman might just be the link that snapped.

CHAPTER

14

I BOUGHT THE CHEAPEST iPhone I could find—by a distance.

"I have a couple of old 'eights' left in the storeroom," said the shop assistant. "I suppose I could let you have one of those."

He had been trying his best to sell me the most recent top-of-the-range model for over a thousand pounds. I tried to explain to him that it was far too expensive, but he wasn't to be deterred. Eventually, I stood up and started to walk out of his shop. Only then did he change his tune.

"How much?" I asked.

"As a company, we don't sell the eights anymore, so I'll have to look it up. The two I have left somehow never got sent back to the warehouse."

He went into the back of the shop but soon reappeared.

"You can have one for a hundred and sixty pounds," he said to me quietly, "as long as you take a thirty-day preloaded SIM with it."

I looked at his fellow shop assistant, who was busy with another customer.

"A hundred for cash," I replied, equally quietly.

"Hundred and forty." He was almost whispering.

"A hundred and twenty is my top and final offer. And for that, you also have to set it up for me."

"Okay," he said. "Deal."

I walked down the road to the cashpoint outside Lloyd's Bank while he unpacked the phone from its sealed box and inserted the SIM card. But only when I was completely satisfied that the phone was operating properly, did I hand over the hundred and twenty in cash.

He again disappeared into the back and shortly returned with my receipt, which, I noted with amusement, was only for the pre-loaded SIM, at ten pounds.

"That SIM gives you ten gigabytes of data on 4G, and thirty days of unlimited calls and texts to UK numbers," he said. "After that, you'll need to renew to make calls or send texts, but unused data will roll over."

"How do I renew?"

"You can do it online via our website, or bring it back here."

"Will it automatically download all my stuff from iCloud if I enter my Apple ID?"

"Sure, but do it when you're connected to Wi-Fi, or you'll just instantly use up all your data."

"Okay, thanks. I will."

*   *   *

With my new phone safely stowed in my trouser pocket, I made my way back to my office without incident.

Nigel was still there.

"Ah," he said as I went in. "The wanderer returns at last. The chairman's been looking for you."

He made it sound like I was in trouble.

I walked down the corridor to the chairman's office and knocked on the door.

"I hear you've been looking for me," I said, opening it with trepidation.

"Ah, yes, Theo, I have. Come on in."

At least he was smiling, which I took to be a good sign.

"I have looked up Starsign Bloodstock for you. It seems it is a small Irish entity from Cashel, in County Tipperary."

"Does the registration give any names of the individuals involved, such as its directors?" I asked.

"No, but that's not at all uncommon for non-incorporated businesses in Ireland. We deal with them quite a lot. Many are just small farms with one or two broodmares."

"So it could be anyone?" I said, exasperated. "Someone just invents a business name and hides behind it. Do they have a bank account?"

"They must have, but I have no details. It appears that they have requested payment for the horse, if sold, by cheque."

"Is that normal?"

"No, not normal, but it's also not that unusual. We encourage all payments nowadays to be made via direct bank transfer. Makes it much easier to comply with the money-laundering requirements. I am sure we will have asked Starsign for their bank details, but a few payments are still made by cheque, as of course they all were not that very long ago."

It still sounded very suspicious to me.

"I suggest you set aside your concerns of this matter now," the chairman said. "It is time to concentrate on your preparation for Books Two, Three, and Four."

"Okay," I said, not meaning it. "But can I please have that letter from you confirming that I have informed you of my belief that Elliot Mitchell and Brian Kitman are together guilty of collusive bidding? You said yesterday that you would get your secretary to type it up this morning."

He sighed. "Is that really necessary?"

"Yes," I replied. "It is. Otherwise, I will have no option but to seek legal advice from the Bloodstock Industry Forum Panel Lawyer, as printed in our catalogues."

I could tell he wasn't at all happy with my answer. The panel lawyer was there for anyone to approach if they had doubts about the probity of a sale, a sort of bloodstock-industry-paid-for whistle-blowing service.

"Very well," he said with another sigh. "Will a handwritten one suffice?"

"Yes. I suppose so."

He sat at his desk and wrote on a piece of the sales company–headed notepaper. He handed it to me, and I read it.

This is to confirm that Theodore Jennings has indicated to me that he believes that Elliot Mitchell and Brian Kitman were guilty of collusive bidding at the Book 1 sale earlier this week. After a thorough investigation, I have found no compelling evidence to support Theo's assertion, but as requested by him, I provide this note as a record of his discussion with me.

He had signed and dated it.

I folded it up and put it in my pocket with my new phone.

"Thank you."

As a legal document, it probably wasn't worth the paper it was written on, but it made me feel better, even if I didn't accept that the chairman had performed much of an investigation, and certainly not a thorough one, as he had stated in his note.

I went back to my office to continue my preparation for the upcoming sales. Nigel was still there, and he looked up as I came in.

"Why are you limping?" he asked.

I hadn't realised I had been. It was obviously time for more paracetamol.

"I twisted my ankle last night," I said. "I tripped down the steps at the back of my flat."

"You mean Alex Cooper's flat," he corrected, rather pleased with himself.

"Okay, Alex Cooper's flat. So where do you live?"

"Why do you want to know?"

"No reason. I'm just curious."

"That's your problem, young Theo. You're far too curious in all sorts of ways."

He laughed, but I tried to ignore him and concentrate on the yearlings' pedigrees.

"I live on Studlands Park Avenue, off the Fordham Road," Nigel said after a while. "Just past the Tesco supermarket and the Burger King."

"Nice," I said.

"Not really. It's very industrialised round there, and the Fordham Road is so busy, especially in the mornings. It can take me ages even to get out onto the roundabout."

I found the whole conversation somewhat strange. We had never "chatted" like this before. Was he trying to befriend me so that I didn't complain about him again to the chairman?

I was about to get up and go out again, when he stood up.

"Fancy a coffee?" he asked.

I looked up at him. In three years he had never once asked if I wanted a coffee. Previously, he had always just gone and fetched one only for himself.

"Why Mr Nice Guy all of a sudden?" I asked.

He leaned his head to one side, as if thinking. "I'm not sure. Perhaps I underestimated you."

Perhaps he had thought he could stamp on me, just like stepping on a spider, but I had bitten back. That was because I was no ordinary spider, more like a scorpion.

"Thank you," I said. "White, with no sugar."

While he went out to fetch the coffees, I logged on to the company Wi-Fi on my phone. I selected the correct buttons in the settings, and as if by magic, all my contacts, my calendar, my apps, and even my photos downloaded from the cloud.

I was back in business.

I added Janis's number to my contacts and included it in my favourites.

Suddenly life felt good again.

Such a pity it didn't last.

*   *   *

At the end of the afternoon, I waited for Alex to come and collect me from my office before walking home with him.

"How's the ankle?" he asked as we passed the point where I had been attacked.

"Quite sore. I'm going to stay in tonight and rest it."

"We could have a takeaway Chinese from The Fountain, if you like? I'll collect it."

"That would be great."

So Alex and I spent the evening at home, eating Peking duck pancakes followed by beef in black-bean sauce with fried rice, while I sat on the sofa with my left leg raised up on a pillow placed on the coffee table.

"Did you have a good day," I asked him.

"This Friday is always a bit of a nothing day between the sales. I spent most of the afternoon shifting bloody great packs of Book Two and Book Three catalogues from the stores into the main building. It's not right. I'm supposed to be here to be trained to become an auctioneer, not to act as a bloody manual labourer."

I laughed at his turn of phrase, and he eventually smiled back.

"So are you ready for the weekend?" I asked.

He sighed. "As ready as I'll ever be."

"Have you got your father a birthday present?"

"I'll stop and buy him a bottle of whisky on the way. He likes his single malt." He sighed again. *"Here you are, Dad—get drunk on this because I'm gay."*

"Stop it," I said sharply. "There is no reason for you to say anything to your parents. Not yet anyway."

"Why not? Perhaps I'll announce it in the middle of the birthday lunch: *"Hello, everybody, hands up if you're gay like me."* At least it would make it a party to remember."

"You will do no such thing. How long have your parents known you?"

He looked confused that I should ask. "Obviously since I was born."

"Exactly. So, after twenty-four years they must know you pretty well. Maybe even better than you know yourself. You might be surprised at what they really think. Perhaps your mother keeps asking if you have a girlfriend because she knows, deep down, that you might be gay, and she's waiting for you to say so." I paused. "She surely must have some inkling, if only because you have never had one. Maybe it would even be a relief for her to know for sure, one way or the other."

He looked at me. "You're joking, right?"

"No. I'm not. But you need to tell them when you, and you alone, are ready, and not just because you are with them this weekend. Leave it for now. You need to be content in yourself first."

"What do you mean by that?" he asked.

"You said to me yesterday that you have always suspected that you're gay."

"Yes. Well, I think I am."

"You don't seem very certain. I suggest you have a relationship with someone, to see if it makes you happy."

"You mean with a man?"

I laughed. "Yes, of course with a man."

"How?"

"Is there a gay bar in Newmarket?"

"I doubt it. There's not very many openly gay people in horse racing."

That was true.

"Then go to Cambridge," I said. "There must be some gay bars there, what with all those students."

"I'm not so sure," he said slowly, pondering.

"But you must be sure, Alex, and especially before you say anything to your mum and dad."

As I must also be sure, I thought, *about Mitchell and Kitman before I say anything to the police.* And I nearly was.

CHAPTER

15

I PARKED MY CAR outside Janis's family home in Soham at five
minutes to midday on Saturday morning, having used the maps
app on my new phone to find it.

I was dressed in an open-necked white shirt and my second-
best suit, the trousers of my best one having been deposited on the
way at the local "invisible mender," although he had claimed that
they were really beyond repair, even for him.

"Just do your best," I had urged him.

"It would have been easier if the cuts had been made down
the seams," he had mused, shaking his head. "Give me a week
and I'll see what I can do."

Alex had departed for his weekend in Stourbridge after breakfast, seemingly a little happier than he had been the previous
evening.

"Remember," I had said to him, as he was leaving, "don't say
anything to anyone."

"That seems to be your mantra," he had replied with a smile.

Janis's front door opened before I had a chance to ring the bell.

"I saw you arrive from my bedroom window," she said, smiling. "I was waiting for you."

"So, are you ready?"

"I will be in a minute. You'd better come in first."

For inspection, I thought.

Janis led me down the hallway to the kitchen, where a woman that I took to be in her fifties was standing by the stove, in an apron, stirring whatever was in a saucepan on the hot plate.

"Hello, Mrs Thompson," I said, extending my right hand. "I'm Theo Jennings. I work with Janis at the sales company in Newmarket."

She wiped her own hand on her apron and shook mine. As she did so, she literally looked me up and down, and seemed to approve of what she saw. She smiled, but it lacked any warmth and didn't reach her eyes.

"Janis tells me you are taking her to Newmarket races."

"Yes," I said. "And then afterwards for dinner at Unico's."

"How lovely. And what time is your reservation for dinner?"

"Six thirty."

It was the only time, and at the only restaurant, that I could find a free table in all of Newmarket.

"Good," Mrs Thompson said. "So Janis will be home by nine at the latest."

"I thought we might go for a nightcap at the Bedford Lodge Hotel after dinner, if that's all right. I promise she'll be home by ten thirty."

"I think nine o'clock is quite late enough. I don't want her coming to any harm."

"Janis won't come to any harm, Mrs Thompson. I will make sure of that."

Although how could I make sure of it? I thought, when I couldn't even prevent myself being struck by a hit-and-run driver in my own driveway.

In the end, she agreed to allow Janis to be out with me until nine thirty.

"Phew," I said, when we were both safely in my car with the doors closed.

"You did well," Janis said, waving to her mother, who stood in the front doorway as I drove away. "All morning she has been umming and ahhing about whether to let me go at all."

"But you're a grown woman, not a child. You should be able to make your own decisions about where you go and with whom."

"Mum makes it quite clear that while I am still living under her roof, I have to abide by her house rules."

"And what if you don't? She's hardly going to throw you out."

"I couldn't do that to her," Janis said miserably.

I began to have some sympathy for Darryl, Janis's former boyfriend.

"Okay," she said, snapping out of her moroseness, "where are we going?"

I fleetingly looked across at her. "To the races, unless you have somewhere else in mind." My mind was running away with places I would like to take her, most of which involved a large double bed and a chilled bottle of champagne.

"I meant whereabouts at the races. Which enclosure?"

I swallowed my disappointment.

"The Premier Enclosure," I said with a smile.

"Ooo-er, who's a clever boy, then. I'd heard they were all sold out."

"They were, but I managed to get a pair of complimentaries. It seems the sales company is sponsoring one of the races, and part of the deal was to have some Premier Enclosure free tickets. Barbara on Reception gave them to me, as all the directors are going to a box for lunch."

"Perhaps we can gatecrash it," Janis said, laughing mischievously.

But perhaps not, I thought. I'd pushed my luck far enough this week.

I parked in the Premier Enclosure car park—free pass also provided by Barbara.

"Help," Janis cried. "I can't get out." She was pulling furiously at the broken door handle.

"That doesn't work. I'll open it from the outside."

I climbed out of the driver's door and then went swiftly round to her side and let her out. "Sorry about that. I don't usually have passengers, so I haven't bothered to get it fixed."

I locked the car, and we made our way in through the entrance archway and into the Premier Enclosure itself.

"Would madam care for some luncheon?" I asked in my most grandiose tone.

"That would be delightful, Jeeves," she replied, equally affected. "What's on the menu?"

"Burgers, bangers and mash, or fish and chips with curry sauce," I replied in full East End Cockney. "All created in high-class mobile kitchens—or food vans, to you and me."

Janis laughed.

"Or we could just have the meal that's included in our entry tickets."

"Sounds wonderful."

We made our way to the Carvery Lounge and even managed to acquire a table next to the window, thanks to some early birds who were already finished and just leaving as we arrived.

"This building was once the weighing room and jockeys' changing rooms," I said, "before they built the big new ones over on the far side of the paddock."

"When was that?"

"Years ago. Twenty-five at least."

We ate a sumptuous lunch of roast beef and Yorkshire pudding, together with roast potatoes, cauliflower cheese, carrots, parsnips, broccoli, and leeks.

"That was lovely," Janis said, putting down her knife and fork and clutching her full stomach. "I can't think I'll need another big meal in just six hours' time."

"I could cancel my dinner booking," I said. *And go to bed instead,* I thought fleetingly.

"No, leave it. I'm sure we'll want a little something by then." She smiled at me. "So what will win the first?"

We picked up our provided racecards and looked at the list of runners in the seven-furlong contest for fillies only, all of them three years old or older.

I noticed that number two, Halaveli, was trained by Brian Kitman. I scanned through the cards for all seven races. In total, there were four Kitman-trained runners during the afternoon, including one, Saffron Lady, in the big race at 2:40.

"Let's go and see the horses in the paddock," I said.

We went out of the old weighing room and across the freshly mowed grass towards the new one. There, we leaned on the white rail and watched the thirteen runners circulating.

"Which do you fancy?" Janis asked.

I thought of saying that I fancied her but . . .

"Number two," I said. "Let's move round a bit."

We moved to our left, bypassing a group of racegoers who had obviously had quite a liquid lunch and were quite worse for wear already, even before the first race. We found another space on the rail, this time quite close by to the connections of Halaveli, who were standing on the grass just inside the ring.

Brian Kitman was standing with two others, an older man in a tweed suit and a woman in a brown hat. The horse's owners, I thought. Presently, a jockey wearing blue and yellow silks came out of the weighing room and joined them.

Kitman was a tall man with a ramrod-straight back, and he towered over the diminutive jockey as he gave his last-minute instructions on how to ride the horse in the race.

The jockey had his back to me, with Kitman facing him, and me.

I stood up as tall as I could and stared at Kitman's face, and as often seemed to happen, his eyes drifted up over the jockey's blue-capped head and locked onto mine.

Twist, twist.

I lifted my fore and middle finger up to my own eyes, then pointed them straight at Kitman in the universal "I'm-watching-you" gesture.

Even at a distance of ten yards, I could see his face go pale under his trilby. He continued to stare straight at me, his eyes flickering slightly in his anxiety, before the lady in the brown hat touched his arm and he suddenly transferred his attention to her, as if she'd been speaking to him but he hadn't been listening.

An official rang a bell, and Kitman, together with the jockey, went over to horse number two as it continued to walk along. The jockey gathered the reins, and Kitman gave him a leg up, tossing his lightweight frame up onto the saddle in one smooth, easy, well-practiced movement.

As the horse moved away, Kitman stopped and turned round to look back at me. I hadn't taken my eyes off him for one second, and once again our eyes met. I just nodded at him, a very slight nod, hardly perceptible, but he saw it all right.

Twist, twist.

"Come on," Janis said, taking hold of my hand. "Let's go and have a bet."

We went through the main Millennium Grandstand and out to where the bookmakers were standing in a row, shouting their odds. She put five pounds to win on number seven, simply because she liked its name—Sunshine Lily—while I put five each way on Halaveli, each of us receiving a printed ticket in exchange for our money.

I noticed that neither of our choices was the favourite, Sunshine Lily being offered at sixteen to one, while Halaveli was priced at elevens on most boards. The favourite was much shorter priced, at just three to one.

"Where shall we watch it from?" I asked.

"Let's go down at the front," Janis said eagerly. "I love it when you can actually feel the horses' hooves thudding into the ground."

"How often do you come to the races?" I asked, quite surprised.

"Almost never these days, but I did a lot as a small child. Dad adored his racing, especially over the jumps. He used to love going to Huntingdon. He'd always take me with him, and we'd go down the course and stand next to a fence to watch the horses, and to feel them as they went past. It was very exciting."

"Does he still go?"

"Not anymore." She paused, as if deciding whether to go on. "Dad had his problems after the murders. Like a lot of people did in Soham. He started drinking far too much, and also he began to gamble heavily. So it was best if he didn't go to the races again."

The evil man who had murdered those girls had destroyed so many other lives in addition to the two young ones he had actually taken.

Neither Sunshine Lily nor Halaveli won the race in spite of Janis and I cheering them home at the top of our voices. The favourite won by two clear lengths, while the remainder of the field flashed past us in a single bunch, the vibration of their hooves on the turf reaching our feet with ease.

"Never mind," Janis said, pulling a sad face. "There are still six more races."

The official result was announced on the public address system.

"Halaveli was third," I said. "I backed it each way, so I won."

Janis clapped her hands together in excitement.

"How much?"

I looked at my printed slip. "Sixteen pounds for the place. But I put ten pounds on altogether, so I'm six pounds up. You lost five, so, together, we're still ahead by a pound!"

She beamed. "Let's celebrate."

"In a while," I said. "I want to see the horses come in to the unsaddling enclosure first."

We rushed back through the grandstand and arrived just before the horses.

There was quite a crush as many happy punters tried to get close to the place designated for the winner, to cheer her in, but I wanted to be elsewhere, right next to the "third place" pole, where it was much less busy. Hence Brian Kitman saw me as soon as he arrived with the horse's owners.

He stopped dead and frowned.

Twist, twist.

*   *   *

The second race on the card was the one sponsored by our sales company, where all the runners had to have been auctioned by us as yearlings at our sales last year. The weight each of them was to carry on their backs was determined by their sale price—the higher the price, the greater the weight.

Peter Radway, the company chairman, was in the paddock before the race, greeting some of the connections of the twenty-seven two-year-old horses that were vying for a share of the hundred-and-fifty-thousand-pound purse.

Brian Kitman did not have a runner in this race, so I wasn't particularly looking out for him, but there was a major bonus, as far as I was concerned, with the appearance in the paddock of Elliot Mitchell. He was standing right in the centre with two men aged about forty, each of them wearing a slim-fit dark suit and sunglasses.

As I watched, Peter Radway walked over to them, and I could tell that Elliot was introducing him to the others. Hands were shaken all round.

I felt a slap on my left shoulder and half turned my head—Liam Barton.

"Bejesus, doesn't it make you proud to see our boss hobnobbing with the rich and famous?"

"Who are they?"

"The nearest thing we have in Ireland to royalty. Pop stars. Members of an Irish boy band from the early 2000s. Had a whole string of mega hits, especially in the States. They're new to horse ownership, mind. Elliot bought this one for them at our last year's October Book Three sale, and I reckon he's now after more of their business, and more of their money."

"Which one is theirs?" I said, looking down at the racecard I was holding.

He laughed. "Which do you think?"

I scanned through the list of runners. Number four caught my eye.

"Platinum Album?"

"One and the same."

The horse's owners were named in the racecard as Ronan Drew and Shane Clayton. I'd never heard of them, but I turned to Janis, who was standing on the other side of me from Liam.

"Have you ever heard of Ronan Drew and Shane Clayton?" I asked her.

"Yeah, of course," she replied excitedly. "They're members of Ultra High. I absolutely love them. I worshipped them as a teenager."

"That's them over there, standing with Elliot Mitchell and Peter Radway."

Much to my chagrin, Janis switched all of her attention from me to them, almost swooning over them.

"Can we go and meet them?" she asked almost breathlessly. "Can we? Can we? Please. Please."

"I don't see why not," I said. "Let's give it a go." And it would get me close to Elliot Mitchell, and that was my aim, even if it wasn't Janis's. "Are you coming, Liam?"

"I think I won't be. I have other people to see."

"Okay, but there is one other thing I'd like to ask. Have you ever been to Cashel, in County Tipperary?"

He slowly shook his head. "No way. I'm from Donegal, remember, way up in the north, even farther north than Northern Ireland. From there it's a long way to Tipperary." He sang it, like the song, laughing. "Why do you ask?"

"Because that's where Starsign Bloodstock are based. You know, the consignor of the three-million colt."

Janis was getting impatient, and she kept pulling at my sleeve.

I took her by the hand, and we walked purposefully over towards the gap in the rail used for pedestrian entry to the paddock. It was guarded by a stern-looking official from the racecourse.

"Don't stop, and don't look at the gateman," I said to her quietly. "Just keep walking as if you have every right to be here."

I held Janis's hand tightly and marched through the opening without looking at the official.

"Hold on a minute, sir," he said firmly, trying to reach for the sleeve of my jacket. "Have you got a badge?"

"We're with the sponsors," I said, back over my shoulder, as I stood eagerly looking for a gap between the horses in order to cross into the centre.

I could sense the gateman's indecision and almost hear his thought processes as he weighed up his options: Did he stop us and make a fuss or just let us go in? A fuss might be embarrassing for him if he was wrong and we were indeed entitled to enter.

No fuss won.

"All right, sir," he said. "But mind the horses."

A gap opened up between two of them, and we quickly went through it, across onto the grass in the centre.

I noticed that Peter Radway had moved on, away from Elliot Mitchell and the two men, to speak to other owners. Perhaps that was a good thing.

As Janis and I walked over towards her musical heroes, I noticed that they had been joined by Nick Walton, the local New-market trainer of the horse, someone I knew well by sight, as he was a regular bidder at auctions.

"Hi, Nick," I said, approaching him. "Theo Jennings from the sales company."

I held out my hand.

"Oh, hello, Theo," he replied with a slightly inquisitive look in his eyes.

"Just thought I'd put in an appearance," I said. "I was the auctioneer who sold this colt last year."

"Oh," Nick said, relaxing. "Well done."

I might or might not have been the one who sold the colt—I couldn't remember—but it was a good line anyway, and it seemed to do the trick.

"Who are the owners?" I asked innocently.

Nick introduced me to the two men in the slim-fit suits as the man who had auctioned their horse, and in turn I introduced Janis, who could hardly contain her excitement.

"I adore your music," she said to them. "Especially *Big Thunder Morning*. Totally love it. Play it all the time. My dad's a fan too. He loves all music. In fact, my name is Janis with an *i-s* at the end because he named me after Janis Joplin."

The two men seemed to be quite taken with her and were clearly enjoying her adulation.

"Would it be all right to have a photo?" Janis asked.

"Sure," they said.

Janis gave me her phone while she stood between her idols.

As I lined up the shot, Elliot Mitchell came up behind me.

"What the fuck are you doing here?" he asked into my ear.

I took the photo—several of them in fact—then turned my head to Elliot.

"I'm here to watch you," I said, whispering back.

Twist, twist.

16

MUCH TO ELLIOT Mitchell's obvious huge annoyance, Janis—with an *i-s*—and I were asked by Ronan and Shane—we were now on first-name terms—to come up to their box at the top of the main grandstand, to watch the race.

There were about ten other guests already there, mostly from the music business, with one or two I even recognised, and I was introduced to them all as the man who had sold the horse to Ronan and Shane.

"So you're a horse breeder," the woman on my left said loudly.

I smiled at her. "No, I was just the auctioneer that sold the horse at the sales."

Everyone laughed—everyone, that is, except Elliot Mitchell, who scowled.

"Drink?" Ronan asked.

"Just a small white wine, thank you," I replied. "I'm driving later."

Janis had a white wine as well, a large one, and she seemed to be in seventh heaven. I wondered how I was ever going to take her just to a local pizza restaurant for dinner after rubbing shoulders with this lot.

"Come on everybody," Shane shouted from the door to the balcony. "The race is about to start."

We all moved outside.

* * *

Platinum Album didn't win.

At one point it had looked like he might, and everyone on the balcony had been shouting and cheering for all they were worth, but he was beaten on the line by another carrying far less weight and with a much faster finish, deflating the excitement around me as instantly as a pin bursting a balloon.

"I suppose being second is not too bad," Ronan said to me with obvious disappointment as we went back into the box together.

"You still get prize money for coming second," I said. I looked at the racecard. "More than thirty grand of prize money."

It didn't cheer him up much.

"It's not the money that's important," he said, sounding like someone who has plenty of it. "It's the number-one slot that means everything. Same as in music. Number one, or nowhere."

"But Platinum Album might be the number one next time he runs. Racing's not just a one-time affair. He's still a very young horse with plenty of runs left in him. You never know—he might even be a world beater next summer."

He smiled at me. "But Elliot says that we need to pay a lot more money for our horses—that's if we want to own winners."

Elliot would say that, I thought.

"Expensive doesn't always equate to good in this game."

"He wants us to come with him to the sales this coming week, to buy four or five more."

"And will you?" I asked.

"We can't. I'm currently in the studio recording a solo album, and Shane's back in Ireland for a family gathering."

"There'll always be next year," I assured him. "Plenty more yearlings then."

"Elliot says he's quite prepared to buy the horses for us without our being there. And, after all, he is the expert." He laughed. "I mean, we wouldn't know a good one from a bad one without them racing against each other, now would we? They all look just the same to us." He laughed again.

Very rich, totally equine ignorant, and also not present at the sales.

They were exactly the sort of clients that all bloodstock agents dreamed of.

I looked through the glass front of the box, where Elliot was still outside, deep in conversation with one of the other guests.

I liked Ronan. For all his success and fame, he seemed very down to earth.

"Just be careful," I said to him. "You can spend a huge amount of money very quickly in the horse business."

Especially with Elliot Mitchell doing the bidding, I thought.

Ronan looked me in the eye. "Are you telling us not to go ahead?"

"No, I'm not saying any such thing. Why would I? My job relies on people buying horses. I'm just saying be careful. Learn some more about it. Enjoy running the one you have for a while. Maybe get another, or even two more, rather than splashing out on four or five all at once."

* * *

Everyone in the box went down to greet Platinum Album in the unsaddling enclosure, and Janis and I went along with them, but this time we stayed outside the white rails.

Word had clearly got round that music celebrities were afoot, because the crowd by the "second place" pole was very much larger than that for the winner.

Both Ronan and Shane were interviewed on camera by a national television host as if their horse had been victorious, while the owner of the actual winner had to console himself with the knowledge that he'd just collected eighty thousand pounds, which was more than he'd actually paid for the animal in the first place.

"Horses away," shouted an official, and the still-steaming heroes were led out, on their way back to the racecourse stables and a well-deserved rest.

Most of the box guests also drifted away. And while Ronan and Shane were still surrounded by press photographers on one side of the enclosure, Peter Radway presented the trophies to the winning connections on the other.

"Come on, Janis," I said. "Let's go and see the horses in the paddock for the next race."

I took her by the hand and steered her away, but she kept glancing back over her shoulder, perhaps longing for Ronan or Shane to summon her back.

But of course, they didn't. It was time to move on.

"That was great fun while it lasted," I said. "Have you looked at the photos I took?"

She took out her camera and opened the pictures. Thankfully, I hadn't cut off their heads, or caught any of them with their eyes shut, and she seemed to perk up a bit, even smiling at me.

"The other girls in the office are going to be soooo jealous."

We walked along and found a space on the paddock rail.

"This is the big race of the day," I said. "The Sun Chariot Stakes."

"They surely don't pull chariots," Janis said, making a face.

I laughed. "That would be a sight. No, the race is named after a horse called Sun Chariot. It won the fillies' Triple Crown back in 1942."

"What, during the Second World War? I'd have thought that all racing would have stopped."

"Most of it had, but a small amount was allowed to continue, to maintain the Thoroughbred bloodlines, because of course no one knew then how long the war was going to last."

The five annual Classic races for three-year-olds, including the Derby, the Oaks, and the St Leger, had all been run during the war at Newmarket, on the July course, as Epsom had been commandeered by the army as a training base, and Doncaster had been used as a prisoner-of-war camp. Aintree was also used to house prisoners, and Ascot became a German refugee internment camp, while many other racecourses around the country had been ploughed up to grow food.

"This racecourse," I said, "where we are now, was converted into an RAF base, with aircraft taking off and landing on the grass where the horses now race."

"Amazing," she said.

There were just nine runners in the Sun Chariot Stakes, all fillies or mares, so the centre of the paddock was a lot less congested with owners and trainers than it had been for twenty-seven of the previous races. According to the racecard, Brian Kitman's horse—number six, Saffron Lady—was owned by a syndicate, so it should be easy to spot him.

I searched and eventually found him standing in the midst of a large group of mostly middle-aged men, all of them wearing bright scarlet and blue scarves.

But Kitman had his back to me.

"Come on," I said to Janis. "Let's move round a bit."

"But I like it here," she replied, sitting down on one of the fixed stools.

"Okay," I said, stifling my slight irritation, standing just next to her.

So we stayed where we were, but I needn't have worried. Brian Kitman turned right round, as if searching. When he saw me, he stopped turning and stared at me. I stared back.

The nine jockeys appeared from the weighing room and walked over to the owners of their respective horses for the obligatory introductions and final instructions before the race. The one that joined the Kitman group was wearing bright scarlet and blue quartered silks. *Hence the scarves,* I thought.

An official rang the bell as the signal for the jockeys to get mounted, and as luck would have it, Saffron Lady was at that moment walking down the side of the paddock towards us.

The scarlet-and-blue-clad jockey walked over, and the trainer gave him a leg up onto the horse's back. As the horse moved on, Kitman was left standing just a few yards away from us.

"Go away," he shouted at me angrily. "Leave me alone."

"It's a free country," I replied much more quietly, but still loud enough for him to hear. "I can stand wherever I like."

"Leave me alone," he shouted at me again, clearly getting agitated.

"Tell me how the colt died," I said quietly but clearly. "Then I'll leave you alone."

He turned abruptly and marched away.

Janis looked up at me. "What the hell was all that about?"

"It's a long story."

"It's a long afternoon."

"I'll tell you after this race. Now let's go and have a bet."

We went through the grandstand to the betting ring, and Janis put another fiver to win on a horse she liked the name of, while I did the same on Saffron Lady, which I noticed was the betting favourite at six to four.

"Don't tell my mum that I've been gambling. She'd kill me."

Not a suitable turn of phrase, I thought, given quite a number of different circumstances.

"Five pounds isn't going to get you into trouble, and we're still ahead, remember."

"Only by one solitary pound."

We went up into the grandstand seats for the race, this one over a straight mile, starting away to our right, with the horses racing mostly head-on towards us. Fortunately a huge-screen television had been positioned opposite the grandstand, so we could tell which horse was leading right from the start.

The nine horses jumped out of the starting stalls pretty much in an even line, but the race soon developed into a tactical affair, with some of the jockeys dropping their mounts in behind others as they raced along the nearside running rail.

The straight mile on the Rowley course is largely flat, with only a few small undulations during the first five furlongs. Only after the horses reach "the bushes," a pair of large hawthorn bushes planted on the right-hand side of the track a little over two furlongs from home, do things change. Then the course runs gently down-hill for a furlong, into "the dip," before rising back up again steadily all the way to the finish line.

Only as the closely bunched field passed the bushes, did the race begin in earnest, with horses at the rear of the group being edged out wider, to give them a clear run for glory.

As they ran down into the dip, they were five or six abreast, each being ridden hard, but the climb to the line sorted them out, with the bright scarlet and blue silks of the favourite, Saffron Lady, easing away for a three-quarter-length victory, much heralded by the cheering crowd.

Brian Kitman, for all his faults, certainly knew how to train winners, and winners of big races like this. Why on earth was he also involved in killing a horse as part of some sordid insurance fraud?

Perhaps I should go and ask him.

* * *

We went down to the unsaddling enclosure, but by the time we arrived, there was already a three- or four-deep crowd around the rail next to the place reserved for the winner. That, together with all the scarlet-and-blue-scarved members of the rapturous syndicate celebrating inside the enclosure itself, meant I couldn't even get into Brian Kitman's line of sight, let alone near enough to speak to him.

"How about a drink?" I said to Janis with a smile. "I have more winnings to spend."

"It's not fair, you betting on the favourite," she said in mock disapproval.

"What do you mean? I won seven pounds, fifty pence, didn't I? That makes us three pounds fifty up overall. Let's celebrate with champagne—at least a thimbleful of it anyway."

She laughed. Such a happy sound.

We decided to go back to the Carvery Lounge rather than stand at one of the bars, and we were almost at the door when I was roughly grabbed by the shoulder, from behind.

"What the fuck did you say to Ronan Drew?"

Elliot Mitchell was in a total rage, the veins standing out sharply on his forehead.

"Go away, Elliot," I said, and began to turn back towards the entrance to the lounge, but he wasn't having that. He grabbed my arm hard and swung me back again to face him.

"What did you tell him?" he demanded.

"I just told him to be careful—nothing more."

"You're lying," he snarled.

I could tell that Janis next to me was getting quite agitated, the nails on her left hand digging hard into the palm of my right.

"Go away, Elliot," I said again. "You're frightening the lady."

He ignored me.

"I've been working on both Drew and Clayton for months, and now you've gone and flushed all that effort down the toilet, you bastard. I could bloody kill you for that."

I could feel his spittle landing on my face, and I was worried that he *was* about to try and kill me, there and then.

And I also wondered if it had been he who had already tried once and failed.

"You should be encouraging people to buy horses at the sales, not putting them off," he shouted. "That's your bloody job."

I suppose he was right, up to a point.

"Who's side are you on anyway?" he demanded.

Not his, clearly.

CHAPTER

17

E LLIOT MITCHELL DID go away eventually, but not before he had created quite a scene.

By that time, Janis had pulled me through the door into the Carvery Lounge, where we sought refuge from the tirade of abuse still aimed in my direction from outside.

"My," Janis said after we had sat down at a table and had been served our drinks—a gin and tonic for her, and a Diet Coke for me. "You *do* seem to have upset some people today. That's the second person who has shouted at you in the past half hour."

I smiled at her. "I don't mind if all they do is shout at me, even if they make stupid threats to kill me. But it was the fact that somebody did actually try to do it on Thursday evening that really upsets me."

I told her about the car trying to run me over, and having ended up in Addenbrooke's Hospital with a dislocated ankle. She was both shocked and frightened for me, as was I.

"Are you sure it was deliberate?" she asked, taking another sip of her gin.

"Absolutely."

"Do the police know?"

"Yes, but they seem to believe it couldn't have been carried out on purpose. They appear to be treating the whole thing as a simple hit-and-run, rather than attempted murder."

"But why would anyone want to kill you?"

"That's also what the police asked me," I replied. "But you've just heard Elliot Mitchell threaten me."

"Yes, but that was because of something you did only today, not on Thursday or earlier."

It was a good point.

"At the time, I thought that it might have been Nigel Stanhope in revenge for me reporting his bullying and sexual comments to the chairman, but now I'm thinking it must be something to do with that three-million-guinea colt that was killed."

She looked confused. "But we were told in the office yesterday that the post-mortem had shown that the horse died from natural causes. Some sort of heart attack."

"That is what some people would like us to think, but I don't believe it."

"Why not?"

I wondered how much I should tell Janis.

Could I trust her? Would she even believe me? Or would she think I was just some sort of crazy weirdo that she'd be much better off keeping well away from?

In the end, I decided that if I couldn't trust her, I couldn't trust anyone, and I would have to take my chances on the weirdo thing.

We watched the fourth race on the racecourse television sets in the Carvery Lounge, rather than chance being confronted again by Elliot Mitchell. There were seven runners this time, all two-year-olds, and not one of them was trained by Brian Kitman. They competed over the same straight mile course as in the Sun Chariot race, and two of them fought out a close photo finish, but somehow the excitement of the racing had faded, at least for Janis and me.

"Can I please have another drink?" she asked.

I collected her another gin and tonic from the bar, and then I told her everything.

I began with the auction of the dead colt, explaining how the bidding had already gone way above what most people had believed was an appropriate level for an animal with that pedigree before Kitman and Mitchell had then continued to push the price right up to the three-million-guinea mark.

"Perhaps they both wanted it very badly," Janis said. "Or maybe they just didn't want the other one to get it."

"That's what I had thought at the time, but that soon all changed."

I told her about the conversation I had overheard in the gents', and her mouth fell open.

"But is that allowed?"

"It most certainly is not," I said. "It's called collusive bidding and is strictly against the sales rules, and also against the law. I tried to tell the chairman about it that night, but he was unavailable. But when I found out the next morning that the horse had been discovered dead in its box, I went straight to the chairman and told him then."

"What did he say?"

"He kept asking me if I was sure, or could I have been mistaken, or had I misheard what was actually said. I told him I was absolutely certain, but I don't think he wants to believe it's true. But at least I insisted that he organise a vet to do a post-mortem."

"Which showed nothing unusual."

"Exactly. That was a disappointment, but I still remain certain that they killed it somehow. They bid it up way above what it's really worth, insured it at that inflated auction value, then killed it for the payout."

"But Elliot still has to pay us the bid price for the colt, even though it's now dead, so how does he gain anything?"

"I'm not sure, but I believe it has something to do with the entity that consigned the colt for sale in the first place—Starsign Bloodstock. It's hidden behind a cloak of secrecy, and I wouldn't be at all surprised if Elliot Mitchell hasn't got something to do with it."

"But how can you prove that?"

"I can't. Not at the moment. Indeed, I can't prove any of it. That's why I keep watching them. And I've let them know I'm watching them, in the hope that one of them will crack under the pressure. I thought it would be Kitman, but having seen Elliot get so angry just now, it might well be him."

"Just as long as they don't crack you first."

"Yes," I agreed. "There is that little problem."

* * *

Brian Kitman had a runner in the fifth race, and I suggested to Janis that we might go and see the horses in the paddock.

"I'd much rather not," she said.

"Fine. You wait here, and I'll go on my own. I'll come back here to watch the race with you on the television."

"Please don't go," she said in a rush. "I'd feel much happier if you stayed here with me."

I could see that she was visibly upset.

Was it, I wondered, because she didn't want to be left alone? Or was it because she feared for *my* safety?

"Okay," I said, smiling at her in reassurance. "I'll stay, but we can hardly spend the rest of the afternoon in here."

"Can't we just go home now? Or at least leave the racecourse? I don't want to be around here anymore."

"But there are three more races to be run."

"I don't care," she said. "I want to go now."

"All right. We'll go."

I reached over the table and took both her hands in mine.

"I'm so sorry that I've frightened you."

She didn't deny it.

I was cross with myself.

What had been such a fun afternoon had suddenly become anything but. And it was all my fault. My fault for telling Ronan Drew to be careful when I could have simply remained silent and let Elliot Mitchell rip him off. And my fault for riling Brian Kitman to the point of him shouting at me across the paddock rail.

And all for what?

I was no nearer proving what they had done, or had not done, and I had almost certainly put myself into even greater danger than I had been before—that is, if you could be in greater danger than to have someone try to kill you by running you over.

*   *   *

We walked briskly out of the Carvery Lounge together at five minutes to four, while the fifth race was actually in progress, in order to lessen the chances of bumping into anyone.

I was pretty sure that Brian Kitman would be somewhere with his owners to watch their horse run in the race, so I wasn't worried about him, but Elliot Mitchell could be anywhere, and he might have been watching and waiting for us to appear.

We made our way directly to the nearest racecourse exit, which was also conveniently the shortest route to the Premier Enclosure car park.

We were not quite running, but not far off it, and I thought about what the nurse at the hospital had said to me on Thursday evening: *"Absolutely no running or jumping for at least two weeks."*

Tough. Needs must.

And my sore ankle was the least of my worries at the moment.

As we passed through the exit archway, we slowed, and I looked back over my shoulder. No one was following us.

"Watch out for any moving cars," I said to Janis. "Or a stationary one with someone sitting in it."

She gave me a look of real concern.

"Just to be on the safe side," I said, smiling at her to try and diffuse the nasty moment.

My Audi was in the fifth row, and we carefully weaved between the other parked cars towards it. But nothing was on the move, and no one jumped out at us from a hiding place.

We made it safely, and Janis climbed into the passenger seat, slamming the door shut, while I walked round to check that all the tyres were still inflated. They were.

I climbed in beside her and locked all the doors.

"There," I said, taking her hand. "No problem."

She suddenly started crying.

"I'm sorry," she said between sobs. "I think I'm a bit tipsy."

"It's all right. Don't worry. It is your body's natural reaction to the release of stress." *Plus the alcohol,* I thought. "Come on. Let's get away from here."

I started the Audi and drove it out of the car park.

"Do you want me to take you home?" I asked.

She didn't answer immediately, but I set the nose of the car towards Soham, nevertheless, driving up the High Street, past the Jockey Club Rooms, before turning left at the Queen Victoria Golden Jubilee Clock Tower onto Fordham Road. In the silence, I drove on past the Tesco supermarket and Burger King, which made me think of Nigel Stanhope.

Only when we were past the flyover across the A14 Newmarket bypass, did she answer my question.

"I'm sorry," she said again. "I realise how much trouble you must have had to get a table in Newmarket on a Saturday, especially on the raceday Saturday between Books One and Two, but I really don't want to spend the evening in a restaurant with lots of other people all around. Not after what happened earlier."

"It's okay," I replied, not feeling that it was at all okay.

"But is the offer of having a takeaway still open?" she asked.

I nearly drove off the road into the ditch.

"Of course. What would you like?"

"Nothing yet. I'm still full from my lunch. Could we not just go to your flat for a while?"

Nearly into the ditch again.

"Yes, of course," I said, thanking my lucky stars that I had made my bed and washed up the breakfast things before leaving for the invisible menders.

I turned the Audi round at the next junction and drove back towards Newmarket.

We almost returned to where we had started, before I turned left into the driveway behind Beaumont Court, rather than right towards the racecourse.

"Is this where you were hit by the car?" Janis asked as I drove slowly past the red-brick ends of the garage blocks.

"Yes," I said. "Just about here."

She visibly shivered. It had the same effect on me.

I parked the car in a free space at the end of the driveway and went round the car to let Janis out of the passenger side.

"Don't you have a garage?" she asked.

"There's only one garage per flat, and Alex has it for his car. I just have to take my chances on there being a free outside parking space."

Hand in hand, we safely negotiated the four steps down towards the building entrance.

"And you're absolutely sure Alex is not here?"

"He left after breakfast this morning. I watched him go, and he's not due back here until tomorrow night."

But I did wonder how things were going with Alex's parents in Stourbridge. I just hoped he hadn't had a flaming row with them as soon as he'd arrived, and was already on his way back.

I opened the front door of number twelve and stood to one side to allow Janis to go in first, only because it didn't seem appropriate to carry her over the threshold, not on this first visit.

"I could give you the extended tour," I said, "but it would only take me about ten seconds."

The flat actually had five rooms plus a hallway that joined them all together—two bedrooms, one bathroom, a sitting room, and a kitchen.

"Would you like some tea?" I asked. "Or a coffee?"

Or perhaps some champagne and then bed?

"Tea would be nice."

I went into the kitchen and filled the electric kettle while Janis went on her own self-conducted tour of the flat.

"Can I use your bathroom?" she called out from the hallway.

"Of course," I called back.

I worried that the lavatory might be dirty or that I hadn't put the top back on the toothpaste, but I heard no screams of disapproval.

I was pouring the boiling water over teabags in two mugs when she came into the kitchen and stood next to me.

"It's nice."

I shook my head. "It's hardly nice," I said. "But it's functional,"

"And it is owned by Alex Cooper."

"Yes. He charges me rent for my room, which helps him pay the interest on his mortgage."

"Wouldn't you rather have a place of your own?"

"Of course I would," I said. "I've been saving for a deposit ever since I've been here. But the amount I need to save seems to rise much quicker than the amount I actually have."

"Tell me about it," she said. "I reckon I'm going to be living at home with my parents forever."

We laughed and I turned towards her, taking her in my arms.

"Careful now, Mr Jennings," she said in a mocking tone. "You're not trying to take advantage of me, are you?"

"Not at all," I said, pulling away. "I'm sorry."

"Don't be sorry. I was enjoying it." She put her arms round me. "After all, it was my idea to come here."

"So it was."

She reached up and kissed me firmly on my mouth, with her lips open.

After several long, glorious seconds, she pulled away.

"That was very forward of you, Miss Thompson," I said. "You must be feeling better."

"I am, thank you, Mr Jennings. Much better."

She smiled up at me, then leaned her head against my chest, putting her fingers though the gaps between the buttons on the front of my shirt, and undoing them.

"Are you suggesting, Miss Thompson, that we should go to bed together?"

"I'm suggesting no such thing, Mr Jennings. But we could sit side by side on the sofa and have our tea, if you'd like."

"I'd like that very much."

So we did, but our tea went cold before we got around to drinking it.

18

I DROVE JANIS BACK to Soham in good time to meet her mother's nine-thirty curfew.

In the end, we hadn't even had a takeaway.

I had found some eggs in the fridge, and Janis had cooked us each a ham and cheese omelette, standing at the cooker in the kitchen, wearing nothing but my now-crumpled white shirt, unbuttoned down the front, while I watched her.

We hadn't gone to my bed either, preferring to lie entwined together on the sitting room carpet, with the electric fire on.

Even though we were five minutes early arriving at Soham, Mrs Thompson was already standing in the front window, looking out for us.

"Now, don't forget to phone me as soon as you are back in the flat," Janis said to me earnestly before we got out of the car. "I want to know that you have arrived safely."

"Right," I said. "I'll call you. I promise."

I went round and opened the passenger door for her, and then we walked up the path together. Mrs Thompson appeared at the front door before we got there.

"Good evening, Mrs Thompson," I said.

"Have you both had a good time?" she asked.

"An excellent time," Janis replied. "And you'll never guess who we met at the races—Ronan Drew and Shane Clayton from Ultra High."

Mrs Thompson didn't seem any wiser than I had been.

"Thank you for a lovely day," I said to Janis, giving her just the slightest little peck on the cheek. "I'll see you at work on Monday."

Both mother and daughter stood in the doorway and waved at me as I climbed back into the Audi and drove away.

It had turned out to be a much better day that I could ever have expected. An excellent one, in fact.

I smiled to myself at the memory of making love with Janis on the sitting-room floor. I think it had been a hugely satisfying experience for both of us—it certainly had been for me—as we had discovered the delights of each other's bodies. There had been nothing clumsy, awkward or embarrassing about it, being much more loving and tender than any of my previous sexual experiences.

I thumped the steering wheel in front of me in total joy and contentment.

Now all I had to do was get home safely to make the day perfect.

* * *

As I drove out of Soham towards Newmarket, I thought back to the other events of the past couple of days—the attack on me in the Beaumont Court driveway, me bumping into Mitchell and Kitman having a secret conversation behind the horsebox, and then my taunting of them both at the races, and their hostile and aggressive reactions.

I had to admit that having someone try to kill me had been quite a shock. It had raised the stakes to a new level, even if the attempt had been unsuccessful.

I had come to the conclusion, rightly or wrongly, that Nigel Stanhope could not have had anything to do with it, even though I had given his name to the policeman. It was surely too extreme a reaction simply to get back at me for reporting his unwelcome behaviour to the chairman.

So my thoughts now were that it must have been either Mitchell or Kitman, with Mitchell being the odds-on favourite. I had already seen at very close quarters the anger he could generate, and I had been seriously concerned for my welfare outside the Carvery Lounge earlier at the racecourse.

I had little doubt that, having tried and failed once, he would almost certainly try again. Especially after today. But how?

I glanced up at the Audi's rearview mirror.

A pair of headlights was close behind me.

I turned right at the roundabout onto the main Newmarket road, and the headlights behind did exactly the same.

I suddenly became convinced that I was being followed.

I sped up but the car behind me sped up too, so I slowed down again, almost to a crawl, hoping the car would overtake, but there was a continuous stream of fast-flowing traffic coming the other way preventing that.

At the next roundabout, I drove right round it, twice.

The car that had been behind me didn't follow but simply went straight on, speeding away into the distance.

I laughed at my foolishness.

Why would anyone need to follow me when they would know perfectly well where I was going? They would surely just wait for me at home.

But I'd rather be foolish than dead.

* * *

When I turned in behind Beaumont Court, I did so with the Audi's lights already switched off, stopping in the driveway entrance so that I could see right down to the far end.

I remained there for several minutes, allowing my eyes to become accustomed to the darkness, searching for any movement in the shadows thrown by the meagre outside lighting.

There was nothing.

I turned the Audi's headlights on again, but not a single thing was caught moving in the beams, not even a cat or a fox, let alone a would-be assassin.

Content that there was no one about, I drove down to the end and parked the car in the same free space as I'd used earlier.

Again, I sat in the dark for a minute or two, allowing my eyes to readjust.

I reached over into the back seat and picked up the large golf umbrella I had left in the car at the races, just in case the weather had taken a turn for the worse later. It wasn't much of a weapon, but it was better than nothing.

I slowly got out of the car, closing the door as quietly as I could.

Speed or stealth? I asked myself. Which was the best option?

In the end, I went for a combination of the two.

I moved slowly and silently as far as the four steps, negotiated them carefully so as not to aggravate my ankle, then I ran to the building entrance.

In my haste, I couldn't get the key properly in my front-door lock, but I managed it eventually and let myself in, slamming the door shut behind me and locking it. I leaned against it, breathing heavily.

No one had been there.

Had I been overreacting?

Maybe. Maybe not.

Better to overreact than to be overcome, and end up dead.

My phone rang. The display showed Janis's number.

"Hello," I said answering it.

"Oh, thank God," she said at a rush. "I've been worrying myself sick. You've been so long. Why didn't you call me?"

She seemed quite cross.

"But I've only this second walked in. I'm still standing in the hall. I took it easy on the way, that's all. Everything is fine. Everything."

"Good." I could hear her taking a few deep breaths to recover her composure. "Well, you certainly seem to have been a hit with my mother. She's been going on about how you are such a well-mannered young man. In particular, she was quite taken by you coming round to open the car door for me when we got back." She laughed. "Needless to say, I didn't tell her why."

"Thanks."

"Anyway, she told me to ask if you'd like to come and have Sunday lunch with us here tomorrow. She said she would like that."

"But would you like it?" I asked.

"Very much so. Although I don't think we'd better do what we did this afternoon." She giggled. "Not on our sitting room carpet anyway, not with the rest of my family watching."

She giggled again, and I giggled with her.

"It was lovely," I said. "Truly lovely."

"Mmm, I agree." She paused. "So, will you come?"

"I'd love to. What time?"

"Come about one, although we don't normally sit down until nearer two."

"Any particular dress code?"

"Not really. Perhaps not ripped jeans or a T-shirt with Che Guevara's face printed on it." She laughed. "You don't want to tarnish your clean-cut reputation that quickly. God, if my mum only knew what we've been up to." More giggles. "She'd have a fit and banish you from the house forever rather than inviting you here for lunch."

"So who will be there?" I asked.

"Six altogether, including you. Mum and Dad; me and my younger brother, David, who's twenty-two, plus my gran—that's Mum's mum. Dad will go over in the morning and collect her from her care home in Ely. She comes to lunch most Sundays, then she invariably falls asleep on the sofa in the front room for a couple of hours before Dad takes her back."

"How old is she?"

"Eighty-five, but she's still got all her marbles." She laughed again. "Gran will definitely give you a run for your money, especially about your politics."

"What should I say to her?"

"Oh no, I'm not helping you out on that one. You'll have to wait and see, and work it out for yourself."

I could have gone on talking to her all night, but she said she had to go because her mother was calling her.

"Give me a call in the morning," I said. "While you're still in bed."

"You naughty boy."

"What's naughty about that?" I asked, but she just laughed once more.

"Okay, Mum, I'm just coming," she shouted away from the phone. "Sorry, Theo," she then said into it. "I must go."

"Sleep well," I said.

"I think I will." And with that, she hung up.

I stood there in the hall, holding my phone and longing to be with her.

Was this true love or just an infatuation?

Either way, I would enjoy it while it lasted, provided I could stay alive long enough.

* * *

I spent Sunday morning doing what I normally did on most Sunday mornings: domestic chores.

I changed the sheets on my bed and put a wash load in the washer/dryer in the kitchen. Then I vacuumed my bedroom floor and also the carpet in the sitting room, smiling again at the memory of what had taken place there yesterday.

Janis had called me at seven thirty.

"I'm still in bed," she'd said.

So had I been.

"I wish you were here with me in mine," I'd said to her.

"Yeah, me too." She had paused. "But did it really happen?"

"It certainly did."

"All that alcohol you plied me with at the races must have lowered my defences."

"Are you now wishing it hadn't happened?"

"No, not at all. It was lovely. But I'm not usually like that. So forward, I mean. I hope you don't now think badly of me because of it."

"Badly of you?" I'd said, surprised. "Of course not. Why would I? You made all my dreams come true."

"So you're still coming to lunch?"

"You bet, as long as you're happy that I do."

"Very happy."

We had chatted on for a good half an hour more until I could put off my chores no longer. I wanted to get my things washed, dried and put away before I went out, so that the place looked respectable for Alex's return. It was no more than I would have expected of him if the flat had been mine.

*   *   *

I pulled up promptly at one o'clock outside the Thompson household in Soham.

Janis must have been looking out for me again because she came bounding out of the front door as I was still getting out of the Audi.

She threw her arms around my neck and kissed me passionately—it was quite a welcome, and one I hadn't been expecting.

"Be careful," I said, glancing across at the house. "Someone will see."

"Mum's busy cooking in the kitchen at the back, and David went with Dad to collect Gran. They won't be here for at least another ten to fifteen minutes."

That was okay, then. I hugged her tight and kissed her back, until she pulled away.

"Are you all right?" I asked.

"Yes, fine. I just don't want the neighbours to see us being too passionate. Everyone is as nosy as hell around here. People eyeball everything, just in case."

"In case of what?" I asked, but I realised that I probably already knew the answer.

"You know . . . to be witnesses in case something was to happen here again. You mark my words, someone will have your car's number plate written down by now."

"But how can you live like that?"

"You get used to it."

I suppose people can actually get used to anything.

Janis and I walked up the path to the still open front door.

"Remember," she whispered as we went into the hall, "be good."

"Yes," I whispered back. "Like I was yesterday afternoon on the carpet."

She giggled. "Stop it."

We went on into the kitchen, where Janis's mother had a multitude of pans steaming on the stove.

"Hello, Mrs Thompson," I said. "Thank you so much for inviting me to lunch."

She again looked me up and down, and my choice of blue checked shirt and cream chinos didn't seem to offend her too much.

"You're welcome, young man. And please call me Sarah." Then she turned back to her saucepans. "Janis has been telling me all about your day at the races. It seems you had a very exciting time."

"Very exciting," I agreed.

"Janis, will you please lay the table. Theo, perhaps you could help her."

"Certainly, Sarah," I said, smiling.

The kitchen was large and had obviously been extended outwards at the back into the garden. It also doubled as the dining room, with a rectangular bleached pine table in front of large French windows that opened out onto a paved patio.

Janis and I laid the six places and had just finished when the others arrived back with Gran, who seemed quite spritely for a lady of eighty-five, marching into the kitchen to inspect the new addition to their lunch party.

"Hello," she said. "And what is your name?"

"Theo," I replied. "It's short for Theodore, like the American president."

"But they don't call you Teddy?"

I must have looked slightly confused, but she soon put me right.

"Theodore Roosevelt, the American president, was always referred to as Teddy, even though it seemed he hated the name. He was the youngest man to ever assume the US presidency, even younger than Jack Kennedy. He wasn't elected president then, of course. Not until later. But he was the vice president when McKinley was assassinated, so he took over."

"You seem to know a lot about it," I said, impressed.

"Reading American history is my hobby," she said. "That and doing crossword puzzles. There's not much else to do when you get to eighty-five."

She laughed loudly, almost a cackle.

Mr Thompson and David came into the kitchen, and we shook hands, even though I felt that David took an instant dislike to me. Maybe he was trying to protect his sister's honour, although it was a bit late for that.

"Janis tells me that your father is a science teacher," Mr Thompson said as a way of starting the conversation.

"He was," I replied. "Physics. But he died a little over three years ago from a brain tumour."

"Oh. I'm so sorry."

A conversation stopper.

After a suitable pause, he tried again.

"Which school was he at?"

"Radley College," I said. "Just south of Oxford. He taught there for nearly twenty years. Ended up being Head of Science."

Mr Thompson nodded. "I know of Radley College by reputation, of course. But I've never actually been there."

"It's very beautiful. I was also there as a pupil."

"Lucky you," David said in a tone that I felt was a cross between envy and disapproval, mostly disapproval.

Yes, I thought. *I had been lucky*, but I'd also worked damned hard to win the top scholarship, which was the only reason I'd been able to go there in the first place.

I ignored David and concentrated on Mr Thompson.

"Janis tells me you're a science teacher too."

"Yes, that's right. At Ely College. It sounds impressive, but it's not as grand as Radley. We're a state-funded eleven through eighteen comprehensive academy."

"Which of the sciences do you teach?"

"I teach all three to the younger pupils as part of their general science course. But I specialise in biology at GCSE and A-level."

"Lunch is ready," announced Mrs Thompson. "Sit down, everyone."

Janis and I sat side by side, our backs to the French windows. David was opposite me, with Gran across from Janis. Mr Thompson took the end between David and me, leaving the other for his wife.

"How lovely," I said as a large, golden roasted chicken was placed down on the table.

"I hope you're not a veggie or a vegan," David said, almost laughing.

"No chance of that," I said.

His father started to carve the bird while dishes of roast potatoes, carrots, broccoli, peas and cauliflower appeared, as if by magic.

"Would you like a drink, Theo?" Mrs Thompson asked.

"Yes, please," I replied eagerly. "Thank you."

I could really do with one.

"Water or orange squash?" she said.

Janis could hardly contain herself.

"My late husband and I always had a sherry or two before our Sunday lunch," Gran said wistfully.

A sherry or two sounded like rather a good idea to me at the moment. Not necessarily my first choice of tipple, but it would be better than water or orange squash.

"But no chance of that here," Gran said, facing me but flicking her eyes in the direction of her son-in-law. "Not anymore. Isn't that right, Sarah? Lead him not into temptation."

The son-in-law in question ignored her and went on carving while Sarah stood waiting for my answer.

"Water will be just fine," I said. "Thank you."

Janis had told me yesterday at the races that her father had started drinking heavily after the murders, but I hadn't realised that alcohol was now banned from the household. Clearly another of Mrs Thompson's house rules. No wonder a single glass of white wine, plus a couple of gin and tonics, had had such an effect on Janis.

Lunch progressed, with all of them seemingly taking it in turns to ask me questions about my life, my family, my likes and dislikes—everything—all of which I tried to answer truthfully and with good grace.

But there was definitely something rather odd about the whole occasion, not that I was able to work out precisely what it was. Perhaps it was the way Mrs Thompson kept stroking Janis's forearm that I found disturbing.

"Do you believe in God?" Gran asked me suddenly.

"That's a very personal question," I said, but I could see from her expression that she still wanted it answered. "No, I don't think I do."

"You don't *think* you do?" David said sarcastically. "What sort of answer is that? Either you do or you don't. Thinking doesn't come into it."

I looked across the table at him. "But surely individual thinking has everything to do with it. Not all religions rely on a belief in some higher power, a god, which directs our lives and will ultimately pass judgement on our souls. No one questions that Buddhism is a religion, but Buddhists don't believe in any god at all."

"So you're a Buddhist," David said in a slightly mocking tone.

"No, I'm not, but I have studied some of Buddha's teachings. He argued that the idea of an all-powerful 'god' was created by mankind solely out of fear, especially the fear of death and its great unknown. Most religions have played on that fear for thousands of years to control their followers—to make them live by their rules—with threats of eternal pain and damnation if they don't. Throughout history, differences in religious belief have caused endless persecution and war, resulting in untold human suffering. And it's still happening today, not least because everyone fervently believes that 'God' is on their side."

I ceased speaking and looked around the table.

All five of them had stopped eating and were staring at me.

"So, no," I said. "I don't think that I do believe in God."

We all sat there in silence for several long, long seconds.

"Wow!" said Janis, finally. "And Gran hasn't even asked you yet if you vote Labour or Tory."

19

I FINALLY ESCAPED FROM the lunch from hell about four thirty, with my voting choices still kept to myself, but very little else.

Janis came out with me to the car.

"I'm so sorry," she said. "I didn't expect them to give you quite such a grilling. I should have given you more warning."

"It's all right," I said. "In fact, I rather enjoyed it."

"And you certainly shut them up with your answer about believing in God. I absolutely loved it." She laughed. "I've never seen Gran lost for words before."

"I don't think your brother likes me."

"Oh, don't worry about him. He doesn't like any of the boys I've brought home over the years. In fact, I thought he warmed to you a bit by the end. More than he ever has to anyone else. At least he said goodbye, and that was a first."

"So others have been put through the same ordeal?"

"Afraid so. It's a sort of rite of passage. Most of them don't last the course, and one boy disappeared completely without trace immediately afterwards. He wouldn't even answer my calls." She laughed again. "But I really hope that won't happen with you."

"Not a chance."

"And I'm sorry about the drink thing."

"You could have warned me. I very nearly brought a bottle of wine with me."

She laughed once more. "I'm so glad you didn't. Another boy did that once. My mother simply opened it and poured it straight down the sink. He didn't come back either, but I didn't fancy him anyway." She paused. "Not like you."

She glanced up at the house, and I did the same. We couldn't see anyone standing in the windows, but that didn't mean we weren't being watched.

"Let them see," she said. "I don't care."

She reached up on her toes and kissed me on the mouth.

"I do care," I said. "I care very much."

And I kissed her back.

*　*　*

Alex arrived back at the flat at half past nine as I was sitting on the sofa with my left ankle raised on a cushion on the coffee table.

"How did it go?" I asked.

"Nightmare," he said, flopping down into one of his deep armchairs. "All my parents' boring old friends were there. I think I was the only person under fifty, apart from a couple of trophy second wives in their thirties." He laughed. "And they all got pissed. If the cops were outside with breathalysers when they left, they'd have had a field day. God knows if they all got home safely."

"I assume you didn't drink anything."

"No, not a drop—not alcohol anyway—and I left before most of the guests did. And that was at seven o'clock, and they'd been hard at it for over six hours by then."

"And how about last night?" I asked.

"God, that was awful too. I got the usual third degree from my mother about whether I had found a girlfriend, but I remembered what you'd said, and I just told her that no, I hadn't. But I think my dad might have guessed. When Mum was out in the kitchen this morning, and the two of us were sorting the drinks in the dining room, he told me quietly not to worry about her. They would be very happy, he said, just as long as I was happy."

"What did you say to that?"

"I just told him that I was happy."

And I was happy too, I thought.

* * *

The Book 2 sale started an hour earlier than Book 1, at ten o'clock, and while not quite as prestigious, the whole place would be busier, with more prospective purchasers able to afford the expected lower prices.

As before, I was scheduled to be fourth in the auctioneer's roster, due on the rostrum around eleven thirty, depending on how quickly lots were sold and how many horses were withdrawn.

Vendors could easily gauge the interest there was in each of their particular yearlings by the number of times the horse had been vetted over the weekend. If they didn't believe there was a good chance of reaching their hoped-for price, they tended to withdraw the lot, rather than have it knocked down for a song, or even left unsold. Then they might re-enter it for a later sale in November or December, in the hope of it doing better.

I arrived at my desk at half past seven to go over the catalogue notes for the horses I had been allocated to sell, practicing in my head how I would introduce each lot and at what price I would start the bidding, always mindful of the vendor's reserve, if any.

Nigel Stanhope walked in at a quarter past eight.

"Good morning, Theo," he said, remarkably jovial for early on a Monday. "I always look forward to the Book Two sale. Still some great horses to sell, but far less anxiety and more happy faces from both vendors and buyers than were here last week."

I was still slightly perplexed by Nigel's more friendly demeanour towards me, but I nodded in agreement and went back to studying the equine pedigrees and bloodlines. But fifteen minutes later, I stood up and went down the corridor to the Accounts Department. My purpose was twofold—primarily to see Janis, and secondly, to ask Geoff Pollard whether he could find any records of Starsign Bloodstock.

Janis wasn't yet in her office, but Geoff was in his.

"Excuse me, Geoff," I said, putting my head round his door. "Do you have any records to show if Starsign Bloodstock have ever consigned any yearlings for sale before the one that died last week? I haven't been able to find out anything about them. Peter says they are registered with us, but there are no details of any individuals on the registration. I was wondering if they have a trading account with us."

He consulted his computer, tapping away at his keyboard.

"Here we are," he said after a few moments. "Starsign Blood-stock. Seems it's an Irish operation out of Cashel in County Tipperary."

"Yes, Peter has already told me that."

"As far as I can see, that was the first yearling they have consigned for sale with us, but there have been others, mostly in the horses-in-training sales. They don't have a trading account as such, but we have a mailing address for us to send them payment in due course, once we have received the funds from the purchaser."

"So Starsign Bloodstock was the vendor?"

"Not necessarily. It is quite normal for us to pay agents, who then pay the vendors, having deducted their own fees."

"What is their actual mailing address?" I asked.

"I'm afraid I can't give you that without their strict permission because the data is protected by GDPR, the General Data Protection Regulations, and as our designated data controller, I might be liable."

"Is there anything else with the address?" I asked. "Such as the names of any individuals?"

He studied his screen again. "No, nothing like that. Sorry. And GDPR would have prevented me telling you the names even if there had been."

"Thanks anyway, for looking."

Thanks for nothing, I thought. Frustration.

I withdrew my head and found Janis standing behind me in the corridor.

"Hello," she said, smiling. "Have you recovered from yesterday?"

"Just about. What did they say about me when you went back in?"

"Gran was really taken with you. At least that's what she said before she went to sleep on the sofa. And they *did* all see us kissing by your car. Mum told me sternly that I should not have been so brazen with you until I knew you much better. Little does she know."

"What are you doing after work?" I asked. "Do you fancy another drink at the Bedford Lodge? Say around seven thirty? I will have to stay here until after the day's sale ends."

She pulled a face. "I can't. Mum has some sort of fundraising event this evening at the local hospital, which she has to attend for her work, so I've agreed that I would cook supper for Dad and David."

"Can't they cook supper for themselves?"

"You must be joking. Dad can't even boil an egg, and David's just useless at everything."

"Surely they could put something in the microwave?"

"How about tomorrow?" she said. "And I could try and arrange with Mum to stay out later."

I smiled at her. "That would be lovely. But call me tonight after you've finished your *MasterChef* impression."

She gave me a quick kiss and then went into her office to join the other Accounts staff while I went back to mine to join Nigel and to continue my preparations for later.

I thought of Janis and smiled to myself.

Things were pretty good.

* * *

At five minutes to nine, the chairman marched in.

"Theo," he said. "My office. Now." And then he walked out again.

I looked across at Nigel, who pulled a face and shook his head slightly, as if indicating that he didn't know what this was about. Did I believe him?

I went along the corridor and into the chairman's office.

"Shut the door," he said.

I did so, and he didn't invite me to sit down.

"I had Elliot Mitchell in this office half an hour ago, ranting on at me about you. He claims that you were stalking both him and Brian Kitman at the races on Saturday and that you purposefully undermined his relationship with some of his clients, telling them not to buy any yearlings at the sales this week. He also said that you openly accused him of killing that three-million colt."

I stood there in silence.

"Well?" the chairman said angrily. "What have you to say for yourself?"

"I didn't tell his clients not to buy *any* yearlings," I said calmly. "I just advised them to be careful, and maybe not to give Elliot Mitchell carte blanche to buy them four or five when they were not going to be here during the bidding." I paused. "Apart from that, what Elliot says is pretty much the truth."

That last part of my answer seemed to take some of the wind out of his sails.

"So you don't deny you were stalking Elliot and Brian Kitman?"

"I wouldn't have actually called it *stalking*. I just told them both that I would be watching them, that's all. So I did. And I don't suppose Mitchell told you that he physically attacked me and also verbally abused me during Saturday afternoon. Quite vicious, he was too."

"What has got into you this last week?" he asked.

"What has got into me, Chairman, is that Elliot Mitchell is a crook, aided and abetted by Brian Kitman, and you are doing nothing about it because you won't confront either of them about their collusive bidding up. And yes, I did accuse Mitchell of killing that colt because I am quite certain that he did, whatever

Andrew Ingleby and his post-mortem report might say. In fact, I'd go so far as to say that Mitchell is rather pleased with himself for having managed it in a manner that has been undetectable, and the sooner we ban him from entering these premises ever again, the better."

"He, in turn, demands that you be removed immediately from the auctioneer roster. Indeed, he insists that you should be summarily dismissed for conduct prejudicial to the good name of British bloodstock, and of this sales company. Otherwise, he says he will not purchase any more horses at our sales."

"Good," I replied. "We would be much better off without him."

"It's not as simple as that," the chairman went on. "Elliot is very well respected and much liked throughout the bloodstock industry. His opinions are listened to, and he is held in high regard by a large number of our potential purchasers."

"I can't imagine why."

"And what's more, he's the chairman of the British Bloodstock Agents Association, and he threatened to instruct all its members not to make any bids while you are on the rostrum."

I stared at him, worried now for the first time about my future. "They surely wouldn't agree to that."

"I can't take that risk, and nor can I expect our vendors to take that risk either."

"So what are you going to do?" I asked, dreading his answer.

"You are suspended from employment with this company with immediate effect. You will leave these premises at once and not return unless specifically invited to be here by me. All your planned shifts on the rostrum will be covered by others. There is a full company board meeting next Monday, and the directors will also act as a disciplinary panel on that day, to consider whether you are to be reinstated or dismissed."

From the tone of his voice, there was not much doubt which outcome he would be in favour of.

"You're making the wrong decision," I said to him. "You should be calling Mitchell's bluff and suspending him from acting as an agent here, and permanently. And I demand to be able to defend myself at the disciplinary hearing."

"I don't believe that is necessary, but I will consider your request."

"You'll have do more than just consider it," I said to him. "I think you'll find that it's my legal right to be present. And I will be consulting beforehand with an employment lawyer."

"That is your prerogative."

"Damn right it is."

The chairman then reached down to his desk and picked up an envelope. He handed it to me.

"This is the formal notification of your suspension. Give me your company ID card, and also remove your tie."

Reluctantly, I took my ID card out of my pocket and handed it to him. Then I removed my tie, with the company logo embroidered all over it, and held it out to him. He took it and placed it in the top right-hand drawer of his desk.

He then made a very brief telephone call, the purpose of which became apparent when a member of the company security team came into the room.

"You will be taken to your office to clear your desk of your personal effects," said the chairman. "And then you will be accompanied off the estate. All the security staff will be instructed to call the police if you are seen to re-enter. And while suspended, you are not to communicate with any other company employee. To do so might severely prejudice your disciplinary hearing. Do I make myself clear?"

"Perfectly clear," I said, even though that last bit could present me with quite a problem, as I lived with one of the company's employees and was romantically attached to another.

I was not quite frogmarched back to my office, but pretty close to it, the security man never letting me wander more than a few inches from his grasp.

We went in, and I stood by my desk, removing a few of my own things from the drawers and putting them into a plastic bag that the security man gave me for the purpose. As I did so, he checked every item, just in case I was taking something with me that was company property.

"What the hell is going on?" Nigel asked.

"Mr Jennings is leaving," said the security man.

"Are you saying he's been fired?" Nigel retorted.

Neither the security man nor I said anything.

"Theo," Nigel said urgently to me, "have you been sacked?"

"Nigel, I've been told that I'm not allowed to talk to you. Or to any other company employee, for that matter. But suffice to say, I've been suspended, pending a disciplinary hearing next week. And I have no doubt that I will be sacked then."

"What on earth for?" Nigel asked, standing up.

"For telling the truth."

"That's enough," said the security man brusquely. "No more talking. Come on, Mr Jennings. It's time to go."

It felt as if I was being led to the scaffold for my execution.

I WAS CEREMONIALLY DEPOSITED outside the main security gate on The Avenue, rather than leaving by my usual route, which was via the pedestrian gate on Queensberry Road.

I felt totally bereft, standing there alone on the street, holding my pathetic plastic bag that contained just a few pens, a ruler, a calculator, and the Oxford United coffee mug that my mother had given me at Christmas.

Not much to show, I thought, *for three years of full employment.*

But not only had the sales company been my employer over those three years, it had also become my whole life.

Right from the start, I had been on warm and easy-going terms with all my colleagues, Nigel Stanhope excepted, and had made many firm friendships. I had also got to know many of the prospective buyers, their agents, and the vets.

I had enjoyed travelling up and down the country on company business during the high-summer months, visiting breeders and stud-farm owners, to inspect their new crops of yearlings. Over time, many of those people had also become my friends.

But most of all, I was bereft because I had been forced to leave Janis.

Could the company really justify stopping me talking to my girlfriend?

Surely not.

I took my phone out of my pocket and wrote her a text.

Don't speak to anyone. Please call me as soon as you can, but make sure you are somewhere private. I love you. Theo.

I suddenly hesitated before sending it, looking specifically at the last few words.

Was it right for me to tell her that I loved her when we'd only been seeing each other for less than a week?

Not that I didn't believe it myself.

I was quite certain that I loved her.

I thought of her absolutely all the time and physically ached to be with her. Just the idea of us being together gave me an all-over warm feeling, and not just in those parts of my body that I might expect.

But did I really put *I love you* on a text to her?

Would she recoil from it because she felt I was being too presumptuous?

While I was still considering my options, my thumb must have subconsciously touched the "Send" button because the message was suddenly being dispatched through the ether just as it was, before I'd had a chance to change it.

I stood waiting for some considerable time, and worrying, until my phone finally rang.

"What's wrong?" Janis asked, anxiety clearly audible in her voice.

"Can anyone hear you?" I asked.

"No. I've gone outside. I'm near the blood-test boxes."

"Good," I said. "I wanted to tell you something myself, before you heard it from anyone else."

"Tell me what?" If anything the anxiety had grown.

"That I've been suspended from my job."

"Oh my God, Theo, why?"

"Elliot Mitchell complained about me because of what happened at Newmarket races on Saturday, and the chairman took his side."

"But that's so unfair." I could tell that she was both angry and distressed. "Mitchell was the one in the wrong, and I'm going to go and damn well tell everyone that, including Peter Bloody Radway."

"Janis, please don't do that," I said urgently. "You will only get yourself into trouble."

"But it's not right."

She was crying.

"I've been told that I must not communicate with any of the company's employees, not before a disciplinary hearing next Monday, so if you go and complain to Peter Radway now, you will only get me into more trouble, as well as yourself."

"But it's not fair," she said between sobs. "And you and I are definitely going to communicate, whatever the bloody company says, because I love you too, very much."

Every cloud, I thought, however dark, has a silver lining.

*　*　*

I started walking slowly back to the flat in Beaumont Court, carrying my plastic bag.

What did I do now? I wondered. Did I finally take up building railway bridges?

As I turned left into the High Street and began to climb the hill, my phone rang again. I answered it.

"Theo, it's Alex. I've heard what has happened to you. It's awful."

"Alex, before you say any more, you should know that I'm not meant to be speaking to you," I said. "I've been told not to be in contact with anyone from the company."

"I know." He paused. "That's what I'm really calling about."

"What?"

"The chairman told me that it could seriously compromise my future position in the company if I continued to share a flat with you. I'm so very sorry, Theo, but I must ask to you move out."

"When?"

"Today. Preferably before I get home."

I was pretty sure that our tenancy agreement provided for more notice than just a few hours, but I wasn't about to argue the point because I could tell he was upset enough already.

"I'll be gone before five o'clock," I said.

"Thank you. I'm so sorry." I could tell that he was choking back tears.

"Yeah, I know. Don't worry."

I was about to hang up, when I had a thought.

"Alex," I said. "What sort of lawyer is your father?"

"He's a solicitor."

"Yes, I know that, but what aspects of the law does he deal with?"

"All sorts. Wills, contracts, house conveyancing, divorce—you name it, he does it."

"Is he any good at employment law?" I asked.

"I'm not sure. But if he isn't, he'll certainly know someone who is. He knows everyone."

"Could you text me his number?"

*   *   *

I spent much of the morning in a semi trance, packing up my stuff and wandering around the flat in a state of total disbelief.

But I also made a few calls, and some concrete plans.

At one point, I stood in the sitting room, looking down at the carpet in front of the electric fire, wishing that things could be different, but at the same time very happy at the memory of what had happened there just two days previously.

Janis called me during her lunch break, when she was well away from any other listening ears.

"I'm so angry I could scream," she said.

"Me too," I replied.

I told her about me also having to leave Alex's flat.

She was horrified.

"Who told them you lived there?"

"It's not exactly a secret. Nigel Stanhope knows, for a start. He goaded me about it last week, remember. Even you knew."

"Nigel is such a bastard," she said with feeling. "I'd still bet that this was his doing. Where will you go?"

"To my mother's place."

"Where's that?"

"In Radley, south of Oxford. My parents bought the house years ago when Dad first went to work at the College. She just stayed on when he died. I'll stay there, at least for tonight."

"And after that?"

"Well," I said, "I feel that the only way I'm going to sort this mess out is to prove that Elliot Mitchell is up to no good, and I believe the key to that must be in Ireland. So I've booked myself onto the midday flight tomorrow from Heathrow to Dublin."

"Oh!" She sounded almost distraught. "I've always wanted to go to Ireland."

"Then come with me. Take a couple of days of annual leave. I'm sure I could book another ticket."

"I can't," she said.

"Why not?"

"I wouldn't be allowed to take leave—not just like that, not without any notice, and especially not at the moment. This is our busiest week of the whole year."

"Then tell them that your long-lost Irish granny has suddenly died, and you have to go to her funeral, and it's on Wednesday. You could hardly give them notice for that."

She laughed. "I couldn't do that."

"Then sign off sick."

"I can't." She paused. "It's not only that." She said it slowly.

"So what is it?" I asked. "Is it me?"

"No, of course it's not you. I would absolutely love to go with you. But . . ." She paused again. "It's complicated."

Now it was my turn to pause. I said nothing. I just waited.

"You know how Mum is. You saw it for yourself. Well, let me tell you, she is infinitely better now than she used to be."

I still said nothing.

"She had a complete mental breakdown after the murders of Holly and Jessica. She became totally convinced that I would be the next one to be killed, and she even suffered from vivid hallucinations of my murder. Throughout large parts of my childhood, and for most of my teenage years, she was in and out of various hospitals—you know, psychiatric hospitals. Gran always came to live with us whenever Mum had to go away, to look after us. Sometimes for months and months at a time. What with Mum locked up in a secure hospital ward and Dad trying to drink himself into an early grave, it was not a great time for any of us."

"I'm so sorry."

"In fact, I think it's quite amazing that I have turned out to be as normal as I am." She laughed, as if trying to release the tension. "But Mum's mental health is still like the sword of Damocles that hangs permanently over all our heads. So we try very hard to do nothing to rock her boat. That's why Dad ignored Gran yesterday when she was provoking him over the sherry." She sighed. "Going off to Ireland with you tomorrow sounds totally fabulous, but without giving Mum at least three months' notice to get used to the idea, it would likely capsize her boat altogether."

"Yes," I said. "It is definitely complicated."

"But please don't run away from me," she said in a rush, with a touch of desperation in her voice. "I should never have said anything."

"I'm so glad you did," I replied. "It helps me understand. And no, I'm not going to run away from you—well, maybe to Ireland for a couple of days—but I will come back, I promise, because I love you, Janis Thompson."

*　*　*

I packed all my clothes into one large suitcase, which I placed in the boot of the car, while the rest of my things were mostly in multiple plastic bags strewn across the back seat.

As I was loading the final few items, a police car swept into the driveway and pulled up nearby. PC Langford climbed out of it.

"I've been trying to call you," he said. "Your phone is permanently switched off." He said it in an accusatory tone, as if it were my fault.

"But the number I gave you at the hospital is for the phone that I lost last Thursday night. I never did find it."

"Ah," he said. "That explains it."

"So what have you discovered?" I asked, standing where I was and purposely not inviting him into the flat.

"Not much, I'm afraid," he said. "I inspected the vehicle owned by Mr Stanhope, and I am satisfied that it was not the one involved."

"How about the crack you found in his windscreen?" I asked.

The policeman seemed surprised I knew about that.

"Mr Stanhope told me you had been to see his car," I said. "And that you had taken some photographs."

"Yes, I did. But our forensic team have studied the pictures under a microscope, and they are satisfied that there is some tiny cratering of the glass surface, which indicates that the damage was caused by the impact of a small hard item, possibly a stone, as Mr Stanhope maintained, and not by striking a person."

"So what else have you got?" I asked.

"I'm sorry to say that we have no other leads to follow at present," the policeman said. "That's partly why I am here, to ask if you've had any further thoughts of who might have been responsible."

"As a matter of fact, I have," I replied. "Two people that have shown considerable animosity towards me over the past few days."

The policeman removed a notebook from his pocket.

"And what are the names of these two individuals?"

It was time to twist the chain a little bit more.

"Elliot Mitchell and Brian Kitman," I said. "Mitchell is a bloodstock agent, and Kitman is a racehorse trainer, both of them based here in Newmarket. Each of them shouted abuse at me at the races on Saturday, and for no good reason. Mitchell even threatened me—*"I could bloody kill you"* were his exact words. And there were several witnesses to him saying that."

PC Langford wrote it all down in his notebook.

"And why did Mr Mitchell threaten you exactly?" he asked.

"He accused me of undermining his position as a bloodstock agent with some of his clients."

"And did you?"

"Not at all. Why would I? My job as an auctioneer of horses relies very heavily on bloodstock agents."

Or at least it had until today.

"Is there anything else you would like to tell me?" he asked.

"Only my new phone number."

I certainly wasn't going to mention anything to this policeman about me being suspended from my job, or why, just in case he thought I was making things up, simply to get even.

I gave him my new phone number, and he also wrote that down.

"Right, Mr Jennings," he said. "I will follow up on these leads, and I will contact you on this new number if I need anything further from you, such as a sworn statement, or if you need to have a formal interview at the station."

He snapped his notebook shut.

"So will you be going to see both Mr Mitchell and Mr Kitman?" I asked.

"I certainly will," he replied. "Just as soon as I have obtained the details of their vehicles."

Twist, twist.

* * *

I finally drove my Audi out of the driveway behind Beaumont Court at ten past four, but not before I had spent a productive and enjoyable half hour on the phone with Alex Cooper's dad.

The text from Alex, with his father's number, had arrived just as PC Langford was driving away, and I'd called it straight away.

"The best employment lawyer I know is a man called Ted Ackerman," Mr Cooper said. "I trained with him at the College of Law in York, almost forty years ago now, but we've been best of mates ever since."

He shared Ted Ackerman's contact details by text.

"I'll give Ted a ring now and warn him that you'll be calling. Alex spoke to me earlier about what had happened to you. He actually rang to make sure that under the present circumstances I would be happy for him to give you my number, which I was. Hence, he had to tell me about it. I'm very sorry."

"Thank you," I said. "I just need some legal advice, that's all, to know what my rights are."

"Then Ted is definitely your man."

"Where's his office?" I asked.

"In London. Near Blackfriars Bridge."

That worried me. "Is he very expensive?"

"Hugely." He laughed. "But I will ask him to give you half an hour of his time on the phone for free, and then you can decide whether to proceed. He owes me a favour or two anyway."

"Thank you, Mr Cooper. That's very kind."

"Please call me Martyn. That's Martyn with a *y*."

"Right, thank you, Martyn. Alex told me you had quite a birthday lunch party yesterday."

"We certainly did." He laughed again. "Some of our guests didn't go home until nearly midnight. I thought they'd never leave. Hence, my wife and I both had dreadful hangovers this morning." He laughed once more. "You must get Alex to bring you over here sometime after all this employment stuff is sorted. We're only two and a half hours from Newmarket."

"Thank you," I said again. "I'd like that."

We disconnected and I stood there looking at Ted Ackerman's number on my phone, but I decided against calling him straight away, to give Martyn Cooper a chance to speak to him first.

So, with one last wistful look back at my home for the past three years, I climbed into my car and set course to my mother's house in Radley, towards a new phase of my life, whatever it might hold for me.

21

Early on Tuesday morning, after another restless night, I spent some time talking to Ted Ackerman on the phone before I left for the airport.

"Employment law is like a minefield," he said by way of introduction. "Step just a few feet off the designated safe path, and you can easily get blown up."

I outlined my current situation to him in some detail, or at least how I saw it.

"What do the company's policies state with reference to undermining company clients, particularly the bloodstock agents?" he asked.

"The company policies?" I said. "I have no idea. I don't think I've ever seen any policies."

"I see. Don't all employees get given a booklet containing the company policies when they join? Best practice also dictates that policies should be updated at least once every two years and redistributed to staff, either physically or by email. All employees should then have to confirm in writing that they have read them."

"I can't remember ever being given anything like that, and certainly not having to sign that I'd read it."

"So you are not aware whether you have contravened a particular policy or not, or even if such a policy exists?"

"Absolutely not."

"That is good," he said. "In employment law, unlike in criminal cases, ignorance is a valid defence. Employers have a duty to ensure that all their employees are aware of company policies. It is not the responsibility of employees to have to search for them. But you must have been advised of the disciplinary procedures?"

"No."

"Not even yesterday?"

"No. I was only informed that there would be a disciplinary hearing by the company directors next Monday, and they would decide if I was to be reinstated or dismissed. I even had to request that I be present to defend myself, because the chairman told me he didn't believe it was necessary."

"That's naughty," Ted said. "You have a legal right to be present at a disciplinary hearing."

"That's what I told him."

"You also have a legal right to be accompanied."

"By a lawyer?" I asked, half wondering how much it would cost me to bring him all the way from London to Newmarket.

"Well, no. Strangely, the law doesn't actually allow for an employee to be accompanied by a lawyer, not unless the employer agrees to it, and most of them won't. But you do have the right to be accompanied by a work colleague or by a trade union representative."

"I'm not a member of a trade union."

"A work colleague, then. Do you have anyone in mind who could accompany you? You will need to give your employer reasonable notice of who it will be. And you should have been given the details of the full disciplinary procedure, dates of previous written warnings, and so on."

"I've had nothing, certainly nothing in writing, except for a short note handed to me yesterday to confirm that I had been suspended from my employment forthwith and that I was banned from entering the company premises or from communicating with any other company employee prior to the disciplinary hearing."

"Then they must be using the *gross misconduct* procedures."

"Gross misconduct?"

"Yes, there is provision in law for an employee to be immediately suspended or dismissed for gross misconduct, without the need for any previous warnings to have been given, either verbally or in writing."

"What constitutes gross misconduct?" I asked.

"Various things, including theft or wilful damage of property, physical violence, gross negligence, or serious insubordination such as deliberately disobeying your manager's instructions, combined with rude, aggressive or threatening behaviour."

"I definitely haven't done any of those."

But had I been guilty of serious insubordination by continuing to question the sale and death of the three-million-guinea colt, even after being told to forget it and move on by the chairman? Although I had never been rude, aggressive or threatening towards him.

I suppose my behaviour at the races might have been considered as threatening by Mitchell or Kitman, but only if they had something to hide.

"Well," Ted said, finally, "if everything you have told me is true, I think that if things go against you at the hearing next Monday, you should have a reasonable claim for unfair dismissal. But I have to warn you, even if you eventually win your case at an employment tribunal, it doesn't mean you would necessarily get your job back. Over the years, I have known many companies who believe that the possibility of being ordered to pay compensation by a tribunal is a risk worth taking to rid themselves of a troublesome employee."

"But I'm not a troublesome employee," I said.

"You might be in the eyes of your boss."

*   *   *

My flight from Heathrow landed at Dublin Airport at quarter past one on Tuesday afternoon, after a quick seventy-minute hop across the Irish Sea.

I had watched through the aircraft window as we crossed the Welsh coast just south of Anglesey, and I'd wondered what on earth I was doing.

Was this simply a wild goose chase?

The dead colt had been bred in Ireland—its dam, Lucky Lass, having been covered by the stallion, Foxtrot Mike, at Holycross Stud, near Thurles, in County Tipperary. And Starsign Bloodstock, the colt's consignor, was also based in Tipperary, at Cashel, just twelve miles south of Thurles, although I still didn't have their actual address.

So the key to unlocking the mystery had to be in Ireland, in Tipperary, but goodness knows how I'd find it. I had a crazy idea of just wandering around the streets of Cashel, shouting *"Starsign Bloodstock"* over and over again at the top of my voice, in the hope that someone might have heard of it.

But if I weren't doing this, what else would I be doing? Probably just kicking my heels at my mother's house. At least, this way I felt like I was doing something vaguely useful, even if it did turn out to be a futile exercise.

I picked up a small rental car at the airport, took the M50 west around the city, and then the N8 southwest towards Cork.

Janis had called me as I was in the Heathrow departure lounge, and she had still been very distressed.

"I still can't believe it's happened," she said. "All the girls in Accounts are absolutely furious. We've been specifically told not to talk about it between ourselves. But of course, we are."

"Don't get yourself into trouble."

"I don't care. It's so unfair."

"Let's see what I find out in Ireland."

"Why are you going there exactly?"

"I want to find out more about Starsign Bloodstock, the entity that consigned the dead colt for sale. They are based in a small town called Cashel, although I'm not quite sure where, so I'll ask around in the hope that someone has heard of them. I also intend to visit the stud farm where the sire of the colt stands, to see if they can give me a pointer towards the true vendor of the colt, or at least the name of the breeder that owned its dam."

"Where are you staying?"

"I've booked a room for tonight in a bed-and-breakfast place in Cashel. After that, I'll see. I should be back at my mother's on Thursday, or Friday at the latest. It all depends on how I get on."

"I do so wish I was with you."

"Yeah, me too."

*   *   *

I drove into Cashel at half past four and easily found my bed-and-breakfast establishment in a side street across the road from St John's Cathedral.

I checked in to my room, a very small affair with just a narrow single bed; an upright wooden chair; a compact, old-fashioned, varnished wardrobe; and a washbasin in one corner—the bathroom was along the landing—but it was clean enough and also had a partial view of the cathedral.

As I was unpacking my bag, my phone rang.

It was Janis again.

"It's sixty-four Main Street," she said breathlessly.

"What is?" I asked.

"The address given to us by Starsign Bloodstock. In Cashel. I know I shouldn't have been looking for it, and it took me ages, but I eventually found it deep in the accounts computer system, in the VAT records. I didn't want to email it to you or even put it in a text because both of those are traceable."

"Where are you now?" I asked her.

"On my way to meet my mum at the hospital. It's okay. No one can hear me. I love you."

"And I love you too. Thank you so much for this. But please be careful."

"I will be careful. I must dash. I'm late."

She hung up.

Sixty-four Main Street.

Perhaps I wouldn't have to go shouting around the streets of Cashel after all.

* * *

Number 64 Main Street, Cashel, was a small, yellow-painted, terraced townhouse sandwiched between a dental surgery and a branch of the Allied Irish Bank, and there was nothing on or near its bright red front door to indicate that it was the headquarters of an international bloodstock business.

I rang the doorbell.

After a few seconds, the door was partially opened on a security chain by an elderly man. From what I could see of him through the narrow gap, I took him to be in his late seventies or early eighties.

"You'll not be selling things now, will you?" he said.

"No," I replied, almost with a laugh. "I'm not selling. I'm actually looking for a business called Starsign Bloodstock."

"Starsign Bloodstock?" he repeated. "Now would that be in Cashel?"

"Yes. In Cashel. And this is the postal address I have for them—sixty-four Main Street."

"To be sure, this is number sixty-four, all right. What name did you say?"

"Starsign Bloodstock."

He closed the door slightly, and I could hear him shouting at someone else deeper in the house. "Eileen, there's a man at the door. Something about Starsign Bloodstock."

Presently, the door was opened again, much wider, and this time by a small white-haired woman wearing a flower-printed apron.

"I'm so sorry," she said with a smile. "My old boy gets quite confused these days. Starsign Bloodstock did you say?"

"Yes. Mrs . . .?"

"Murphy," she said. "Eileen Murphy. But you've had a wasted journey here, so you have. There's nothing to collect, nothing at all."

"Collect?" Now it was my turn to be confused.

"The post. As I said, there's nothing here to collect because nothing has been delivered since you collected last time."

"Oh, right," I said, suddenly understanding.

Sixty-four Main Street, Cashel, was simply an *accommodation address* for Starsign Bloodstock, an unofficial poste restante, where mail could be sent, for it to be personally collected later.

"But, just because nothing's arrived," she said sharply, "doesn't mean I don't still want paying, so I do."

"Yes, of course," I said, smiling at her. "Remind me, how much is it? I haven't been here before."

"One of the other fellas promised me twenty euros a month, but I think it should be increased, what with food prices going up so fast, and all. And I'll be owed for three months at the end of this one."

"*One* of the other fellas?" I asked.

"That's right. One of them fellas that comes here to collect the mail."

"How many fellas are there exactly?" I asked.

"I knows of two of them. You're the third."

"Well," I said, "I suppose I could pay you what you're owed. Then I'll ask about an increase for next time."

I pulled three twenty-euro notes out of my pocket, grateful that I had been to a cashpoint at the airport, and gave them to her. She grabbed the money and put it quickly deep into the pocket on the front of her apron before I had a chance to change my mind.

"You don't happen to know the name of the fella who offered you the money?" I asked her. "So I know to ask the right person."

"He called himself Seamus," she said. "But I don't think that was his real name, because he wasn't Irish. English, he was, just like you."

I took my phone out of my pocket and googled images of Elliot Mitchell.

"Was it this man?" I asked, showing her one of the pictures.

She studied it closely.

"It might have been him," she said. "But my eyes are not as they were."

I showed her another image of Mitchell, this one full face, taken ironically in the sale ring at Newmarket, and she agreed that this one did look much more like him.

"How much more like him?" I pressed her.

"I would say that it is definitely him, to be sure."

To be sure.

"In that case, I'll have a word with him when I get back," I said. "And I expect he'll let you have more money next time he comes."

That is, if he isn't already in prison by then, I thought.

If Elliot Mitchell had been collecting the Starsign Bloodstock mail from here, then I had him bang to rights.

Quite apart from the collusive bidding up with Brian Kitman, the Bloodstock Industry Code of Practice also specifically stated that agents were not permitted to act for both the purchaser and the vendor in the same sale, due to a serious conflict of interest.

To say nothing about the potential, in this case, for insurance fraud.

If I could show that Mitchell was in line to receive some, or even all, of the proceeds of the sale of the colt, via his involvement with Starsign, then the insurance company was going to be asking him some very difficult questions before they paid out on his claim for the horse's death—that's if they ever did.

And I was quite sure the police would be interested in talking to him too.

But who was Eileen Murphy's other fella?

* * *

I spent the evening in an Irish pub in Cashel town, drinking Guinness and consuming a large plate of colcannon, a local dish of mashed potato, cabbage, and smoked pork sausages, and very tasty it was too.

"So what are you here for in October?" the barman asked me as he pulled me a second pint of the black stuff.

"Just taking a few days of holiday. I've never been to Tipperary before. I'm keen on horse racing, particularly the breeding of racehorses, so I thought I'd come and see where it all happens."

"So you'll be going to the races at Thurles later this week?"

"I certainly will," I agreed, even though I wouldn't be. "But I'm going to a stud farm tomorrow."

"Coolmore?" he asked.

"No." I laughed. "Nothing as grand as that."

Coolmore Stud was currently the headquarters of the world's largest centre for the breeding of Thoroughbred racehorses, and one of the most successful, and it was just twenty minutes by car down the road from Cashel, in Fethard.

"I'm going to a small place just outside Thurles, called Holy-cross Stud."

The barman had nodded. "I know it. Patrick O'Connor's place. He's done well with that stallion of his recently, so he has. He's got plenty of mares already booked for the next breeding season, and at good money."

"Foxtrot Mike?"

"Indeed. Couldn't sire a bloody carthorse for years, then hits the jackpot with that current two-year-old champion."

I nodded. "Lucky Mike."

"Bloody lucky it was too, if you ask me. A freak, more like. Bit like winning the lottery."

"You don't happen to know who owned its dam?" I asked him. "Lucky Lass, I think her name was."

"That would have been Fergus Ryan."

"And do you know where I could find him?"

"Indeed I do," said the barman. "He's just down the road from here. In Cormac's Cemetery. He died this last August. I went to his wake."

"Oh." I said. "What did he die from?"

"Cancer, it was. Prostate cancer. He'd had it for years, so he had, but it got really bad in the summer. Poor man."

"So who owns the horse now?" I asked.

"That must be his widow, Grace Ryan."

"And where does she live?" I asked.

"Where she and Fergus always lived, at Six Barn Farm, in Kilkarney."

My ears suddenly pricked up, in spite of the Guinness.

The blue rug, which the three-million-guinea colt had been wearing when it died, had had "Property of Six Barn Farm" stitched along its edge in small red letters.

22

I HAD A BETTER sleep than I'd had for any of the seven nights during the previous week, in spite of the narrowness of the bed—that and the continual chiming of the hours through the night by the cathedral clock.

I lay awake in the bed, listening to the clock strike seven, thinking back to the time I had spent here so far and my plans for the coming day.

Even if I discovered nothing else during my visits to Holycross Stud and Six Barn Farm, it would still have been worth coming.

What I had to do now was to firm up the evidence that Elliot Mitchell was indeed involved with Starsign Bloodstock and was therefore in breach of the Bloodstock Industry Code of Practice. And to do so before my disciplinary hearing on Monday, not that I believed for one second that the chairman was going to be pleased that I'd been right, and him wrong, all along.

"Would you care for a full Irish breakfast, Mr Jennings?" asked my host when I went downstairs to the dining room at a quarter to eight.

"That would be splendid," I answered.

My full Irish breakfast consisted of much the same as a full English: bacon, eggs, sausage, mushrooms, baked beans, and grilled tomato—but with the addition of something called *white pudding*, which was similar to black pudding, but without the pig's blood, and it was delicious.

I was just finishing this huge feast when my phone rang.

"Have you heard the news?" Janis asked in a rush as soon as I answered.

"What news?"

"Elliot Mitchell has killed himself."

"What! I don't believe it."

Elliot Mitchell had never seemed to me to be the sort of person who would ever consider taking his own life. Even if forced into a really tight corner, I would have expected him to try and bamboozle his way out rather than to kill himself. But maybe my continual twisting of the chain, including a visit by PC Langford to inspect his car, had finally caused his link to snap.

"It's true," Janis said. "Hanged himself."

"My god, where?"

"In the same box where that colt died. Suspended from a beam, he was, apparently, with a knocked over bucket beneath his dangling feet."

"Wow!"

"There was a bit of a panic here yesterday when he couldn't be found. Some of his clients had been drinking with him in the bar at six o'clock on Monday afternoon. They were looking all over for him, but he wasn't even answering his phone. I nearly called you to warn you that he might be following you to Ireland. But now we know why they couldn't find him. He must have done it on Monday night, and he was in there, hanging, all day yesterday. That particular stable block hasn't been used since last week, for obvious reasons, and he was found this morning when the steam cleaners arrived."

She paused and drew breath.

"Everyone here seems to be quite cut up by his death—that's everyone except me. I saw what he was really like—at the races last Saturday."

But what would Elliot Mitchell's death mean for me?

Part of me felt slightly cheated. I had finally discovered something to show that he was involved in criminal activity, but I would never have the chance to make him squirm or pay for his transgressions.

I also wondered if it was a good thing or a bad one for my upcoming disciplinary hearing. Elliot Mitchell had certainly been my chief detractor, but would his death make all his accusations go away?

Probably not. Not now.

And would my insistence on continuing to reveal his own wrongdoing now look like I was simply speaking ill of the dead, and of someone who had committed suicide, to boot?

I wondered about what I would do if I were the chairman.

Quite clearly, for the good of the business, the sooner the sorry tale of the dead colt was finished and forgotten, the better. The company would now be unlikely ever to receive the three million guineas for its sale, but it wouldn't need to pay out anything to the vendor either, so the only real loss would be the hoped-for five per cent commission on the three million—a hundred and fifty thousand guineas.

It was a sizable sum to lose, but it was small in comparison to the more than ten million guineas in commission that the company was expected to earn over the full October yearling sales. Especially when you consider that the hammer price of the colt had been artificially inflated, making the commission on its sale so much greater than had been anticipated anyway.

I could foresee that the chairman and his fellow directors would want to sweep everything under the carpet as quickly and discreetly as possible. And that might still include getting rid of me as an employee, so I would not be a continual reminder to them of the wretched affair, even if I promised not to walk around the offices wearing a T-shirt with "I TOLD YOU SO" blazoned across it in big letters.

"So what are you going to do?" Janis asked, bringing me back from my wandering thoughts. "Will you come home now?"

"As I'm over here, I might as well still go and see the stud farm. It might help my cause if I can show that Elliot Mitchell had been up to his neck in criminality."

Or it might not.

*   *   *

I checked out of my bed and breakfast, threw my overnight bag onto the back seat of the rental car, and drove the nine miles north to the village of Holycross and its eponymous stud farm.

For the past three years, I had spent much of my summer months visiting stud farms and breeders up and down England, and not one of them had looked like the stud at Holycross. Indeed, I had driven past it twice before I even realised it was the place I was looking for, and then only because I spotted a small, cream wooden sign, hanging at an acute angle beside the front gate, with "Holycross Stud" painted on it in small, badly faded black lettering.

I turned in through the gate onto a short driveway that ran alongside a grey pebble-dash bungalow, set close to the road behind a four-foot-high white stone wall, which was badly in need of a lick of fresh paint. On the other side of the bungalow, beyond a conifer hedge, stood a barn with a corrugated-iron roof, much of it the worse for wear through rust.

As I was climbing out of the car, a large man wearing a brown raincoat, Wellington boots, and a cap, came out of a door on the side of the bungalow.

"And what would you be after now?" he asked sharply.

"You must be Patrick O'Connor," I replied in a much more friendly tone.

"Indeed, I am," he said. "But I asked you what it is you'd be after?"

He sounded quite hostile, and I could tell that this wasn't going to be an easy conversation.

"I came to ask about your stallion Foxtrot Mike," I said in my most disarming manner.

"What about him?" he asked.

"Is he well?"

Even I could tell that it had been a foolish question, and Patrick O'Connor was clearly not the sort of man to suffer fools gladly.

"I think, mister, you had better get right back in your car and go away."

Perhaps he was right, and I was about to do as he suggested, when I turned back to him.

"Do you know a man called Elliot Mitchell?" I asked.

"What about him?" he asked again, this time with considerably more interest.

"So you *do* know him. At least you did. He killed himself yesterday."

Mr O'Connor didn't seem that concerned.

"He was a pompous ass," he said, almost under his breath.

"He certainly was that," I agreed. "When did you last see him?"

"August."

"What did he want?"

"What he always wanted. And what you want too, I shouldn't wonder."

"Which is what?"

"To lease my Foxtrot and have him moved to what Mitchell called a more prestigious establishment. Bloody cheek. He came back here month after month, ever since that two-year-old won his maiden by six lengths on the first day of the season, back in March."

"Lucky Mike?" I said.

"That's the one."

Lucky Mike had run five more times since that first race win, at the Curragh racecourse just outside Dublin, and he had won them all easily, including the Coventry Stakes, the premier race for two-year-olds at Royal Ascot, and in a record time.

A freak, the barman in the pub in Cashel had called him, but he would cement his reputation as one of the greatest ever two-year-olds if he could win the Group 1 Dewhurst Stakes at Newmarket on the coming Saturday. And he was already the short-priced favourite for the first of next year's Classics.

"Each time Mitchell came, he would up his offer a bit, not that it was ever very much. I told him to get lost, the horse wasn't available, but he kept coming back anyway. Arrogant prig, so he was."

"So he was, indeed," I agreed. "Mr O'Connor, I promise you that I am not here to try to buy, lease, or move your stallion."

"Then why *are* you here?" he asked pointedly. "What are you after?"

"I already have what I came for. More than."

He looked at me with a quizzical expression. "And what was that?"

"Confirmation that Elliot Mitchell had been here. And now I know that he was here multiple times, and why he came."

Our mutual dislike of Elliot Mitchell seemed to override his antipathy towards me, at least for the moment.

"And why is that important?"

I wondered how much I should tell him. Not much, I decided.

"Just trust me that it is. I believe Mitchell was up to no good, and this is another piece of the jigsaw puzzle that I need to piece together to prove it."

"But now he's dead," Mr O'Connor said. "So what's the point?"

It was a good question.

"Because it would make me feel better."

"Fleeced you, did he?" He laughed, but not in a malicious manner, more in sympathy.

"Yeah," I said. "Something like that."

I began to climb back into the rental car.

"So would you like to see him now you're here?" O'Connor asked. "Foxtrot Mike."

I stood up again. "I would love to."

He led me behind the bungalow, through a gap in the conifer hedge, and into the barn with the rusting roof.

In the corner of the barn was a makeshift stable with half-height wooden walls, with railings above, and there he was, Foxtrot Mike, standing quietly in the middle on some straw bedding.

He was not a big horse, but he looked well, and he was well groomed.

"Is he your only stallion?" I asked, looking around at the rest of the empty barn.

"That he is. He's only been a sideline, really, more of a hobby, at least up to now. My main business has been cattle."

O'Connor went over to the sliding door of the stable and opened it a fraction. Foxtrot Mike came over to him, and he stroked its head with obvious affection. I thought the horse was remarkably docile for a stallion, some of which could be very difficult to control.

"He's been out in my top paddock for much of the summer, with the heifers, but I've brought him back in now because he's been eating too much fresh grass for his own good. What with the mild weather we've been having, the grass is growing again as if it's springtime, which is great for the cattle, but not so for this fellow." He tickled the horse between its ears. "It affects his feet, and I have to get him back into tip-top shape to start his work again come February." He gave the horse a friendly slap on the neck. "Then you'll have some fun, won't you, my boy?"

"Have you a full book?" I asked him.

"Bursting at the seams, I am." He smiled broadly. "Over a hundred mares booked so far, and more clamouring to come. I'm planning to take on another stud groom in January, just to cope."

"What's his stud fee?"

He looked sideways at me.

"It was only two thousand euros this year, but I've put it up to twelve for next, so I have."

That still sounded amazingly cheap to me, considering that Foxtrot Mike had sired the best two-year-old currently racing in Europe and had over a hundred mares already waiting for his services, with more still to come. Frankel, in comparison, commanded a fee of over a quarter of a million pounds for each mare covered.

I looked again at the horse in question. He was totally uninterested by the rise in price of his semen, instead happy just to pull a few strands of hay from his net.

No wonder Elliot Mitchell had tried to lease him.

I would too, given half a chance.

Patrick O'Connor laughed. "Thanks to this boy, I'll be able to reroof this barn next summer. And if he gives me another champion, I'll reroof the house as well."

He gave the horse a final gentle slap on its neck, then closed the sliding door of the stall.

"But one of last year's crop will never be a champion," I said seriously.

"I know. I heard. A full brother of Lucky Mike too. Bloody shame. Couldn't believe it when I found out." His good humour had suddenly evaporated.

"Who told you?" I asked.

"Grace Ryan," he said. "She had owned it with her late husband."

"But at least it was sold before it dropped down dead."

"And Grace is very grateful for that."

Not that she was likely to get the full proceeds of the sale, I thought—not unless the insurance company did eventually pay out or she was able to make a claim against Elliot Mitchell's estate. That was assuming he had died with at least three million worth of assets.

"But even so," Patrick said, "that colt won't now be able to prove his worth on a racecourse. And that's a big blow for me too, especially if he had turned out to be as good as his brother."

"We will never know," I said, thinking that only extremely rarely, if ever, did lightning strike twice in exactly the same place, and perhaps the colt's death had been a good thing for Patrick O'Connor after all.

23

Six Barn Farm, in Kilkarney, had also seen better days, and it took me even longer to find than Holycross Stud.

The maps app on my iPhone stubbornly refused to believe in the existence of a Kilkarney, close to Cashel, in County Tipperary, trying instead to send me over a hundred miles southwest to a town of the same name in County Kerry.

It was just one of the joys of rural life in Ireland.

I did find the farm eventually, but only after having to stop to ask a man riding a bike, and also a woman out walking her dog.

The farm buildings were set well back, away from the road, down a long lane, which had no convenient name plate at its end, so I wasn't sure I was in the right place even when I arrived, especially as I couldn't count six barns in the farmyard—only two.

I parked the car as close to the farmhouse as I could, and climbed out.

The place was all rather ramshackle, with small piles of rubble dotted around and an old broken armchair lying on its back by a wall.

If I'd thought that parts of Holycross Stud could have benefitted from a lick of paint, then they would need more than that here. The wooden window frames in the farmhouse were well beyond just painting, with rot having taken a strong hold.

I walked over to the open back door and knocked on the frame.

"Is anyone home?" I shouted into the building.

There was no immediate answer, but after a little while, a woman appeared.

"Grace Ryan?" I asked.

"That's me. Now what can I do you for?"

I was not quite sure what I had been expecting, but whatever it was, she wasn't it. I suppose I had imagined her to be a small, elderly lady, being a widow, and with a name like Grace, but she was, in fact, a large, robust, middle-aged woman, wearing a check shirt and red jumper above a green tweed skirt, thick stockings, and bedroom slippers.

"I'm here about Lucky Lass," I said.

"What about her?"

"Is she in foal this year?"

"What if she is?" she said. "Neither she nor the foal are for sale, so piss off."

I should have learned by now that all the folk around here would think that a stranger—an English stranger, no less—was on the make, after something they didn't want to give or sell—except that everyone would have their price.

I should learn to be more direct.

"Elliot Mitchell," I said, clearly and loudly, expecting a hostile response.

But she smiled. "Mitch? What about him?"

"You know him?"

"Of course," she said. "Lovely man. How is he?"

"I'm sorry, but I'm here to tell you that Mitch died suddenly yesterday."

She took a step back and steadied herself against the frame of the door.

"How dreadful," she said. "I was only talking to him a couple of days ago." She was genuinely upset, and there were even tears in her eyes. "You had better come in."

She led me through the hallway into her kitchen.

The general sense of dilapidation, clearly visible from the out-side, continued inside, but the kitchen itself was tidy enough and warm, thanks to an old-fashioned cream AGA on the far wall.

She went over and leaned her back against the rail on its front.

"How dreadful," she said again. "That has really upset me."

"I'm so sorry."

She looked up at the ceiling and took a couple of deep breaths. Then her eyes returned to mine. "But life must go on," she said, as if trying to snap herself out of her melancholy. "Would you like some coffee?" she asked. "I was about to have one myself when you arrived."

"Thank you," I said. "That would be lovely. Milk, no sugar."

She lifted one of the AGA lids and put the kettle on the hotplate.

"I can't believe that Mitch has gone, just so suddenly like that, when he was still so young. My Fergus would have been sad too. He and Mitch had become good friends."

She spooned instant coffee into two mugs, poured boiling water from the kettle over them, and then fetched some milk from a fridge under the counter.

"I'm sorry about the loss of your husband," I said, taking my cup.

"Thank you," she said. "Fergus also went well before his time." She was silent for a moment, as if remembering back to happier days. "So that is why you've come here, to tell me about Mitch?"

"Partly," I said. "And also to sort out the question of Lucky Lass's colt, you know, the one that also died."

And both of them found dead in the same stable, I thought, *the colt and Elliot Mitchell, and exactly one week apart.*

She nodded. "That was a real shame. Such a nice young horse. I can't believe that it just dropped down dead like that, and for no reason. Mitch called me on Saturday to tell me all about it."

He would have told her his version, I thought.

"But there is still the question of payment to be sorted," I said.

"Now what question would that be?" Grace asked.

"The question of payment to you for the colt, now that Elliot Mitchell has died."

"But we've already been paid. The money is in the bank."

I was confused. Why would the sales company have paid the vendor before receiving the funds from Elliot Mitchell or from the insurance company? And surely that hadn't all happened yesterday or today, not with Elliot being dead.

"When exactly were you paid?" I asked.

"Oh, it must have been back in June. Fergus was still alive." She paused again. "Fergus was the one who was so keen on getting the sale completed, so he would know for certain that I had some money after he was gone—you know, to pay for his funeral and to live on until I could sell the farm."

I was still confused.

"So are you saying that you didn't own the colt when he went to the sales in Newmarket last week?"

"Oh no. We'd sold him long before then."

"Who to?" I asked.

"A syndicate, I think it was. Fergus dealt with everything, him and Mitch."

"Can I ask how much you sold him for?"

She smiled. "A quarter of a million euros. Who'd have thought it? More than we could have ever imagined. Especially with his bad hocks."

"Bad hocks?"

"He had some bone chips in his hocks. I saw the X-rays."

But the set of thirty-two X-rays of the colt's joints, supposedly taken within twenty-eight days of the sale and then lodged at the sales company as part of the vetting process, had been perfect in every way—not a bone chip to be seen.

"Who showed you these X-rays?" I asked.

"That would have been Mitch. He arranged for them to be taken."

One of two possible scenarios came to mind. Either the X-rays lodged with the sales company were not actually of this particular colt, or the ones Grace had been shown were not. And it was too late to take any more X-rays to find out which it was.

"Does the name Starsign Bloodstock mean anything to you?" I asked.

"They were the agents that acted for the syndicate. I'm sure Mitch mentioned them. He did all the negotiating for us. And he forced the syndicate to up their offer twice before he was happy with the deal."

Elliot Mitchell had probably been laughing himself silly behind their backs, I thought, and all the way to the bank.

"Who actually paid the money into your account?"

"Mitch did. The syndicate paid him, and he then paid us, less his commission, of course."

Of course.

"How much commission did he charge?"

"He said his standard rate for private sales was ten per cent, but he was prepared to take only seven and a half, as he could see that we needed the money."

How gracious of him—*not*.

The customary rate for bloodstock agents' commission on a sale was just five per cent.

And it seemed to me that he had taken his seven and a half per cent commission from these trusting people when he, himself, had been the actual purchaser of the colt, notwithstanding what he had told Grace and Fergus about the existence of a mysterious syndicate and their supposed agents, Starsign Bloodstock.

It was totally despicable, but nothing now surprised me about Elliot Mitchell, other than the fact that he had killed himself.

"Are you aware," I asked Grace, "that the colt went through the sale ring in Newmarket before it died, and was sold?"

"Mitch did mention something to me about that on Saturday, when he called me, but he also told me that because the horse had died within twenty-four hours, the sale had been voided."

"That is not actually the case," I said. "All sales in the ring are final on the fall of the auctioneer's hammer, as long as the horse subsequently passes its wind test, which your colt did."

There were a few special circumstances under which a sale could be voided and the horse returned to the vendor, for example, if it had been wrongly described in the catalogue or was found to have certain traits and habits that had not previously been revealed, such as wind sucking or habitual box walking. However, dropping down dead within twenty-four hours of the hammer falling, or even within twenty-four seconds, for that matter, was not one of them.

"And did Mitch tell you how much it was sold for in the sale ring?"

She shook her head.

"Three million guineas," I said. "That's over three and a half million euros. And I know that for sure because I was the auctioneer who sold it."

Grace stared at me, and she seemed to have some difficulty breathing.

"Are you all right?" I asked her, concerned.

I went over and took her arm, guiding her to one of the upright chairs around the kitchen table. She sat down heavily.

"Three million, you say?" she said, finally.

I nodded.

"But who would have paid that much for it, with its bad legs and all."

"It was knocked down to Elliot Mitchell for three million guineas," I said, although I didn't know whether he was buying it on instructions from somebody else, but I doubted it.

"Mitch?" she said, in a sort of trance. "But he certainly knew about its legs, from the X-rays. He told us that because of the bone chips, the colt was only worth about two hundred thousand euros, absolute tops, but he had managed to force the syndicate up to two hundred and fifty thousand."

"Do you still have those X-rays?" I asked.

She shook her head. "I think Mitch took them away again."

I was quite sure he had.

But if the X-rays of the colt that Mitchell had shown to Grace and Fergus Ryan had been faked—or were of another horse altogether, one that did have bad hocks—and the colt in question had had perfect joints, as shown on the X-rays lodged with the sales company, *and* it had indeed been Elliot Mitchell who had bought the colt from the Ryans in the first place, why had he not just let it go through the sale ring without bidding on it? It would have made its expected million to a million and a half, and that would have provided him with a fine profit.

The alternative was that the set of thirty-two X-rays lodged at Newmarket had been the ones of a different horse, and the colt had indeed had bone chips in its hocks all the time. Now, Mitchell was forced to buy it at the auction, because if anyone else had, they might have soon discovered that its hocks were not as shown on the X-rays, and then Mitchell would have been in deep trouble.

However, having bought it, the colt then had to die, and its carcass be rapidly disposed of, because any future potential purchaser, trainer, or even the insurance company, could have easily discovered the fraud by having it re-X-rayed. Mitchell couldn't take the chance of that happening.

Also, by collusively bidding the hammer price up to way over its true value and then insuring the colt at that inflated figure, he had greatly increased his potential profit. And if I hadn't overheard the conversation between him and Kitman, he might have got away with it.

So, in fact, Mitchell might not have scammed the Ryans, after all. Perhaps he had even done them a favour by paying them over the odds for their horse.

The problem was, now that both Mitchell and the horse were dead, there seemed little chance of proving anything.

24

I SPENT MY SECOND night in Ireland at a hotel close to Dublin Airport, sleeping soundly without a cathedral clock chiming bell to be heard anywhere.

Ironically, I had been unable to find a single empty seat on any flights to London on Wednesday evening because they were full of Irishmen going over to the Future Champions Festival at Newmarket racecourse, all of them seemingly in support of Lucky Mike in Saturday's Dewhurst Stakes. But I had finally managed to secure one on the 10:50 British Airways flight to Heathrow the following morning.

After eating dinner in the hotel bar, I called Janis.

"So what did you find out?" she asked.

"You won't believe it," I said. "I am pretty sure that Elliot Mitchell already owned that colt before he bid three million for it in the sale ring."

"But that doesn't make sense. If he already owned it, why bid for it?"

I explained my theory of how he had bought the colt cheaply from the Ryans, falsified its X-rays, and then grossly inflated its value by collusive bidding up with Brian Kitman, before making a claim on the insurance, potentially netting him more than two and three-quarter million pounds in the process.

"Wow!" she said when I finished. "No wonder he killed himself."

"But why would he? He didn't know on Tuesday that I would find this out. He didn't even know I was coming to Ireland. I didn't tell anyone apart from you."

"And I told no one," she said quickly.

"Not anyone in your office?"

"Absolutely not." She seemed a little affronted that I should think such a thing. "I told no one, I promise. Not even my mother."

"Good," I said. "I didn't really think you had."

I should never have doubted it.

"So where will you go now?" she asked.

"Back to my own mother's place, I suppose. I have nowhere else."

"So when will I see you?"

"I have to be in Newmarket on Monday for this disciplinary hearing. I'll try and sort out somewhere to stay on Sunday night, but not in Alex's flat, obviously. I'll let you know when I've found somewhere."

With luck, all the racegoers, those who had filled up all the flights, and would do the same to every available Newmarket hotel bed, would be leaving for home on Sunday morning, freeing up some space for me.

"How were things at the sales today?" I asked.

"Really strange. Flat, I would say. Everyone was talking about Elliot Mitchell rather than concentrating on the horses. And you'll never guess."

"Guess what?" I asked.

"Nigel Stanhope has been going round saying that with Mitchell now dead, you should be reinstated as an auctioneer. He says it's not fair to have fired you on Mitchell's say-so, not when Mitchell has then killed himself."

Now it was my turn to say *"Wow!"*

"I've not technically been fired—not yet anyway—only suspended."

Suspended, but thankfully, not by the neck.

* * *

Janis called me again as I was checking in for my flight at Dublin Airport on Thursday morning.

"All hell has broken loose here," she said almost in a whisper. "The police arrived en masse at half past eight this morning, and they've cancelled all of today's sale. The company staff have been all been put together in the restaurant, and everyone else has been corralled into the sale-ring building, either in the seats or sitting on the floor. We've been told we will have to stay in there until we've been interviewed, and we've also been told not to use our mobiles, but everyone is, of course, texting like crazy below the tables in silent mode. I told a policeman that I was having my period, and I had to go to the ladies'. That's where I am now."

"What's happened?"

"One of the girls in the office, Anne-Marie, texted her boy-friend. He works for the police. He replied that a post-mortem has shown that Elliot Mitchell must have already been dead when he was strung up in the stable, because there are no signs of him having been strangled."

No red dots of petechiae in the whites of his eyes, I thought.

"It seems they have also found a small hypodermic needle puncture in his chest, right over his heart," Janis said. "The police are currently doing drug tests, and his death is now being treated by them as murder."

Why was I not surprised?

* * *

My phone rang as soon as I turned it back on after the flight from Dublin to Heathrow.

It was from my voicemail, and there was a new message from PC Langford asking me to call him urgently. I dialled his number.

"Where are you?" he demanded.

"Heathrow Airport," I replied.

"Where are you going?" he asked with concern in his voice.

"Nowhere," I said. "I've just landed. I've been to Ireland."

"Theodore Jennings," he said very formally, "you are to approach the nearest uniformed police officer in the terminal building and tell them to immediately contact Suffolk police. You are to remain there, with the police, until told otherwise. Do you understand?"

"Why?" I asked.

"Just do it now."

"Am I being arrested or something?"

"No, but Suffolk police are very keen to interview you."

"Why?" I asked him again, even though I could guess.

"Just do it now," PC Langford repeated. "Or a warrant *will* be issued for your arrest."

I walked out from Arrivals into the main terminal building and spotted a pair of uniformed policemen, each with a machine gun slung across his chest.

"Excuse me," I said to them. "I have been instructed to present myself to you and to tell you to immediately contact Suffolk police."

"What is your name, sir?" one of them asked.

"Theodore Jennings."

One of the two stood right next to me while the other moved a few paces away and spoke into his personal radio. I tried to hear what he was saying, but without success, and I couldn't have heard the reply anyway because it would have come via his earpiece. After a while he came back.

"They're sending a car for you," he said. "We are to take you to the airport police station, and you will wait for it there."

"Where is the airport police station?" I asked.

"On the northern edge," the officer replied.

"What about my car? It's in the Terminal Five long-term car park."

"It can stay there," he replied. "Suffolk said you are not to be left alone."

That didn't sound very encouraging, but I had no choice.

The policemen took me out of the terminal building, one walking on each side of me, as if I were a dangerous criminal. A police car arrived, and I was put in the back, with one of the officers, and driven round the perimeter road to the airport police station.

There I was taken into the custody suite and presented in front of the custody sergeant.

"Name?"

"Theodore Jennings," I replied.

The sergeant tapped it into his computer.

"Reason for arrest?"

"He's not under arrest, Sarge," replied my shadow. "We are just to keep him here until Suffolk arrive to collect him. They're sending a car."

"And what if I don't want to stay?" I said.

The sergeant's gaze transferred from his computer screen to me. "Then, Mr Theodore Jennings, you will be arrested, under Section Forty-Six, Subsection Two, of the Police Reform Act 2002, for obstructing the police in the line of their duty."

I wondered if he knew the whole of the Act off by heart, and decided that he probably did.

"Okay, then," I said, with a smile. "I'll stay."

The sergeant looked again at his screen. "Put him in cell number two."

"Hey, I thought you said I wasn't under arrest," I complained.

"We won't shut the door," said the sergeant. "There's nowhere else for you to wait."

I was escorted down the corridor to cell number two by my shadow, and as the sergeant had instructed, he left the door open, and to be fair, he also allowed me to keep my bag and my mobile phone.

I sat down on the blue plastic-covered mattress on the concrete bed and leaned against the wall, wondering how long it would take for the police car to come all the way from Suffolk.

I had driven the journey from Newmarket to Heathrow many times, and at night with no other traffic on the roads, it took under two hours—straight down the M11 and around the M25.

But the car was probably coming from the Suffolk police investigation centre in Bury St Edmunds, or even their headquarters in Ipswich, both of which were farther away from Heathrow than Newmarket. And I didn't even know if the car had set off yet, or how many traffic holdups there would be along the motorways on a Thursday afternoon.

I rather hoped they might put on their blues and twos to get here quicker, but I somehow doubted it.

The time passed very slowly, but it did give me the opportunity to think.

* * *

So Elliot Mitchell had been murdered.

But why?

And by whom?

Two simple questions, but neither of them had a simple answer.

Peter Radway, the sales company chairman, had said to me that Elliot was much liked throughout the bloodstock industry, but I was sure he would have made lots of enemies too, especially if he had been up to similar tricks before, as he had with the dead colt—buying a horse cheaply from its breeders and then bidding it up high in the sale ring, for his own profit.

But had he really upset a breeder enough for them to want to kill him?

It reminded me of the question that both PC Langford and Janis had asked of me: *"Why would anyone want to kill you?"*

Why indeed?

Until very recently, I had come to the conclusion that it must have been Elliot who had tried to run me over in the driveway behind Beaumont Court. But now I was not so sure. Had it actually been him? Or had it been someone else entirely?

In fact, was the same person responsible both for the murder of Elliot Mitchell and the attempted murder of me? And if so, what was it that they feared either Elliot, or I, could reveal about them that warranted such drastic action?

* * *

The police car from Suffolk didn't arrive at the Heathrow Airport Police Station until nearly five o'clock in the afternoon, by which time I was almost climbing up the cell walls in frustration.

I repeatedly visited the BBC News app on my phone, but there were no reports about any Newmarket murder, and the sales company website just stated that the yearling sales had been temporarily suspended, without giving any reasons.

I had sent texts to Janis at three and four o'clock, asking how she was doing, but had received no reply, so I tried to call her, but again without success.

It was PC Langford who arrived to collect me, and he came into the cell as I was again searching the news app.

"I told my inspector that I knew what you looked like and that if I came, we could be sure of getting the right man."

"The right man for what?" I asked. "What's all this about?"

"You are wanted for questioning?"

"About what?" I asked, deciding not to tell him that I already knew.

"You will find that out when I get you back to Bury St Edmunds."

"But all you had to do was ask, and I would have driven there myself. My car's here at the airport, in the Terminal Five long-term car park."

"It will have to stay there," said the policeman.

"And who'll be paying for that?" I asked.

He didn't reply. "Come on," he said instead. "It's time to go."

We walked out to his car in the police station yard.

"In the front or the back?" I asked.

"The back," he said, opening the rear door for me.

I suspected that was because he didn't want to have to talk to me, but found that the car was fitted with a metal grille between the front and back seats. I also soon discovered that the inside door handles didn't work. I know because I tried them.

It reminded me of the front passenger door in my own car.

The electric window switches didn't work either.

Hence, I sat imprisoned in the back, looking out of the closed windows at the passing countryside, wondering why the police were so keen to interview me that they had sent PC Langford on a more than four-hour round trip to fetch me.

Someone must have told them that I had been suspended from my job because of a complaint by Elliot Mitchell. Maybe it had even been the chairman. Or perhaps a member of the public had seen the exchange at the racecourse between Elliot and me, and reported it to the police.

According to Janis, Elliot had been with clients on Monday afternoon but had been missing all day Tuesday. At the time, it had been assumed that he must have killed himself sometime during Monday evening or night.

Now we knew that he hadn't killed himself at all, but had been murdered. But that wouldn't have changed the chronology.

No doubt, the pathologist would have given his best guess at the time of Elliot's death, but I knew from Andrew Ingleby's comments about the dead colt that predicting the time of a death was hugely unreliable.

Assuming Elliot was already dead when I boarded my flight to Dublin on Tuesday, how did my alibi stack up for Monday evening and night, or even for early Tuesday morning?

I had spoken to PC Langford outside Beaumont Court mid-afternoon on Monday, then I'd called Martyn Cooper, Alex's dad, before driving to my mother's house.

The traffic around both Cambridge and Bedford had been bad, and I hadn't arrived at Radley until a few minutes after seven—I remembered the time because my mother religiously listened to

The Archers on the radio every weekday, and I'd had to wait for it to finish before I could speak to her.

We had then eaten a supper of spaghetti bolognese together in the kitchen until about nine thirty, when my mother had gone up to bed.

I had sat alone at the kitchen table for a while, planning my next couple of days and booking the bed and breakfast in Cashel, before going to bed myself at about ten, in my old childhood bedroom.

Even though I had slept badly, I hadn't actually got up until about seven thirty, eating breakfast in the kitchen with my mother at eight. I'd then called Ted Ackerman at eight thirty before leaving for the airport around ten past nine. So, only the hours between about ten at night and seven thirty in the morning were unaccounted for, and I'd spent them in my bed.

I suppose couldn't actually prove that I'd been in bed, as I'd been alone. But if I'd driven back to Newmarket in my car during that time, the car's registration would have been picked up by ANPR, the police automatic number plate recognition system.

Surely the police couldn't think that I might have killed Elliot Mitchell. Yet they must; otherwise, they wouldn't have dispatched PC Langford all the way from Suffolk to Heathrow to collect me.

I was quite confident that when I arrived at Bury St Edmunds and was asked about my movements on Monday afternoon, evening, and night, they would quickly realise their mistake.

But exactly how confident was I?

CHAPTER

25

I WASN'T ACTUALLY ARRESTED for murder when we arrived at the Police Investigation Centre in Bury St Edmunds, but it certainly felt like it, at least to me.

PC Langford released me from the back seat of his car, and then he escorted me to an interview room in the middle of the building, with no windows, not that it mattered much, as it was already dark outside.

The room contained a uniformly grey metal table and four matching grey metal chairs, all of which were screwed to the floor. The clock on the wall told me it was twenty-five to nine. There was a CCTV camera high up in one corner, and a black box on the end of the table that was up against the wall.

"Wait here," said the constable. Then he departed, leaving me alone.

I sat down on one of the chairs and waited.

I had tried texting Janis again twice on the journey, but there had been no reply either time. I hoped she was all right.

The most frustrating aspect was not knowing what was going on.

Just before seven o'clock, as PC Langford and I had been passing Stansted Airport on the M11, the news app on my phone had begun reporting the suspicious death of a fifty-two-year-old man from Newmarket, but without giving his name.

Rather worryingly for me, the same report also stated that police sources had indicated that a man of thirty-three was helping them with their enquiries, although no actual arrest had yet been made.

I took my phone out of my pocket and checked the app again, but there was nothing new to report. Probably, I thought, because they were yet to interview the thirty-three-year-old man!

The hands on the clock moved round slowly to nine o'clock, and still no one came. At one point I went over to the door and tried to open it. It was locked from the outside. So even if not formally under arrest, I was definitely being detained.

What I couldn't understand was why I still had my phone. I had always imagined that a suspect's mobile phone was the very first thing to be confiscated and checked for suspicious calls or movements. So why had I still got mine?

Maybe it was because they weren't allowed just to take it without first arresting me. Or were they hoping I would use it to contact an accomplice? Or to try to arrange a jailbreak?

In fact, I was more inclined to use it to order a pizza delivery, as I was starving—my breakfast in the Dublin Airport hotel seeming like a very long time ago.

At ten past nine, two men came into the room, one in a dark suit, and the other in pale chinos and a dark green polo shirt.

"Mr Jennings," said the one in the suit. "Thank you for coming to talk to us."

"I didn't have much choice in the matter," I replied sarcastically.

He fiddled with the black box on the table, which then emitted a long, loud beep.

"This interview is being recorded with both video and audio," he said loudly. Then he gave the date and the time. "This interview is with Mr Theodore Jennings. Present is Detective Constable Clarry, and I am Detective Sergeant Hamilton, both of Suffolk Constabulary. The interview will be conducted under caution. Mr Jennings, you do not have to say anything. But it may harm your defence if you do not mention, when questioned, something which you later rely on in court. Anything you do say may be given in evidence."

"Am I under arrest?" I asked before he could go on.

"No, sir, you are not under arrest," replied the sergeant.

"Then why has the door been locked while I waited for you?"

"So you didn't wander off and get lost." He said it with a smile. "This is a big police station."

Both of us knew he was lying.

"Do I need a solicitor?" I asked.

"I think that depends on whether you have anything to hide."

A solicitor would probably advise me to answer *"no comment"* to anything the detectives asked me, but would that be helpful or simply give them the impression that I was guilty?

Did I have anything to fear from this interview?

They hadn't even told me what it was about yet. Maybe I would wait and see, first, before I demanded a solicitor to be present.

"Why am I here?" I asked.

"To help us with our enquiries," the sergeant answered unhelpfully.

"Enquiries concerning what?" I asked.

"The murder of Elliot Mitchell."

I must have nodded ever so slightly—an involuntary body movement.

"So you knew about that."

"Someone called and told me. At about nine thirty this morning, when I was still at Dublin Airport."

"Who called you?" he asked.

Did I tell him? I didn't want to get Janis into trouble.

"We can always look at your phone records," DS Hamilton said, as if he was reading my mind.

"It was one of the employees of the sales company."

"Janis Thompson?" he asked.

He was obviously one step ahead of me—but then, he was the detective.

"Yes," I said.

"Why were you in Ireland?" he asked, changing tack.

Should I tell him that I was in Ireland investigating Elliot Mitchell? Would that help or worsen my present situation?

"Why don't you just ask me where I was on Monday night?" I said. "I can prove that I wasn't anywhere near Newmarket."

"But your phone was," he said. "A phone registered to your name was connected all evening to a mast on top of Newmarket telephone exchange. And that phone was called at 18:16, again at 18:20, and also at 18:23, and all of those calls were made by Elliot Mitchell. We checked the numbers."

I stared at him.

"But not this one's number," I said, holding up my replacement handset. "The phone you have tracked, and the one that was called, must be the one that I lost in a hit-and-run incident a week ago. Talk to PC Langford about it. He knows. He even called me this morning on this one's number." I held my new phone up again. "He was the policeman who attended the hit-and-run, and I reported to him at the time that my old phone had gone missing. Do a similar position check on this one. It will show you that I was just south of Oxford all night on Monday, from seven o'clock in the evening onwards."

I'm not sure he believed me. If so, he didn't seem particularly phased by his mistake, but it might help explain why the police had been so keen to question me in the first place. But what was Elliot Mitchell doing calling me anyway? And three times? I would have thought that I was the last person he wanted to talk to. At least my lost phone hadn't been used to call him. Then I could have been in real trouble.

"All the best villains," DS Hamilton said, by which I took him to mean all the worst villains, "are never near the scene of a crime when it actually happens. Indeed, it often appears that they are away abroad on holiday. It doesn't mean they actually are, or haven't arranged for someone else to commit the crime for them, and at a time when they have a cast-iron alibi."

"Don't be ridiculous."

Perhaps I should have asked for that solicitor after all.

"Being ridiculous, am I?" the sergeant said, his tone becoming quite hostile. "Why is it, therefore, that all the staff I have interviewed today at the bloodstock sales company in Newmarket have said the same thing? *"Theo Jennings has to be the one who's killed Elliot Mitchell. Theo Jennings had it in for him."*

"I think you will find it was the other way round," I said. "He had it in for me."

As soon as I'd said it, I realised it had been a mistake.

"So is that why you arranged to have him killed? Because his complaints about you have made you lose your job?"

"I didn't arrange to have him killed," I said. "How would I have been able to do such a thing anyway?"

"You tell me, Mr Jennings."

Did this detective really believe that I had contrived with some hitman to have Elliot bumped off in revenge for me losing my job?

If so, why hadn't he arrested me? And why was some tech wizard not already combing through my new mobile phone, searching for incriminating texts or emails between myself and this mysterious assassin?

Was it because there were actually no grounds for arresting me—no evidence whatsoever, other than general tittle-tattle at the sales company and some spurious and inaccurate telephone tracing? Was DS Hamilton simply hoping that I might incriminate myself in my answers to his questions?

If so, it was clearly time to stop answering them.

"As I am not under arrest," I said, "I would like to leave now."

"Interview terminated at . . ." The sergeant looked up at the clock. ". . . 21:27." He then pushed a button on the black box, to stop the recording, before looking across the table at me. "You will wait here."

He stood up and left the room, leaving his sidekick, DC Clarry, sitting silently at the table across from me.

So I had forced the issue.

I would now be either arrested on suspicion of conspiracy to murder, or I'd be allowed to depart; there were no other options, and DS Hamilton had obviously gone to consult with his superiors about which of those two courses he should take.

Either way, I thought, I would not be answering any more of his questions, at least not without a solicitor being present. It was proving far too easy for him to twist and distort what I was saying.

Twist, twist.

I was getting a dose of my own medicine.

* * *

I walked out of the Suffolk Police Investigation Centre at five past ten.

I had loudly demanded that the police organise a lift for me, back to Heathrow, to collect my car, but unsurprisingly, it hadn't been forthcoming.

"So how do I get there?" I'd asked DS Hamilton.

"That's your problem, sir, not mine," he had said dismissively. "Try catching a train."

But that was easier said than done because the last train that could have taken me to London tonight had departed from Bury St Edmunds station ten minutes previously.

So what did I do now?

First up, I tried calling Janis, and although I could hear that her phone was ringing, she didn't answer. The ringtone suddenly stopped, and a disembodied voice announced, "This person's phone is currently unavailable. Please try later, or send a text."

I tried again immediately, but with the same result, without even having been given the opportunity to leave a voicemail message. So I sent her a text.

Janis, please call me. Much love, Theo.

I stood there holding my phone, hopeful and expectant that it would ring, but it remained resolutely silent.

Surely she couldn't still be in the sales company restaurant in Newmarket, or perhaps the police had confiscated all the staff phones, or maybe the police had even turned off the network in Newmarket because the staff wouldn't stop using their phones to send texts.

I tried to console myself with those thoughts while fighting back the overwhelming fear that she was simply not accepting my calls.

But, for the moment, I had other priorities.

From my days hiking in the Himalayas, I knew the five priorities for survival in the wild, not that Bury St Edmunds was particularly wild, not on a Thursday evening at least.

Priority number one was shelter.

The rule of threes also applied: a person can survive *three minutes* without air, *three hours* without shelter in a hostile environment, *three days* without water, and *three weeks* without food.

How hostile was the environment in Bury St Edmunds?

Not very, I thought, although with a clear sky above, the temperature was already dropping fast, and a frost had been forecast.

I had no warm clothing other than a light rain jacket, nor a sleeping bag, so I needed a room for the night.

I fleetingly thought of calling Alex but quickly decided against it, and for two reasons: First, I didn't want him to get into trouble with the sales company for talking to me, and second, he might have actually told me to get lost.

Instead, I tried a hotel-booking website on my phone, but most rooms in Bury St Edmunds were unavailable, no doubt because of the sales and the racing just down the road in Newmarket. However, I did find one spare single in a pub in Crown Street in the centre of the town, about a mile away, so I quickly reserved it before it went off the system.

As I walked there, I tried Janis again, but with the same result as before.

So I sent her another text.

Janis, my love, please call me. I'm in Bury St Edmunds.

My phone rang, and Janis's number was shown on my screen. What joy!

I answered it, but it wasn't her, and it wasn't joyful.

"Stop calling my sister," said a male voice, which I assumed was David Thompson's. "She doesn't want to talk to you. Not now and not ever again. I am blocking your number from her phone."

He abruptly hung up before I had a chance to say anything.

I stood there staring at my phone in disbelief.

How could this be when it had only been three days since she had told me that she loved me? And she'd said it again the following day, on Tuesday evening, and we had spoken happily only this morning.

So what had changed so much in just a few hours?

The detective sergeant told me that all the staff he had interviewed at the sales company had said to him, *"Theo Jennings has to be the one who's killed Elliot Mitchell. Theo Jennings had it in for him."*

Had they all also spent the whole day repeating the same thing to Janis, so much so that she now believed it?

CHAPTER

26

As I walked, I thought.

In just a few days, my whole life seemed to have unravelled round my ears. I had lost my job and my home, and worst of all, it now seemed that I had also lost the girl I adored.

I wondered what else could go wrong.

At least, I still had my liberty, but for how much longer would that continue to be the case?

And why? What had I done wrong?

Absolutely nothing.

I arrived at the pub in Crown Street about half past ten, and having checked into my single room high under the eaves on the third floor, I went downstairs for a drink.

I felt I needed one.

I stood at the bar and ordered myself a gin and tonic plus two packets of crisps and a bag of roasted peanuts. The only topic of conversation amongst the other customers in the pub seemed to be the murder of Elliot Mitchell.

"At least the police have got their man," said someone standing next to me.

"What's that?" asked the man on the other side of him.

"Didn't you hear?" the first replied. "The local cops have arrested the person responsible. He's being questioned by them even as we speak. I hope he rots in hell. In fact, I wish we still had the death penalty for murder. They should string up the bastard."

I assumed that they were talking about me, so I decided to keep quiet and not correct him about the arrest, or rather the lack of it.

Did the whole world now believe that I had killed Elliot Mitchell?

At least no one in the pub yet knew my name, but I was quite certain that would change just as soon as the tabloid press found it out, as they surely would by simply asking any member of staff at the sales company.

Even if they weren't splashed across the front pages, the two words *Theo* and *Jennings* would circulate like wildfire on social media.

Then what would I do?

Another visit to the Buddhist monastery, high in the Himalayas, was becoming more attractive by the minute.

* * *

It would be inaccurate for me to say that I had another disturbed night's sleep, because I hardly slept at all. Instead, I lay on my back in the dark, listening to the creaks and bumps as the roof above me cooled.

During those long hours awake, I thought some more, but everything always came back to the same two basic questions: Who had killed Elliot Mitchell? And why?

I wondered again about some aggrieved breeder who might have been swindled by Elliot out of their rightful profit from the sale of their horses. Would they really murder him in revenge? It seemed a very big step when an easier course would have been to report him to the Bloodstock Industry Ethics Committee and thus destroy his reputation.

What leads someone to murder another human being?

Terrorist murders, such as by suicide bombers of people unknown and unrelated to them, are designed to be shocking and to highlight certain causes in the inevitable publicity, be they polit-ical, racial, or religious. The same could also be said about certain mass shootings, many of which end with the perpetrator turning their weapon on themselves.

Leaving those aside, which I felt was safe to do in this case, where someone had gone to great lengths to try and make it look like Elliot had killed himself, motives for almost all other murders fitted into three main sets of *L*: lust, loathing, and loot.

Perhaps a fourth *L*, love, should be included because a signifi-cant number of murders are committed out of love, to put an end to the victim's suffering and pain, but Elliot's murder didn't seem to fit that criterion either.

So was it lust, loathing or loot, or maybe a combination of them all?

My bets were on the last two, as Elliot's death didn't appear to have any sexual connection, although I had to admit that I was unaware of his romantic liaisons. Perhaps there had been a jealous husband lurking somewhere in the shadows.

But loathing or loot seemed to be much more likely.

Had a horse breeder loathed him so much that murder was the result, or was it all to do with money? And if the latter, what was it about money that required him dead?

It seemed to me that if I was going to be able to salvage any-thing in my life, it was no good just bleating on to the police that it wasn't me that killed Elliot Mitchell. I had to set about trying to find out both who *had* killed him and *why* they had.

* * *

I caught the seven thirty train from Bury St Edmunds on Friday morning, but not the one going towards Ipswich, from where I could have connected with a fast service to Liverpool Street Station in London. Instead, I caught a train going the other way, towards Cambridge, and I got off at Newmarket.

I turned left, leaving the station, and went along Paddocks Drive before turning right into Woodditton Road. I walked alongside—but outside—the wall that marked the boundary of the sales company estate, and climbed the hill, up to the cemetery and the High Street.

I first turned left, and then, at the statue of Queen Elizabeth II with a mare and foal, I went right into Hamilton Road, home to twenty or so of the sixty-six racehorse training stables in Newmarket.

At 8:20 precisely, I walked into Brian Kitman's yard as he was preparing a string of horses to go out onto the training grounds. I had my phone in one hand and my overnight bag in the other.

He saw me immediately and strode over purposefully.

"Get off my bloody property," he shouted angrily.

"You and I need to talk," I said back, much more quietly.

"I'm not talking to you. Bugger off, or I'll call the police." He took his mobile phone out of his pocket and held it up to show me that he meant business.

"What hold did Elliot Mitchell have over you?" I said, ignoring his threat.

"I don't know what you mean."

"Oh, I think you do, and I'm sure the police would be interested to know the answer too. So, go ahead—call them. Let them come."

He hesitated.

"And does the name Grace Ryan mean anything to you?" I asked him.

He stared at me, and there was a distinct touch of panic in his eyes.

"I can't speak to you now," he said quickly. "I'm too busy."

"Make time."

He turned round and looked at the horses currently being mounted by his stable staff.

"Send them out with your assistant," I said.

"Wait here," he said, and walked off, back towards the horses.

I waited and watched as he spoke to one of his staff, and then the string went out through the small gate at the back of the property, straight onto the training grounds on Newmarket Heath.

When the horses were out of sight, Kitman came back towards me.

"In the yard office," he said, turning sharp right.

I followed him into a small room built onto the end of one of the stable blocks. It was a fairly sparse affair, with just a stained wooden desk and three green plastic garden chairs. A large board hung on the far wall, showing the names of all of the horses and the grooms, and with coloured lines between them detailing when each horse was due out for exercise and who was to be riding it.

It was clearly not the main training office, where he would have other staff sitting at computers, doing owner accounts, and sorting out a myriad of other stuff, not least the entries and declarations for races. This was simply a place for the stable staff to find out which horse they were riding, and when.

Kitman sat on the chair behind the desk, and I sat down across from him, putting my bag on the floor and my phone on the table, screen side down.

"Grace Ryan," I repeated.

"What about her?" he asked, having regained some of his composure.

"Whose idea was it to defraud her out of her rightful return for that yearling?"

"She wasn't defrauded," he replied sharply. "Mitch paid her a fair price for the colt. In fact, he probably paid her too much."

"Because it had bone chips in its hocks?"

If he was surprised that I knew about that, he didn't show it.

"But Mitchell then switched the X-rays."

"I don't know what you're talking about. I think I've given you enough of my time." He stood up. "You will have to leave now."

I didn't move other than to cross my legs.

"You can either tell me," I said, "or you can tell the police. And they might also want to talk to you about Mitchell's murder. And I can assure you, that that is not a pleasant experience."

"But I know absolutely nothing about any murder," he said, somewhat alarmed.

Did I believe him? Maybe I did.

"So where were you on Monday evening and Monday night? How's your alibi for the time of the murder? Mine's cast iron—I was miles away. That's why the police let me go."

I could tell that he was slightly rattled.

"But I know where you were on Friday morning, Brian," I said. "I saw you, remember, hiding down at the horsebox loading bays with Elliot Mitchell? Were you planning your next little criminal project?"

"You don't know what you're talking about."

"Don't I?" I said slowly. "Then tell me. What were you doing there?"

He didn't answer, but he did sit down again.

"So," I said, "I now know that Mitchell bought the dead colt from Grace Ryan back in June for two hundred and fifty thousand euros, less the seven and a half per cent commission he also stole from her. For the transaction, he invented a spurious entity called Starsign Bloodstock as the buyer, but Mitchell also owned Starsign, so the purchase of the colt itself was a fraud. Then he switched the set of joint X-rays that were submitted to the sales so that they didn't show the bone chips in its hocks. Fraud number two."

I uncrossed my legs and leaned down on the table.

"Next, you and Mitchell conspired to collusively bid the colt up to three million guineas, insure it at that value, and then kill it. The horse had to die, of course, and the carcass be rapidly disposed of, or the switch of the X-rays would have soon been discovered.

"The insurance company would have to pay for the horse. After deduction of commission, the balance would be sent to Starsign Bloodstock, a cheque dropping through the letterbox of number sixty-four Main Street in Cashel, an accommodation address for Starsign Bloodstock, ready for collection and encashment by no other than Elliot Mitchell. Fraud number three."

I stopped, but Kitman said nothing. He just went on looking at me.

"There are, however, a couple of things I still don't know. First, how you or Mitchell killed the colt in a manner that was undetectable by a post-mortem? And secondly—and which is far more baffling to me—is why you, a highly successful racehorse trainer with a string of Group 1 winners to your name and a hitherto unblemished reputation, found yourself embroiled in something so sordid as a multimillion-pound insurance swindle?"

There was still no response from Brian Kitman.

"So that brings me back to my very first question to you," I said finally. "What hold did Elliot Mitchell have over you?"

I leaned back in the garden chair and waited, recrossing my legs.

"I bet you think you're really bloody clever, don't you?" Kitman said smugly. "But you're not. Mitch was much cleverer than you'll ever be. You don't even know the half of what he did."

"So tell me." I said.

He seemed suddenly to realise that he should have said nothing at all.

"There's nothing to tell," he said, but he was far too late for that.

There clearly was something to tell, but he wouldn't be doing it, at least not without a little persuasion from me first.

"So," I said, "If Mitch was so damn clever, why is he now dead and I'm still alive?" I looked at him for several seconds. "Did you kill him?" I asked.

"Don't be stupid. Why would I?"

"I don't know, but someone did, and I know it wasn't me. So, who else was involved in his little schemes?"

"I think you had better go now," he said, standing up again.

"Or what?" I replied, again without moving. "Are you going to call the police? Or shall I do that?" I reached over for my phone, but I didn't actually pick it up.

"You know nothing."

"I know for a fact that you have been breaking the Bloodstock Industry Code of Practice by collusive bidding. After you bid up that colt to three million, both you and Elliot Mitchell went to the gents' at the top of the stairs in the admin block. Do you remember? In there, you were berating him for nearly leaving you as the high bidder when the hammer fell. Your exact words to him were: *'Bloody hell, Mitch. I thought for a moment you were going to leave me in there at two million six. . . . that young auctioneer nearly dropped his hammer early. I could see it in his eyes as he stared up at me.'"*

I paused and looked at him.

"And you were right, I very nearly did drop my hammer at two million six. You see, Brian, I know exactly what you said to Elliot Mitchell in the gents' because I heard you say it. I was standing in one of the cubicles."

"But they were empty," he said. "I checked. The doors were unlocked."

"So you *do* remember," I said. "The cubicles may have been unlocked, but one of them wasn't empty."

He sat down again, heavily this time.

"Now, Brian," I said, leaning earnestly forward towards him. "I might just go to the Bloodstock Industry Ethics Committee and lay everything I know before them. I am sure that they will find the CCTV footage very interesting viewing, especially that showing the sale ring during the sale of the dead colt. Or maybe that taken during the sale of the Opera House Star colt the following day, when you and Mitchell tried the same trick again. And if I remember correctly, which I do, your body language was most revealing when you thought you'd be left as the high bidder, because initially I wouldn't take Elliot Mitchell's bid. The CCTV in the sale ring covers all the angles, you know, including your favourite bidding spot at the top of the stairwell."

I paused and leaned back again.

"Oh God!" he said, sweating profusely.

He might indeed say, *"Oh God!"*

If the Ethics Committee concluded that he had seriously breached the Bloodstock Industry Code of Conduct, the racing authorities would quite likely also deem him to be not a *fit and proper person* to hold a racehorse trainer's licence.

And that meant he would certainly lose his livelihood, and he might also lose his home because it was in licenced premises.

"Or, then again," I said gently. "I might not even go to the Committee."

He stared at me. "What do you want?" he asked quietly.

But not so quietly, I thought, that it wouldn't have been picked up by the microphone of my mobile phone, which was recording the whole exchange between us—as it had been doing so ever since I had first walked into his yard.

27

"A BICYCLE PUMP? WHAT did he do, hit the colt over the head with it?"

Brian Kitman laughed, which I thought was totally inappropriate in the current circumstances. "No. He used it to inject air into the colt's jugular vein."

"Inject air?"

"You know those metal-spike things which you attach to a bicycle pump to inflate a football. Well, Mitch sharpened one of those until it was like a hypodermic needle. He then injected a whole bloody bicycle pump full of air into the colt's neck. A great bubble of it went straight to its heart. Killed it in seconds, and with no trace. When that vet cut the heart open in the post-mortem, the air would just have floated away. Made it look like the horse died from natural causes."

"Surely the horse wouldn't just stand there and let Mitchell stick a metal spike into its neck."

"Horses get used to having blood taken from their jugular veins. Vets do it all the time. They usually don't even flinch."

"So were you there when he did it?" I asked.

"No. Of course not. He was on his own. But he told me about it afterwards. Almost boasted about how easy it had been. Except that the horse apparently went down so fast it nearly landed on top of him."

Shame it didn't, I thought. *It might have solved a lot of my future problems.*

"Had he done it before?" I asked.

"Not at the sales. He said he'd tried it once in Ireland, during the summer, as a sort of trial run, on an old mare that had outlived her fertility."

What had Janis told me about a hypodermic needle?

I tried to remember and finally got it. A post-mortem had shown that Elliot Mitchell had had a small hypodermic puncture in his chest.

Was his cause of death the same as for the colt?

"So who else was involved?" I asked.

"No one else, as far as I'm aware," he said.

"So how come you were?"

"Mitch said that if I didn't help him bid up the colt, he would bid against me for any horse that I wanted in the future. He also said that none of the horses he bought for any owner would ever come to my stables. He even threatened to tell my current owners that he should be the person buying for them, rather than them leaving it to me."

"Why didn't you report him?" I said.

"For what? It's not against the rules for him to try and get more business for himself. All the bloody agents are trying the same thing. But Elliot Mitchell was the agent with the greatest influence with the owners. I couldn't take the risk."

"But you took a much greater risk in agreeing to bid up the colt."

"Mitch assured me that it was totally risk free. No one would believe that he and I had conspired together—not two of the big boys."

And he'd been right.

During the auction of the colt, I'd thought they were each bidding on behalf of different prospective buyers. Without the overheard conversation in the gents', no one would have ever questioned that they might be colluding together.

Not even me.

And after the overheard conversation, I was still the only person that did believe it, and that was only because it was me that had done the overhearing.

Even the chairman thought I must have been mistaken—assuming that he hadn't already known what was going to happen.

The chairman was due to have been the auctioneer for that particular lot, and I'd only remained on the rostrum because he'd arrived late. So was he also involved?

"So what did Mitch offer you?" I asked Kitman.

"In what way?"

"How much money?"

"He didn't offer me any money."

"So Mitchell stood to make more than two and half million, and he didn't offer to give you any of it. Some friend."

"I can assure you that he was no friend of mine," Kitman said slowly.

"So are you pleased that he's dead?"

"Indeed I am, but it doesn't mean I killed him."

So who did?

* * *

I left Brian Kitman's yard when his horses came back in from the Heath.

The stable staff had started coming to the yard office to confirm their next rides, and Kitman also told me he had to get off to the sales and then to the races.

"One more thing," I'd said to him as I was leaving. "Did you ever go to Cashel to collect the mail for Starsign Bloodstock?"

"Never," he'd replied. "I had nothing to do with any of that."

So who was the other fella?

On the train, I had checked the sales company website, and it said that the sales were resuming this morning at nine o'clock, breaking for the racing at one, and then continuing in the evening. They would also run tomorrow morning, prior to racing;

tomorrow evening; and, if necessary, even go into Sunday to catch up on time lost yesterday.

Kitman didn't tell me much more other than the fact that he thought Mitchell also had other scams on the go.

"Mitch claimed that he was enhancing his pension pot so he could retire early and go live in the Caribbean. He once said something to me about being involved in fixing VAT. But I don't know what it was about or if anyone else was involved."

Janis had also said something to me about VAT—Value Added Tax. What was it??

"So what are you going to do now?" Kitman had asked, clearly worried that he had told me too much.

"Go on looking," I'd replied.

"I mean about me?"

"Nothing. At least not yet. Mitchell is the villain here—plus whoever killed him."

I had recorded all of our conversation, but had done so without Brian Kitman's permission. I knew it wasn't illegal per se to record someone without his or her knowledge. It was what you did with the recording afterwards that mattered. Putting it into the public domain would be a breach of his privacy. Hence, I wasn't sure whether the contents could be admissible as evidence in a court of law, or even at the Bloodstock Industry Ethics Committee.

As I left Kitman's stable yard, I used my phone to call Janis again but simply heard the "currently unavailable" message. So I sent a text, but it said, "Not delivered."

The screen on my phone showed that it was half past nine, and as I walked back up Hamilton Road to the High Street, I wondered what I should do.

My car was still at Heathrow, racking up unnecessary charges in the Terminal 5 long-term car park. So should I go and collect it now?

It would take me several hours to get there—train to Cambridge, change for one going to Kings Cross, tube across London, and then another train from Paddington to Heathrow. Then I'd have to drive back round the M25 on a Friday afternoon, when the traffic on the motorway was always horrendous.

Add to that at least another hour for changing trains and getting the car out of the car park, and I'd likely not be back in Newmarket until six o'clock at the earliest, quite possibly later—and I needed to be here at five.

There was something else I wanted to do then.

So what did I do instead, and for the next seven hours?

First on my agenda was breakfast. The pub in Bury St Edmunds hadn't started serving until seven thirty, by which time I was already catching the train to Newmarket.

I walked down the High Street to the local greasy-spoon café and ordered a full English fry-up.

The place was doing brisk business, with many dressed for the races, some with binocular cases slung over their shoulders, and I had to share a table with two others, a man and a woman in their forties, who were studying form in the *Racing Post*.

"Off to the races?" I asked them.

"We sure are," the woman replied. "Do you have any tips?"

I shook my head. "Sorry. I don't even know what's running."

"Eight bloody races," the man said, scratching his head. "They've divided the maiden fillies stakes. I can't understand why. There are only nine runners in each division. It's not as if they couldn't run all eighteen at once. I mean, there are thirty-two in the Cesarewitch tomorrow, and they also have to go round the bend rather than just down the straight course."

"At least it gives you another race to watch," I said between mouthfuls of fried egg and bacon.

"Another race for the wife to lose my shirt on, you mean." He laughed, and she playfully punched his arm. "Are you going?"

It was a thought. "What time's the first race?" I asked.

"One thirty."

"Maybe," I said, even though, with seven further races, I would certainly have to leave before the last. But going to the races on my own was never much fun, and especially not after having been at the same racecourse the previous Saturday with Janis, with fond memories of what had happened afterwards on the carpet in front of the fire.

"Perhaps we'll see you later, then," the man said, standing up to go. "At the races."

"Yeah," I replied. "Maybe."

After the couple had departed, I remained sitting there alone, staring into the bottom of my empty coffee cup, wondering how my life had crumbled from diamonds to dust in such a short space of time.

I so wished that I had not overheard Brian Kitman and Elliot Mitchell talking that afternoon, just ten days ago. Then, with me being none the wiser, they could have progressed their little scheme to defraud the insurance company. Mitchell would probably still be alive, and my left ankle wouldn't be as sore in the evenings as it had been now for more than a week. And maybe Janis would have still been talking to me.

But what was done was done. What was heard was heard. And there was no winding the clock back or wishing it away.

Even though I thought it highly unlikely that I'd ever regain my job as an auctioneer selling horses, I still felt that I had to press on and discover the whole truth of this nightmare. To do otherwise would always leave a cloud over my future, at least in my mind, even if not in the minds of everyone else.

* * *

In the end, I decided not to go to the races, mostly because I couldn't bear to be with all those people, not when I needed time to be alone to think.

Instead, I went to the National Horseracing Museum—anything to distract me from the dread that I might have lost Janis for good.

The museum, together with the British Sporting Art Trust's magnificent collection of paintings and sculptures, is situated just south of the High Street, within the remaining part of the palace and racing stables of Charles II.

Flanked these days by coffee bars, hairdressers, nail and tan-
ning salons—even a tattoo parlour—Palace House was constructed
for the King in 1671, to the design of William Samwell, and it
remained as a royal residence in the town well into the nineteenth
century, before being sold to the Rothschild banking family.

The building was briefly requisitioned during the Second
World War for use as the RAF officers' mess for the aerodrome on
the racecourse, before it was eventually saved from neglect in 1992
by the local council, supported by English Heritage, and it opened
as part of the horseracing museum in 2016.

On this racing afternoon, it was all very quiet, with most
of their prospective patrons no doubt down the road at the racecourse, and so I had the place almost to myself.

I had lived in Newmarket for more than three years, but I'd
never set foot inside Palace House before. I wandered through the
galleries, even into King Charles's former bedroom, where he had
once enjoyed the favours of his mistress, Nell Gwynne, whom he
had conveniently accommodated in a cottage across the road.

As I admired the British Sporting Art's collection of fabulous
and priceless masterpieces by none other than George Stubbs and
Sir Alfred Munnings, I wondered back to what Brian Kitman had
told me at the end of our meeting.

Did I really believe that Elliot Mitchell had been scamming
his VAT?

If so, it was hardly something that I would have been able to
discover anyway, as I had no access to his financial records. That
would now be up to the executors of his will to uncover, they and
the tax authorities.

I went across Palace Road to the rest of the museum and
meandered amongst their huge assortment of jockey silks, big-race
trophies, and other racing memorabilia, including the six-chamber
revolver that Fred Archer had used to take his own life.

Fred Archer is the most successful jockey that British racing
has ever seen, winning more than a third of the eight thousand
races he rode in during the latter part of the nineteenth century—in

comparison, Gordon Richards, Lester Piggott, Frankie Dettori, and Tony McCoy all won fewer than a quarter, while the great American jockey Willie Shoemaker won barely a fifth.

Having already been champion jockey for thirteen straight years by the time he was just twenty-nine, Fred Archer shot himself while the balance of his mind was disturbed due to the endless starvation diet he was forced to follow to keep his body weight some forty pounds below the normal healthy level for a man of his height.

He was the mega-mega-sports star of his time, and it was said that when news of his death reached London, grown men cried in the street as they queued to buy a special commemorative edition of the *Evening News*.

I looked at the gun behind the glass screen.

I could do with one of those, I thought, for my personal protection.

It was now eight days since someone had tried to run me over in the driveway behind Beaumont Court, and I was still no closer to finding out who. Had it actually been Elliot Mitchell? Or someone else—even the person who had then murdered him?

But why would anybody want to kill Elliot Mitchell just because he was fiddling his VAT? I knew that His Majesty's Revenue and Customs had a reputation for being relentless in their pursuit of tax evaders, but I was pretty sure that they hadn't yet resorted to murder.

So what else was it that had resulted in his death?

28

I WAS IN POSITION well before five o'clock. In fact, I was there by half past four.

I was sitting on a bench in front of the King Edward VII Memorial Hall at the junction of The Avenue with the High Street, and I was as nervous as I had ever been in my life—much more than I had been for my first time on the rostrum as an auctioneer in Australia.

I was nervous on a couple of different counts.

Firstly, would she come? And secondly, and far more importantly, would she speak to me or simply run away?

Janis had told me during our first date at the Roxana Bar in the Bedford Lodge Hotel that she was driven in to work every morning, and at five o'clock she would walk to the local community hospital, where her mother worked, to be driven home again. And the most likely route from her office at the sales company to the hospital would take her past where I was waiting.

But would she be coming today?

The sales on a Newmarket race day were split—morning and evening—so would she be working the evening session on this particular Friday? Or was today the one day a fortnight that she spent at the accounting college in Cambridge? Or was she off sick? Or did she go a different route, such as via Hamilton Road? Or would her mother come and pick her up today? Or had she been offered a lift from one of the others in her office? Or were there any number of other reasons why she wouldn't be walking this way this afternoon?

And even if she did come, would she then stop and talk to me, or tell me to leave her alone? Maybe even scream for help. My heart was pounding at the very thought of that.

I forced myself to calm down.

For the umpteenth time, I checked the time on my phone—16:47.

She wouldn't be here yet, even if she was coming.

I stood up and paced a bit, to relieve the tension in my legs.

Was this the right thing to do, I asked myself, or could it make things worse? Should I act decisively now, or should I give her more time? Should I have just gone and fetched my car from Heathrow and driven it to my mother's house?

And what would I do if she didn't come?

I looked up at the building, which, according to the plaque on the front, had been given to the people of Newmarket in 1913 by the financier Sir Ernest Cassel, in memory of his close friend the late King Edward VII, who had died the previous year.

In the centre, above the windows of the first floor, was a terracotta portrait of the King, surrounded by a wreath.

I wondered why I couldn't have the confidence that he'd clearly had with members of the opposite sex. He had married at age twenty-one to Princess Alexandria of Denmark, and they'd had six children together, but she had clearly not been enough for him. He had been nicknamed "Dirty Bertie" and "Edward the Caresser" by the press, on account of his insatiable sex drive. He'd had literally thousands of mistresses all over Europe, including Lady Randolph Churchill, the future mother of Winston, and even commissioned a purpose-built ornate sex chair, which was kept in the room he rented permanently at Le Chabanais, an upmarket Parisian brothel.

Yes, I bet old Dirty Bertie had never been clumsy and awkward at sex, like I had been.

I checked my phone again—16:54.

The closer it moved to five o'clock, the more nervous I became. 16:56.

I sat down again on the bench because I felt that my presence might be less intimidating to her if I was sitting down.

16:58.

My right leg began to twitch, my heel bouncing up and down with nerves. I moved it, making the sole of my shoe lie flat on the floor. It stopped.

The time on my phone finally changed to 17:00.

I made myself take some deep breaths and tried to relax the tightness in my shoulders.

She won't come, I told myself. *She'll be working late. She won't want to see me anyway. I'm wasting my time. I shouldn't be here.*

17.05 came and went, and there was still no sign.

By now, I had convinced myself that she wouldn't be coming, and I was beginning to lose my nerve anyway.

I even said it out loud. "Of course, she won't come."

But she did, at 17:08.

* * *

I spotted her before she saw me. She was walking along The Avenue towards the junction with the High Street, wearing her blue sales-company uniform.

Just seeing her made my heart leap with excitement, and in that instant, all my nervousness faded away. This suddenly felt like absolutely the right thing to be doing.

She caught sight of me as she was crossing the road at the traffic lights. There was a minor falter in her step, but she didn't stop, and far from running away, she actually ran towards me.

I stood up and took her in my arms.

"God I've missed you," she said, nestling her head into my chest.

Then she pulled away. "But I'm not meant to be with you."

"Why not?" I asked.

"My father says so. He says we've already had enough to do with murderers to last us a lifetime. Mum and David agreed."

"But I'm not a murderer. I wasn't even here at the time. I have an alibi."

"That's what Ian Huntley said. But it wasn't true."

"But mine *is* true," I insisted.

"Anne-Marie's police boyfriend said you were arrested at Heathrow because you were trying to flee the country. Why would you do that if you weren't guilty?"

"Anne-Marie's boyfriend is wrong. I wasn't *fleeing* the country. Quite the reverse. I'd just arrived back in the country, from Ireland. You know that. And I also wasn't arrested. I was simply invited to go to Bury St Edmunds to answer some questions."

I didn't mention that there had been threats of arrest if I didn't accept their "invitation."

"What questions?" she asked. "Why did they think you were involved?"

"Because everyone in the sales company has been telling the police that it must have been me that killed Mitchell because his complaint made me lose my job. But I promise you, I didn't kill him. And the police know that now. That's why I'm not still with them."

"But David said . . ."

"I don't care what David said. He doesn't like me, and he's simply using this as an excuse to stop you seeing me."

She nodded. "He blocked you from my phone."

"So why didn't you unblock it?"

"He said he'd check my calls."

I didn't ask her why she would let him. As she'd once said— her family life was complicated.

She looked at her watch. "I have to go. I've got to meet Mum at the hospital in fifteen minutes."

"I'll walk with you."

She looked around in alarm. "I mustn't be seen talking to you. All the staff were all warned again today not to speak to you either in person or by phone."

"Who by?" I asked.

"The chairman. It was in an email memo he sent round to everyone."

"What else did it say about me?"

"It just said that the police had told him you were helping them with their enquiries into the death of Elliot Mitchell, and we were not to talk to you."

The whole world knew that "helping with enquiries" was police-speak for grilling a suspect in the hope of obtaining a confession. In the eyes of the company staff, I would be guilty unless and until I was proven innocent.

So, that's what I had to do—prove that I was innocent. And the only way of doing that was to find out who was the real killer.

I pulled up the hood of my rain jacket.

"Come on," I said. "We'll go a back route."

One of the advantages of Newmarket being a centre for training racehorses is that a whole network of dedicated horse walks exists through the town to allow the horses to get from their stables to the training grounds without having to fight with the mechanical traffic. And those horse walks would be deserted at this time of day because all the horses would be safely in their stables.

We first went through the memorial gardens behind the hall, and then along one of the horse walks.

As we went, I took Janis's hand in mine.

"I need your help," I said to her.

"What for?"

"To prove that I didn't kill Elliot Mitchell."

"But how can I? Surely that's for the police to do."

"The police aren't interested in proving anyone's innocence, only their guilt. Unless I can find out who really did kill Mitchell, there will always be those who will believe it was me. And I'll need your help to do that."

I told her about my visit to Brian Kitman's yard and how he thought Mitchell was running a dodgy scheme involving VAT.

"What was it you said to me about VAT when I was in Ireland?"

"It was Starsign Bloodstock's address," she replied. "I found it in our VAT records."

"Starsign is Irish, but maybe it's also registered for VAT in the UK. Quite a lot of Irish companies are. And if so, it must have a UK VAT number."

"Is that what you want me to find out?"

"Yes, but you have to be very careful. No one must know you're doing it."

Was it even fair, I wondered, to ask her to do such a thing? Someone had murdered Elliot Mitchell, and the same person may well have tried to kill me, so was it too dangerous?

Should I simply go to the police with what I had learned from Brian Kitman, and let them sort it out? But DS Hamilton had made it quite clear that he still thought I had something to do with the murder.

"You'll be back, mark my words," the sergeant had said as his parting shot to me when I left the investigation centre in Bury St Edmunds. "And then we won't be so nice to you."

If I went to him with the recording of my Kitman conversation, I could see him dismissing it as a smokescreen to what he thought I had actually done. And I would never forgive myself if something happened to Janis because she was caught doing something illegal for me. She would surely lose her job, if not something more serious.

"On second thoughts, forget it," I said to her. "It's not worth the risk of you getting into trouble."

She gripped my hand tighter. "But who else will do it?"

"No, seriously, my love, don't even look. Forget I ever asked. There is someone out there who killed Elliot Mitchell, and I don't want them finding out that you are delving into things you shouldn't be."

"But you think he was killed over VAT?"

"I have no idea, but there must have been some sort of motive. People don't kill for no reason."

She suddenly stopped and turned to look at me.

"Ian Huntley did."

The Soham murders were clearly still very raw for her more than twenty years after they took place. I gave her a comforting hug, then we went on towards the local community hospital.

"You'd better not come in," Janis said as we arrived. "I don't want my mum to know we've been together."

I resisted the temptation to say that surely she was old enough to decide who she could be with or talk to.

"Can I see you tomorrow?" I asked. "How about for lunch?"

"I can't. Mr Pollard has asked all the Accounts staff to go in to work tomorrow, to catch up for Thursday."

"I hope he's paying you extra."

"He's offered each of us a hundred-pound bonus."

"I hope it's a cash bonus," I said. "With no tax deducted."

"You must be kidding." She laughed. "He's a stickler for doing everything by the book, especially when it comes to tax."

I held her hand. "Could you at least unblock me on your phone?"

She hesitated. "David said he'd check."

"Let him," I said. "I had nothing to do with Mitchell's murder. Tell David that."

"He won't believe it."

"Do you?"

"Of course I do," she said, but it didn't sound too convincing.

"How could I have?" I implored. "I was with my mother near Oxford from seven o'clock on Monday evening. She can vouch for that. She lives a good two hours' drive away from here, and you told me that Elliot was seen drinking in the bar at six. Then, early on Tuesday morning, I drove straight from my mother's house to the airport for my flight to Ireland. You called me, remember. I was already in the Heathrow departure lounge. So it's absolutely impossible for me to have killed him."

"David says that you could have arranged for someone else to do it."

I stared at her. "And who could that be exactly? Do you really think I have a list of hired assassins on standby in my contacts list?"

"No, of course not."

"Well then," I said. "That proves I had nothing to do with Mitchell's death."

Except that I probably had everything to do with it.

If it hadn't been for me asking difficult questions about the dead colt, whoever *was* responsible may not have killed him in the first place.

CHAPTER

29

I WATCHED AS JANIS disappeared into the community hospital to meet up with her mother, and my heart ached that I couldn't contact her, and didn't know when I would next be able to.

In spite of my urging, she would still not unblock me from her phone because she was too frightened of her brother, David.

"Please call me when you can," I implored as she walked away from me. "Even though you've blocked my incoming calls and texts, you can still use your phone to call or text *me*."

She didn't turn round.

"Janis Thompson, I love you," I shouted after her. "Just call me. Please. Use a payphone if you have to."

That's if she could even find a public payphone, I thought. I hadn't seen one anywhere in Newmarket during all the years I'd been there.

She strode determinedly across the car park, towards the hospital entrance, without even a backwards glance. Not even once did she turn back to wave.

I felt bereft.

And what did I do now?

If it had been difficult to find a room in Bury St Edmunds yesterday, it would be totally impossible to find one in Newmarket tonight, in the middle of the Future Champions Festival. For miles around they would be occupied with racegoers, many of them eagerly anticipating Lucky Mike's run in the Dewhurst Stakes the following afternoon.

I supposed it was still early enough for me to catch a train from Newmarket to Cambridge, and another from there to Kings Cross. I was pretty sure I could find a room somewhere in London, even on a Friday night, but it would be at a price.

And was that what I wanted to do?

Not really, but what other choice did I have?

Gloomily, I walked away from the hospital, back towards the town centre, returning to the same bench where I had waited for Janis outside the Memorial Hall. Then, instead of going straight down The Avenue to the railway station, I turned right and walked up the hill to Beaumont Court.

I rang the doorbell of number twelve, but there was no reply.

Why had I thought there would be?

Alex would be in the sale ring, doing his job as a spotter at the evening session, and he probably wouldn't be back until ten o'clock at the earliest, especially as they were trying to catch up on the time that was lost on Thursday.

That left me with a dilemma.

The last train of the day from Newmarket to London, via Cambridge, one that would get me into Kings Cross at midnight, left at ten past ten.

If I waited for Alex to get back and then he refused to allow me to stay or, worse still, even to speak to me, I wouldn't have time to get to the station to catch the train, and then I'd be in trouble. Or I could go now and make the train with ease, even maybe catch an earlier one and get into London in time to fetch my car from the airport and drive home to my mother's for the night.

I considered the options and decided to take my chances with Alex, and to wait.

I still had the key to his flat's front door in my pocket, but I thought it would be ill-advised to use it. He might not be best pleased to find me inside. So I sat down on the floor of the vestibule and waited.

*   *   *

I must have nodded off, because I was awakened by a gentle kick on my right leg.

"What the bloody hell are you doing out here?" Alex demanded, standing over me.

I quickly looked at my phone. It showed me that it was 22:10, the exact time that the last train to Cambridge was leaving New-market station.

"I'm sorry," I said. "I need a bed for the night,"

"So why are you out here?" he asked again.

"Because I've missed the last train to London."

I feared he was angry with me for turning up unannounced at his door, but I had misunderstood him.

"But you still have the key," he said. "Why didn't you let your-self in?"

"I didn't like to."

"You silly man," he said, smiling at me.

He reached down and gave me his hand to help me stand up.

"Come on in."

He unlocked the front door, and I followed him into the flat, into the place that had been my home for the past three years.

"I'm starving," he said over his shoulder as he went into the kitchen. "How about you?"

"Famished," I replied, following him. I'd had nothing to eat since my breakfast fry-up, more than twelve hours previously.

"Eggs do?" Alex asked. "It's all I have."

"Then they will do fine."

He scrambled them, on toast, and they were delicious.

"I'm so sorry," he said, laying down his knife and fork.

"For what?"

"Making you leave the flat like that on Monday. I should have told the chairman to bugger off."

"You couldn't do that," I said. "You'd have lost your job in an instant. It's all right. Although I was a little worried you wouldn't let me in tonight."

"Don't be stupid. But I presume no one knew you were coming here."

"No."

"Good." He lowered the blind on the kitchen window. "Then, what no one knows about, no one will worry about." He put our plates in the dishwasher. "So what have you been doing all week?"

"I went to Ireland for two nights," I said.

"Did you, indeed? And what did you discover?"

"What makes you think I was looking for anything?"

"I know you very well, Theo Jennings, and you wouldn't piss off to Ireland in mid-October just to take the waters."

I laughed. "I found out that Elliot Mitchell already owned the three-million colt before it went into our sale ring for him to 'buy' again at a hugely inflated price, so that he could make a fraudulent insurance claim for the higher amount."

"Wow! Does the chairman know that?"

"Not unless he's also involved."

Alex stared at me. "Do you really think he is?"

"He kept telling me to forget what I heard and leave it alone. Was that because he didn't want me to find anything out? Then he suspended me from my job. Was that so I couldn't keep asking questions?"

"I find that difficult to believe," Alex replied.

"But would you have ever believed that Elliot Mitchell could be murdered? Or that someone would try and kill me too? I tell you, the world around here has gone mad, and quite frankly, I could believe anything of anyone at the moment."

I told him about my trip to see Brian Kitman, and then I played him the recording of our conversation.

"You should take that to the police," Alex said.

"Perhaps I should, but I recorded it without Kitman's knowledge. I'm not sure if it would be admissible in a court."

"But the police would surely want to interview him about Mitchell's death. He might be the killer."

"I don't think so. He would never have told me as much as he did. Not if he was a murderer."

"Then who is?" Alex asked pointedly.

*   *   *

I slept in my usual bed, and more soundly than the last time I'd been there.

"We caught up quite a lot yesterday evening," Alex said over Saturday breakfast. "They've asked me to go in this morning, but I'm hopeful I won't be needed for the evening session, even if there is one. I have plans to go to Cambridge."

I looked at him and raised a questioning eyebrow.

"Yes," he said with a slight smile. "I'm going to a pub in the town centre that the internet says is a friendly place where you can meet people—you know—gay people. I'm taking the train." He took a deep breath. "I don't know whether to be excited, nervous, or just downright terrified."

"All three at once, I suspect," I said, smiling back. "You know you can always come home at any time if you feel uncomfortable."

"Yeah. That's if I get there at all. Will you be here later? I could do with some moral support before I go."

"I have to collect my car from Heathrow Airport, but I'll be back later, if that's okay with you? I have to be in Newmarket tomorrow night anyway for the disciplinary hearing on Monday morning."

"It's fine by me," he said. "Just don't stand by the front windows, in case someone from the company spots you."

"Thanks. I won't."

Alex went off to work at eight, and I spent the following half hour or so doing some washing. I'd only taken to Ireland enough changes of clothes for a couple of days, and they had already stretched to five.

I was hanging up the last of my underwear to dry on the radiator in my bedroom when I heard my phone do a triple-tone beep, indicating that it had received a SMS message.

I didn't recognise the phone number that the text had been sent from, but I opened it, nevertheless. It simply read *GB629 0360 48*, with nothing to indicate who had sent it or what the number meant.

I stared at it for several minutes before I realised what it was.

It was a United Kingdom VAT number.

It would be from Janis, I thought, laughing, and she must have borrowed somebody else's phone to send it to me.

I typed the number into a government website, and up popped the name of the company whose VAT number it was: *Starsign Enterprises Limited*. It also gave the address of the company's registered office, and it wasn't in Cashel, nor even anywhere in Ireland. It was in Blackburn, Lancashire.

So Starsign was registered for VAT. That meant that any horse sold by them at the sales and not immediately exported out of the country would attract VAT on the sale price at the standard rate, currently twenty per cent.

It is a strange tax that simply goes round in a circle, provided that all the parties are registered for VAT.

The purchaser of the horse pays the tax to the sales company on top of the full purchase price of the horse. The sales company takes their commission from that sum, plus the VAT due on their commission, and then sends the remaining proceeds, including the remaining VAT, to the vendor or their agent. Both the sales company and the vendor/agent are then responsible for paying their share of the VAT to the taxman as part of their quarterly returns.

Meanwhile, if the purchaser is also registered for VAT, either as a company or through the special government scheme for racehorse owners, then he claims back from the government all the VAT he has paid to the sales company in the first place. So the tax simply goes round in a circle, and in fact, no one ends up having to pay anything.

How could Elliot Mitchell fiddle that?

I looked up Starsign Enterprises Limited on the Companies House website, where all incorporated British firms were registered. There were at least twelve different companies with the word *Starsign* in their names, but only one Starsign Enterprises Ltd, and it had the same registered address as on the VAT website.

So that must be the one.

Conveniently, the listing also included the names of the company directors, together with their addresses and an indication of the nature of the business.

Starsign Enterprises had two directors, but neither of them was called Elliot Mitchell or had any other name that I recognised. And the nature of the business was listed as "sale, maintenance, and repair of cars and light motor vehicles." Not a mention anywhere of horses.

I searched for the company on the internet, and they had their own website. It showed a picture of a large blue garage plus a collection of second-hand cars sitting on the forecourt, with prices in their windscreens. And there was a phone number.

I called it.

"Starsign. Duncan speaking," said the voice that answered. "How can I help?"

"Do you buy and sell horses?" I asked.

He laughed. "I can sell you plenty of horse*power*, if that's what you're after."

"No," I said. "I mean real horses—you know, things that eat hay and have four legs and a tail."

"I know what a bloody horse is, mate," he said, having lost his humour. "And no, we don't sell them, not unless it's on the badge of a Ferrari."

He put the phone down.

I called him back, but changed my voice.

"This is His Majesty's Revenue and Customs," I announced formally when the same man answered. "May I please speak to Elliot Mitchell?"

He didn't reply immediately.

"Is Elliot's surname Mitchell?" I could hear him asking somebody else in the room. "You know, Elliot in the workshop. Young lad. Good with Land Rovers. I've got the taxman on here, asking to talk to him."

I could just about hear a response but couldn't make out the actual words.

"Sorry, mate," said the man coming back to me. "We do have an Elliot, but his surname's Wilson, not Mitchell."

"How strange," I said. "Are you sure you don't know Elliot Mitchell?"

"Never heard of him," the man said. "Is he a mechanic? They come and go pretty regular."

"I must have the wrong information," I said. "Do you have an Irish division?"

"Irish division?" he said. "No, mate, we don't. But we have got a couple of Irish lads working here, if that helps."

"No it doesn't," I said. "Can I just check that I have the right company? Do you know your VAT number?"

"Hold on a minute. It's printed on our invoices. I'll have to find one—my secretary doesn't work Saturdays."

I could hear him rummaging, perhaps in a drawer.

"Here it is. There's a *G* and a *B* followed by six two nine, space, zero three six zero, space, four eight."

"Ah," I said. "That would account for the error. I have the wrong company. So sorry to have troubled you." I hung up.

GB629 0360 48.

Exactly the same number that I had been sent on the text.

Was Starsign Bloodstock something to do with Starsign Enterprises Ltd? Or had the sender of the text—I assumed it was Janis—got the number wrong? But it would be too much of a coincidence for her to have given me the wrong number, one that actually was the VAT number of a company with the word *Starsign* in its name.

Who did I know that was an expert on VAT?

No one. But Alex had once said that his dad knew everyone, so I called his mobile number.

"Martyn Cooper," he said, answering at the second ring.

"Hello, Mr Cooper," I said. "This is Theo Jennings. Alex's friend. I hope it's okay to call you on a Saturday."

"It's fine, Theo. Have you sorted out those employment problems?"

"Not yet. My disciplinary hearing is on Monday."

"Well, good luck with it."

"Thank you, but that's not actually the reason I'm calling you this time. I just wondered if you happen to know anyone who specialises in VAT, value-added tax."

"I know quite a bit about it myself," Martyn said. "I did an accountancy degree before I switched to the law. What do you want to know?"

"Can two different companies have the same VAT registration number?"

"Absolutely not. Every one is unique. The first seven digits are generated randomly, and then the last two are known as the check digits. There's a mathematical way of checking if a number is genuine. But certainly every VAT number is different."

"So how come I know of two separate companies that are using the same number?"

"One of them must be wrong." He paused. "Do they have similar names?"

"Yes they do. One is called Starsign Bloodstock, and the other is Starsign Enterprises Ltd."

"Are you sure it's not a single company simply using two different trading names, like John Lewis stores and Waitrose supermarkets? All of those have the same VAT number because they are actually one company."

"One of them is a car repair shop in Blackburn, and the other a horse bloodstock agency based at Cashel in Ireland. I've spoken to the car repair place, and they have no knowledge of any Irish connection."

"Perhaps the Irish company has an Irish VAT number," Martyn said. "That could be the reason it's the same as the UK one, although Irish numbers should end with one or two letters."

"Both the numbers start with *GB* and are identical, with no other letters."

"Then one of them is lying."

And I reckoned I knew which one it was.

30

"WHY WOULD ANYONE lie about their VAT number?" I asked.

"They are not lying about the number itself," Martyn Cooper replied. "They are lying about whether they actually have one in the first place. It's the oldest trick in the book."

"Please explain."

"Suppose you are Company A, which is VAT registered, and you sell goods or services to an individual or to another company—say, Company B—then you have to charge them VAT, currently at twenty per cent on top of the price. They pay you the total, including the VAT, and then you pay the tax element to the government. Understand so far?"

"Perfectly," I replied.

"If Company B is also VAT registered then it can claim the tax back from the government, so it makes no difference to them that it had to pay it, because they get it all back. However, if Company A is not actually registered for VAT but has told Company B that it is, and given them a false VAT number, then, when the tax is paid by Company B to Company A, Company A simply keeps it for itself, as it has no requirement to pay anything over to the government."

"What difference does it make if Company A is Irish?"

"Not much. Lots of Irish companies are also registered for VAT over here. But it does make a bit of a difference. If the goods come over from Ireland, there will be import tax to pay when they arrive in the UK. But there are ways of getting round that."

"How?"

"Simply take it into Northern Ireland first."

"Is that legal?"

"It's perfectly legal to transport goods across from the Republic of Ireland to the north. The border between them is open, as determined by the Good Friday peace agreement. And it's perfectly legal to bring goods from Northern Ireland to the rest of the United Kingdom. It's just not legal to do both with the same goods, but who's to know? If the goods are a horse, just use a different transport company for each leg of the journey, and maybe have the horse spend a night or two in a stable outside Belfast. I'm convinced it goes on all the time."

"I thought there were customs checks on stuff moving across the Irish Sea between Great Britain and Northern Ireland."

"There are, but everyone seems more concerned about the stuff going west, because it might be going into the Republic, which is a member of the EU, rather than that going east into the UK."

"But why do the two Starsign companies have such similar names?"

He laughed. "Smokescreen, dear boy, smokescreen. Anyone can check a VAT number by just putting it into a government website."

"I know. That's how I found the car repair business."

"If you want to fiddle the system, choose a very similar name, or even the same name as the real VAT registered company with that number. Perhaps spell it incorrectly by just one letter. Then, if anyone does a check on the number, they might well be fooled into thinking it is genuine."

"But don't the Revenue people do audits?" I asked.

"All the time, but you would be amazed at what can slip through. The tax affairs of Company B would appear to an inspector to be in perfect order, with all its input and output taxes correctly recorded, and no one would be checking Company A for its VAT because it's not registered. No inspector would have the time to go through every single transaction of Company B with a fine-tooth comb, checking every VAT number is correct and that the tax was then actually paid to the government. They don't have the manpower. They might do a quick check on the number, but even then, the name Starsign Enterprises could cover a whole range of different activities, including acting as a bloodstock agent, so they would probably accept it at face value."

"Would Company B also have to be in on the fiddle?" I asked.

"Not at all. They would probably just accept Company A's VAT number as being genuine, and if they also did a check, the same thing would apply."

"So let me get this right," I said. "If a horse that was owned by Starsign Bloodstock was sold at auction in Newmarket with VAT, they could simply keep the VAT element for themselves?"

"Yes," Martyn said. "Provided the horse isn't exported after the sale, because then there would be no VAT on it anyway, as it would be zero rated. The horse doesn't even need to be owned by Starsign Bloodstock if they are acting as the selling agents, and they are the ones who are initially paid for it by the sales company. They could simply pass on the correct hammer price to the real owners, less theirs and the auctioneer's commission, and still keep the VAT. Everyone would be happy."

"Except the government."

"Well, yes. In the end, it would be the government that are out of pocket."

And, I thought, *VAT at twenty per cent on a three-million-guinea colt was quite a lot to be out of pocket.*

"Thank you, Martyn. That's been very helpful. And just one other thing, do you know happen to know anything about data protection, in particular GDPR?"

* * *

My car was where I had left it the previous Tuesday morning, in the long-term car park at Terminal 5.

I had caught the ten o'clock train from Newmarket and went to Heathrow, via Cambridge and London, with pretty good connecting times. And the Saturday traffic was light, so I was back in Alex's flat in time to watch the Dewhurst Stakes on the television at three o'clock.

Lucky Mike won the race by two lengths, going away from the field, cheered on by the huge wave of Irishmen over from Dublin Airport. He was clearly quite an exceptional horse, especially when you remember that he'd been sold for a mere eight thousand euros as a yearling.

Alex arrived back at the flat just as the television screen showed Lucky Mike's very lucky owner leading his goldmine into the winner's slot in the unsaddling enclosure, his smile reaching almost to his ears. And well he might smile, I thought. His horse had just won the first prize of three hundred thousand pounds, which was more than forty times what he'd paid for it, by completing the seven-furlong race quicker than the other eight runners, and all in under a minute and a half.

It made me wonder if his full brother would have been even half as good. That is, if he had survived. But probably not. Not with those dodgy hocks.

"Had a good day?" I asked Alex.

"I suppose. Bit boring, really. I hate acting as a spotter. I want to be the auctioneer."

I laughed. "You will be. Give it time."

"The chairman says I can have a slot on the rostrum at the February sale."

"There you are then," I said, smiling at him.

"But February seems a long way away. I was hoping to get a go today in the Book Four sale, especially after . . ."

He tailed off.

"Especially after I got suspended," I said, finishing his sentence.

"Well, yes," he said rather sheepishly.

It was fair enough. I'd have hoped for the same if I'd been him.

"So who has been filling in for me?" I asked.

"Liam Barton. And he's done all right."

"He's a very experienced auctioneer. Nigel Stanhope told me once that when he started at the company, Liam was a regular here on the rostrum. That was before he opted for the quieter life back in Ireland."

Together, Alex and I watched the next race on the television, the Cesarewitch Handicap, with its large field of thirty-two runners.

Cesarewitch is the anglicised version of Tsesarevich, the title once given to the heir of the Russian throne, and the race was originally named in honour of Tsesarevich Alexander, later Tsar Alexander II, who made a donation of three hundred pounds to the Jockey Club. It has been run annually since 1839.

At two and a quarter miles, it is one of the longest flat races on the calendar, and is run over an L-shaped course that cuts through the Devil's Dyke, an eight-mile-long defensive earthwork thought to be of Anglo-Saxon origin, which locally marks the boundary between Cambridgeshire and Suffolk. Hence the Cesarewitch is one of the few horse races that starts in one county and finishes in another.

On this occasion, it was won by a rank outsider, a horse which normally ran over hurdles, getting up on the line to beat the favourite by a short head while carrying twelve pounds less in the handicap.

That wouldn't please Brian Kitman, I thought. He had trained the second.

"Do you need to go back to work later?" I asked Alex.

"No. The sale is finished, thank goodness. We went on until three o'clock, to get the last few lots through. But there weren't many punters left by then because nearly everyone had gone to the races. I felt really sorry for the vendors. Most of the last thirty lots didn't even reach their reserve. So at the end, the chairman announced in the ring that any lots presented after midday today that were unsold or had been bought in by the vendor would be given entry to our December yearling sale at half the commission rate."

How uncommonly generous of him, I thought.

"But at least that means you're free to go to Cambridge tonight," I said.

"I suppose so."

"You don't seem very enthusiastic."

"I don't know. Part of me wants to go a lot, and part of me doesn't want to go at all."

"No one is making you."

"I realise that," he said. "But I need to know. I need to find out."

"Then go. You can always leave and come home again if you feel it's not right.

His fear didn't appear much assuaged.

"Look," I said, "do you want me to come with you for moral support?"

"Absolutely not," he said adamantly. "If I'm going to a bar in Cambridge to meet somebody, there's no point in taking someone else with me. It would make things far too complicated."

"But you can always call me if you're worried," I said. "I'll have my phone with me all the time. In fact, please do call me often, so I know you're safe, and what time train you are catching back, or even if you are not coming back at all. So I don't sit here all night, worrying."

"Okay. I will. Thanks, Mummy!"

He smiled at me with a mixture of excitement and embarrassment.

"I spoke to your dad this morning," I said, thinking it would put him at his ease.

"What about?" he said in sudden renewed alarm.

"Not you," I assured him. "I was asking him some questions about tax, and he was very helpful."

"Your personal tax?"

"No. About VAT on horse sales."

"Oh my God," Alex said, throwing his hands up. "Don't talk to me about VAT on horse sales. I had someone today complaining bitterly to me that they should be paying VAT at something they called the marginal rate on the yearling they had bought, because it had been previously sold as a foal. They claimed they only needed to pay VAT on the difference in the prices, and at a lower rate. I have absolutely no idea what they were on about."

And that would probably have been exactly what Elliot Mitchell and Starsign Bloodstock had relied upon—almost no one really understood the vagaries of the tax system.

* * *

Alex left for Cambridge at six o'clock.

"I don't want to get there late," he said, "because it'll be too busy by then."

"Good idea," I agreed, even though I felt it was more because he was becoming increasingly agitated, and I think he wanted to get going before he lost his nerve altogether. "What's the pub called?"

"The Heavenly Host Inn. It's next door to Cambridge Station."

"Have a good time," I said as he was leaving. "And good luck."

He turned and gave me a look that was half eagerness and half panic.

I laughed.

After he had gone, I wondered what I should do.

As always on a Saturday night, the Newmarket pubs would be busy, but they would be swelled even more on this particular evening by the large Irish contingent celebrating Lucky Mike's win in the Dewhurst Stakes. And no doubt, they would already be well oiled from an afternoon largely spent consuming copious quantities of Guinness in the bars at the racecourse.

And I had no wish to join their drunken party.

I turned on the TV to see what was on. While I was searching through the programme listings, my phone rang. To my delight, it was Janis's number showing on my screen.

"Hello, my darling," I said, but I was suddenly fearful that it would actually be her brother on the line.

It wasn't.

"Hello, Theo," Janis said. "Can you come and meet me?"

"What? Now?"

"Yes. I have something for you."

"What?" I asked.

"More information."

"On what?" I asked.

"On Starsign Bloodstock."

"Oh, great. I'll come straight away," I said. "Where are you?"

"Outside the sales company entrance on The Avenue."

"Right. I'll walk down Queensberry Road towards you."

"No," she said quickly. "Come in your car. You can drive me home."

"Okay. I'll be there in five minutes."

I turned off the television and collected my car keys from my bedroom.

Only as I was on my way out, as I was locking the flat door, did I wonder about Janis's phone call. Something about it had made me feel uncomfortable.

There had been no warmth in her voice. Was that because she was still wondering if I had something to do with Elliot Mitchell's murder? But if that were the case, why would she be prepared to get into my car, for me to drive her home to Soham?

Or was there some other reason?

I drove down Queensberry Road and turned right into The Avenue.

I saw Janis straight away, on the opposite side of the road from the sales company entrance, but she was not alone.

As I drove towards the pair, I saw in the fading daylight that she was standing on the pavement with a man in a dark overcoat, and as I pulled up alongside them, I noticed in the light of my dipped headlights that the man was wearing black shoes.

Plain, black, unremarkable shoes.

But they were shoes that I recognised.

CHAPTER

31

MY PULSE RATE soared as I wondered what to do.

Should I simply drive away?

But that would surely indicate to the man that I knew that it was he who had tried to run me over, and also it would mean leaving him alone with Janis, and that might put her in grave danger.

Did I let him know that I knew? Or play along?

While I was still deciding what path to follow, the man opened the rear door for Janis to get in, and then he himself climbed into the front passenger seat.

I turned my head and looked across at him.

"Hello, Geoff," I said in as friendly a tone as I could muster, while trying to keep any nervousness out of my voice. "This is a surprise. I thought the company staff had been told not to speak to me."

Geoff Pollard, the sales company finance director—my would-be assassin.

He would know all about VAT on horse sales. Of course he would.

"Just drive," he said to me. "I don't want to be seen talking to you here. Go round the back of the town and up onto the Warren Hill training grounds."

I glanced briefly at Janis in the rearview mirror.

"But that's not the way to Soham."

"Never mind," Geoff replied.

"Why don't I take Janis home first? Then we can talk on the way back."

"No," he said adamantly. "She stays for now. She may have some more information for you. You can both go on to Soham together later, after you drop me off in the town."

Did I believe for one second that he would just get out of the car and let Janis and me drive off?

Not a chance.

"Warren Hill training grounds," he said again.

I drove off, and the car started emitting an annoying and incessant little beeping sound.

"Seat belts, please."

Both Geoff and Janis buckled up, and the beeping stopped.

I turned left into Granary Road and went round the back of the town centre and then out on the Moulton Road, to the parking area alongside the Warren Hill gallops.

In the mornings, this car park would be full of vehicles. Some would belong to the trainers, out here to watch their horses at exercise, but many others would be the cars of the "work watchers"—those who spend their mornings with binoculars up to their eyes, studying the progress on the gallops of all the Newmarket horses, in order to provide information to the betting companies, or to sell racing tips direct to the public either by telephone or, increasingly, through online tipping services.

But at six thirty on a Saturday evening in October, as the last of the daylight was rapidly fading away, the place was deserted.

I turned the car round so it was facing down the hill, with the lights of Newmarket laid out below us like a twinkling bejewelled carpet, and the tall Millennium Grandstand at the racecourse, still illuminated after racing, visible in the far distance.

"So tell me what you have found out about Starsign Bloodstock," Geoff said after I'd shut off the engine and turned on the car's interior light.

I shifted in my seat slightly so I was facing him more. "I thought you had information to give me, not the other way round."

"But I need to understand what you already know, so I can fill in the blanks."

"How do you know I've found out anything?"

"Because I discovered this afternoon that Little Miss Inquisitive here has been looking through the Starsign VAT records." He pointed with his thumb over his shoulder at Janis. "She said you asked her to do it."

In fact, I'd specifically told her not to, in order not to get caught. But back then, I'd been worried only about her losing her job, not losing her life as well.

A phone started ringing somewhere in the car. It was not mine. The ring was muffled and coming from Geoff's coat, as if it were in his pocket. He ignored it, and it stopped.

"Come on," he said impatiently. "What do you know?"

I wondered why he wanted me to talk.

Was he still thinking that I didn't know enough to cause him any trouble? Did he believe that I didn't know it was him who had tried to kill me? Was he sounding out whether he needed to take any action against me, and against Janis, to keep things secret?

Or was he just playing with me?

Would it, in fact, make any difference whatever I said?

All I wanted, at the moment, was to get him out of my car while leaving Janis and me still in it, and alive. So what was the best way of achieving that?

It seemed to me that I had two options.

Plan A would be to try and tell him nothing, and maybe he would think I didn't know enough to cause him any trouble, while Plan B would be to tell him everything in the hope that he would realise that the game was up, and there was no point in making things worse by doing anything more.

But of course, either option could go horribly wrong.

If he had murdered Elliot Mitchell, he would surely do everything in his power not to get found out by the police. Including getting rid of Janis and me. And no one else except me knew the whole story. It has often been said that for serial killers it is the first murder that is the difficult one. After that, any further murders are easy.

How would his mind work? And did he have some sort of weapon on him? Maybe even a gun?

I decided to hedge my bets and go with Plan A and give him as little information as possible, at least to start with.

"I don't really know much about Starsign Bloodstock," I said. "They seem to be very secretive. As Churchill once said of Russia, it's a riddle wrapped in a mystery inside an enigma. It's as if they don't want to be found."

Did I sense him relax slightly, or was that just my wishful thinking?

The phone starting ringing again, and once more Geoff ignored it.

So I went on. "Every other bloodstock agency I know has its own website, to attract business, but I can't find anything on the web for Starsign."

I turned and looked at Janis's reflection in the rearview mirror. She was staring back at me with large, frightened eyes. I shook my head—just the very slightest of movements—while nonchalantly pulling a finger across my mouth, and hoped that she would understand my "don't speak" message.

"So any information you can give me, Geoff, would be most welcome."

"There's not much to give," he said. "It's a small Irish outfit from Cashel in County Tipperary."

"Yes, I knew that already," I said. "You told me that on Monday."

"Well, that's about all I know."

Why did I not believe him?

"Well, that's not much good then, is it?" I said in feigned irritation. "If you've nothing else to tell me, Geoff, why are you doing all this cloak-and-dagger stuff just to talk to me? I'll take you back to the town right now, and then I can take Janis home to Soham."

"VAT," he said, staring straight at me.

"What about it?" I replied.

"She was looking up Starsign Bloodstock's VAT records."

"So?" I said, trying to make light of it.

But it must have been like a big warning flag for him when he'd discovered her doing it.

"What do you understand about VAT?" Geoff asked.

"Not much," I replied. "Does anybody? All I know is that the purchaser pays it to the vendor, who then gives it to the government. And then the purchaser claims it back again from the government. So it just goes round in a circle. It's a crazy tax."

Was I convincing him I knew nothing else? I somehow doubted it.

Maybe it was time to try and take the initiative.

"I think we'd better go now," I said. "I can drop you in the town, if you like, Geoff, or you can walk from here."

I reached for the engine "Start/Stop" button on the car's central console, but he grabbed my arm.

"Not so fast," he said. "What did she tell you?"

"Nothing important."

"What was it?"

I didn't answer, and he twisted round in his seat.

"What was it?" he asked Janis forcefully.

She said nothing either.

"Look here, young lady, you could be in real trouble for giving away our client's personal account information without their permission. I can have you fired for that."

"It was only a VAT number," Janis blurted out, close to tears.

"Starsign Bloodstock's VAT number?"

"Yes. And VAT numbers surely aren't secret."

"I see," Geoff said in a way that made me feel that he really did see.

It was clearly time for me to switch to Plan B.

"Except," I said slowly and distinctly, "the VAT number that Janis gave to me isn't the one for Starsign Bloodstock, is it, Geoff?"

He turned back in his seat and looked at me.

"Because Starsign Bloodstock isn't registered for British VAT. That VAT number belongs to Starsign Enterprises Ltd, a car repair shop in Blackburn. Isn't that right, Geoff?"

"I'm sure I don't know what you're talking about," he said.

"Oh, I think you do. You and Elliot Mitchell have been running a little VAT swindle, charging purchasers VAT on the horses they buy, and then keeping it for yourselves. Mitchell only had to ensure that he bought them on behalf of his UK-based principals so the horses weren't exported. Mitchell would spend much of his time in Ireland convincing vendors and trainers to allow Starsign Bloodstock to act as their agent and the consignor of their horses for the horses-in-training sales, and hence be the initial recipient of the sale proceeds. He then would pay the vendor the amount they were expecting and simply keep the VAT element. I suspect he would also bid up the sale prices higher than would otherwise have been the case, in order to maximize the return."

I paused and looked at him, but he just continued staring at me. I wondered what was going on in the brain behind his eyes.

"You made sure that no one could find out about Starsign Bloodstock, claiming that the data protection regulations prevented you even giving out their address. But that's not actually true, is it, Geoff? The regulations don't cover addresses of businesses, only those of individuals. I found that out this morning, from a lawyer. And VAT numbers are not covered by the privacy regulations either, are they, Geoff?"

There was still no response, and in the silence, the phone in his pocket started ringing one more time. He didn't answer it, and after six or seven rings, it stopped.

"You used your position, as both the sales company finance director and the designated data controller, not only to make sure that no one knew anything about Starsign Bloodstock but also to falsify the money-laundering requirements. How else could we have gone on paying Starsign by cheque?"

"You're talking nonsense," Geoff said finally. "How could I have done such a thing without anyone else noticing?"

"Easily," I said. "You run the finance department in such a manner that only you know what is really going on. You keep all the various sections apart and don't allow them to speak to each other. Everything has to go through you."

"It's good company practice. I should know—I'm the current chairman of the Association of Chief Finance Officers."

"So what?" I said. "Bernie Madoff was chairman of the NAS-DAQ Stock Exchange in New York, but he still managed to steal more than sixty-four billion dollars from his investors by falsifying the records of hundreds of thousands of stock transactions that never actually took place. Fabricating a few fake money-laundering checks on Starsign Bloodstock would have been child's play for you, in comparison."

It seemed to me that the more respected the fraudster, the bigger the fraud.

"You wrote out the cheques and simply sent them to an address in Cashel ready for collection. Then you or Mitchell simply waited for them to arrive before collecting them from Mrs Eileen Murphy at number sixty-four Main Street."

There was a slight widening of his eyes when he realised that I knew not only the full address but also the name of the occupant.

"I've never been to Ireland," he said.

I didn't believe him.

"Then everything started to go wrong for you, didn't it, Geoff? I overheard a conversation between Elliot Mitchell and Brian Kitman about collusively bidding up the three-million colt, and hence I started digging into Starsign Bloodstock. I even asked you about it, and that's when the alarm bells started ringing loudly in your head." I paused. "So you tried to kill me. You knew where I lived—my contact details are in the employee records that you hold on your computer. And you could easily work out the route I would be taking home. All you had to do was wait in the dark and run me over, and all your problems would instantly go away."

He went back to staring at me.

"But your plan went wrong, didn't it, Geoff? You didn't manage to kill me, and the police became involved. So what are you going to do now? Try to kill me again? No one will believe it's an accident this time. Not with Janis here too. It will be much better for you if you just get out of my car this instant and walk away."

He didn't move other than to reach inside his coat and pull out not the knife or gun that I had been half expecting, but the bicycle pump with the sharpened football inflator attached.

And he pointed it at my heart from about two inches away.

"Just shut up and drive," he said.

CHAPTER

32

I STARTED THE CAR and drove it back down the Moulton Road towards Newmarket.

"Take the Bury Road," Geoff instructed.

I turned right onto Old Station Road and then right at the roundabout by the Golden Jubilee Clock Tower. I then drove past the Bedford Lodge Hotel and out of town.

"Which way?" I asked as we approached the junction with Well Bottom Road.

"Straight on," Geoff replied.

As I neared the junction, the traffic lights changed from green to red.

"Janis," I said. "When I stop at the traffic lights, get out of the car. Then call the police."

"But Mr Pollard took my phone. That's what's been ringing."

"Get out of the car anyway," I said. "And run away as fast as you can."

Geoff half turned his head. "If you do that, young lady, I will kill your boyfriend, here and now, and then I will get out and also kill you."

Janis emitted a small whimper from behind me, and she did not get out of the car when it stopped.

"Good," said Geoff as we moved off again. "We are just going to go for a little drive. Take the A11 north towards Norwich."

I joined the A11 dual carriageway and sped along.

"Where are we going?" I asked.

"Never you mind."

As he was speaking to me, I might as well ask him some more questions.

"So why did Elliot Mitchell have to die?"

There was no initial response, and I thought he wasn't going to answer at all, but he did, after a fashion.

"Elliot Mitchell was greedy. And careless. I told him not to try it on with that colt, but he was so sure he'd get away with it."

And he almost had, I thought. But he'd been just a bit too careless, he and Brian Kitman both, in the gents'.

"He should have just been happy with the VAT fiddle. It was a nice steady earner, and not so much that anyone would ever notice. But he wanted more. He said he'd seen a house he wanted, somewhere in the Caribbean, for his retirement. He needed a quick couple of million to buy it. And then that colt came along, and he saw a way. Stupid man."

"But why kill him?"

"He was attracting too much attention to Starsign."

"From me, you mean."

"I thought with him dead, the whole thing would blow over."

No chance, I thought. The police don't give up that easily— not for a murder. But maybe he'd believed that everyone would think Elliot really had killed himself.

"What I can't understand is why you didn't simply hand over the Starsign cheques to Elliot Mitchell in your office. It would have saved all the hassle of arranging the accommodation address in Cashel."

"All cheques over five thousand pounds have to be counter-signed by the chairman. Then they are sent out by his office, not mine, and by registered mail," he said. "We have to obtain a receipt from the post office, with the delivery address shown on it, for the auditors."

To prevent fraud, I thought. Although a fat lot of good it had done.

I drove on in silence for a while, wondering what he had in mind for us.

He clearly couldn't just let us go.

I tried to put myself in his shoes—his plain, black, unremarkable shoes. What would I do if I were him?

He clearly couldn't have had a plan in place ahead of time, as he had only discovered this afternoon that Janis had been searching through the Starsign VAT records.

So, first, he had to kill us, and then second, he had to make it appear that he hadn't been responsible. And how could he do that? His DNA would surely be discoverable in my car by the police. Perhaps he would say I had given him a lift home sometime. Anything to account for it. Maybe he'd even set the car on fire. That was the best way of destroying DNA.

So where would he put our bodies?

Leave them in my car? Or dump them somewhere else?

And was there anything I could do to stop him?

He still had the bicycle pump held just above my heart, with the handle drawn out, ready to inject air into me. If a single pump could instantly kill a horse, I hated to think what the same amount would do to me.

Should I try to overpower him? Certainly not while I was travelling at sixty miles per hour along the A11, I thought. It would be careless to avoid being murdered only to be crushed to death in a high-speed road accident. And I had to try and protect Janis at all costs.

"Take the exit for Brandon," Geoff said as I slowed for the roundabout at Barton Mills.

I did as he told me.

I had worked out that it must have been Geoff who had used Elliot Mitchell's phone to call my number on Monday night, just to muddy the waters with the police. But where was my old phone? Did he still have it?

"Where's my phone?" I asked him.

"What phone?"

"The one you took when you tried to run me over."

He didn't say anything, but his silence was answer enough.

The headlights of the car picked out a sign that read "RAF Lakenheath."

"Oh my God!" Janis said from the back seat, choking back tears.

"What's wrong?" I asked.

"Holly and Jessica's bodies were found just outside RAF Lakenheath."

"It's all right, my love. It's only a place. There's nothing to worry about."

And if she believed that, I thought, she'd believe anything.

Although nominally designated as a British Royal Air Force station, it is, in fact, the home of the 48th Fighter Wing of the United States Air Force.

I suddenly had a mad plan of turning sharply into the main entrance of the station, stopping outside the guardroom, and asking the Americans for help, but Geoff seemed to read my mind.

"Just keep going straight on," he said, and he pricked my shirt with the football inflator to emphasise that he meant business.

I drove straight on, past the "Drive on the Left" reminder signs for the US military personnel.

I decided to try and keep Geoff talking in the hope that it was harder for him to kill someone with whom he was currently in conversation.

"So, for how many horses did you keep the VAT?"

"About thirty or so each year. Nothing too flashy or expensive to attract attention, and mostly in the horses-in-training sales."

"Then I'm surprised that I haven't noticed the Starsign Bloodstock name before in the sales catalogue as the consignor."

"We mostly tried to keep it out. We would often announce a late change after the catalogue had gone to press, and I would fix the paperwork so ensure that Starsign was the initial entity paid."

"Neat."

He seemed rather pleased with himself.

"So how much did you make?"

"About sixty-five grand a year each. Not so much that it attracted unwanted attention, but enough to make life a little easier at home, and for holidays in the sun."

"Where did you go?" I asked, desperate to keep him talking.

"My wife has become particularly fond of spending Christmas and New Year in the Maldives."

Lucky her, I thought.

We were still travelling alongside the barbed wire–topped perimeter fence of the airbase, on our left, when Geoff gave his next instruction.

"Turn right just up here," he said.

I slowed the car and turned right onto little more than a dirt track. A sign beside the track stated: "Thetford Forest, Private Road."

I knew a bit about Thetford Forest from occasionally reading the local *Suffolk Norfolk Life* magazine. It had been man-made, created by the large-scale planting of pine trees after the First World War, as a strategic reserve of timber, because so many of the country's great oaks and other trees had been lost due to the wartime demand for wood.

"Keep going down the track," Geoff instructed.

Keeping going was indeed my primary objective. I was quite certain that if I stopped the car, he would stab me with the sharpened football inflator and pump my heart full of air.

And that would be that—at least as far as I was concerned.

So stopping was not on my agenda.

The track went deeper into the forest, the trees on both sides lit up by my headlights as the track turned slightly to the left.

"Here will do," Geoff said. "Stop the car."

Not likely, I thought. I was not going to just meekly stop the car, not here or anywhere. So, instead of putting my right foot on the brake pedal, I slammed it down on the accelerator, causing the car to leap forward at an ever-increasing speed.

"What the hell are you doing?" Geoff shouted. "Stop the bloody car."

By now, we were doing more than forty on the loose dirt, maybe closer to fifty.

Okay, I thought, *if that's what he wants, I will stop the car.*

I picked a solitary tree trunk in the headlights and drove straight at it without slowing down.

I knew it was madness, but this way, at least Janis and I had a chance of surviving.

"Brace! Brace!" I shouted over my shoulder at Janis.

In the last few moments, I let go of the steering wheel with my right hand while at the same time I reached across the central console with my left and unfastened Geoff Pollard's seatbelt.

* * *

I had never been involved in any sort of traffic collision before, and I wasn't really prepared for the ferocity of the impact, or the amount of noise it generated.

One second, all was quiet apart from the whirring of the engine, and in the next, there was a deafening roar as the tree tore through the metal front of the car, combined with the explosive detonation of the five airbags.

When everything around me came to a halt, and silence returned, I was disorientated for a few moments, with a great whiteness blinding my vision. But I quickly realised it was the now-deflated steering-wheel airbag. I pulled it away from my face.

Amazingly, one of the car's headlights remained on.

I looked across at Geoff.

Without his seatbelt fastened, he had not fared as well as I had. If anything, the passenger side airbag had been a hindrance to him rather than a help, sending him upwards into the roof. He was unconscious but gently moaning, which meant he was still alive, and therefore still dangerous.

I needed no better reason than that to get out of the car.

I opened the driver's door and climbed out, slamming the door shut behind me. Then I opened the rear door and looked in, with my heart in my mouth.

Janis was alive and conscious, her terrified eyes as big as saucers as she stared at me.

"You all right?" I asked as gently as I could.

"I'm frightened," she said, almost in a whisper.

"Me too," I said, smiling at her. I reached out a hand to her. "Come on, my love—let's go."

"Where to?" she asked, taking my hand and sliding across the back seat, towards me.

"Anywhere but here."

The Maldives perhaps, I thought.

Suddenly Geoff woke up.

"Stay where you are," he shouted. "I'm warning you."

He was trying to open the passenger door, but to no avail, pulling repeatedly on the broken handle.

"Come on," I said again to Janis, now with more urgency. I helped her out of the car, and we started back along the track the way we had come, walking as quickly as we dared in the darkness.

We had gone only about twenty yards or so when there was a great whooshing sound from behind us.

I turned around.

A fire had started in what remained of the engine compartment of the car. I thought it might have been caused by oil leaking from the damaged engine onto the hot exhaust manifold and igniting.

The headlight had finally gone out, but against the light from the fire beyond, we could see Geoff's silhouette still in the car, and he was continuing to pull hopelessly on the broken door handle, without making any attempt to climb over the central console to escape via the driver's door.

Perhaps he was confused, or maybe concussed.

I wondered what I should do. Did I go back to get him get out? Or did I simply walk away?

"You must go and help him," Janis said.

"Why? He's now tried to kill me twice."

"But you can't just leave him to die in a burning car." She shivered.

I could easily have done, I thought, but Janis was getting very distressed, and the fire was getting noticeably bigger.

"Get farther away in case it explodes," I said to her, pointing along the track. "I'll try and get him out. Here—take my phone." I unlocked it and gave it to her. "Dial nine-one-one. We need the police, the fire service, and an ambulance. Tell them we're down the Thetford Forest track opposite Lakenheath Air Base."

I left her to make the call and went back to the car, but on the driver's side rather than the passenger one. I reopened the driver's door. Geoff stared at me, and now it was his eyes that were terrified.

"Throw out the bicycle pump," I shouted at him.

He just went on looking at me.

"Throw the pump," I shouted again. "Then I'll get you out of the car."

He still had the pump in his hand, primed and ready for use.

He started to hand it to me, but I didn't trust him not to still try to stab me with its hypodermic-like end, so I pulled back.

"Throw it out," I ordered. "Throw it out, right now."

He looked down at the pump in his hand, then he looked across at me.

"Come on, Geoff," I shouted. "It's over. Throw the pump out."

But, instead of throwing it through the open driver's door, he lifted it up and stabbed himself in the chest with it, then pushed down the plunger.

33

I WAS BACK AT the police investigation centre in Bury St Edmunds, in what appeared to me to be the same interview room as before, and with the same two policemen, DS Hamilton plus his silent sidekick, DC Clarry. And so far, it had been a very long interview, going over everything I could remember from the moment Geoff and Janis had climbed into my car.

"So tell us now what happened next," the sergeant said. "After you say Mr Pollard stabbed himself with the bicycle pump."

I could tell from the tone of his voice that he thought the whole scenario to be most unlikely, and I wondered if I should have asked for a solicitor to be present, even though I wasn't under arrest. I was just helping the police with their enquiries, once again.

"When Geoff Pollard pushed in the plunger," I said, "his head dropped onto his chest, and he slumped forward in the seat. I thought he must be dead. So I decided to leave him where he was rather than spend any more time by the car. I was worried that the fuel tank might explode. But then he groaned."

"And where were you exactly, at this time?" the sergeant asked.

"Standing by the open driver's door. Anyway, when I heard him groan, I realised he was still alive, so I went round the back of the car to the front passenger door and opened it. He didn't move, so I reached in, pulled the pump out of his chest and threw it away as far as I could into the trees. Next, I tipped him out of the car, onto the ground, and then dragged him back until we were about twenty-five or thirty yards away. Janis Thompson helped me drag him the last bit because my ankle was hurting. We each had one of his arms."

I took a drink from the glass of the water they had provided.

"And then what?" asked DS Hamilton.

"I couldn't find a pulse in his wrist, so I put him on his back and started chest compressions. Janis gave him mouth-to-mouth. We didn't know whether it was the right thing to do, but we couldn't just stand there and do nothing."

Although the image I had in my head of Janis giving Geoff Pollard mouth-to-mouth resuscitation was something I would much rather forget.

"For how long did you continue?"

"I don't know long exactly. It felt like forever. We stopped once or twice to check if he had a pulse, but basically we kept going until the ambulance arrived. Maybe twenty minutes or so until the paramedics took over. I was exhausted. Then the paramedics loaded him into the ambulance and drove him away."

I drank some more water.

"Did he make it?" I asked.

"The last I heard, they were still working on him at Addenbrooke's Hospital. So there must be some hope."

Hope for what? Did I care if he lived or died? Probably not. Either way would be fine by me.

"Did you find the bicycle pump?" I asked.

"We're still searching for it."

And it would have my fingerprints on it, I thought. But was that a problem? I had already told them I had touched it when I'd pulled it out of Geoff's chest.

And I had more pressing things to worry about.

"I would like to see Janis Thompson now," I said.

We had been separated and brought to Bury St Edmunds in different police cars. I imagined that they were asking her the same questions as me, but in another interview room, to check that our descriptions of events matched.

"All in good time," said the sergeant, using more police-speak.

"But now is a good time," I said. "Janis was completely terrified when I crashed my car into the tree, and I want to check that she's all right and not hurt. So I'm not answering any further questions until after I see her."

"Then you will wait here," DS Hamilton said. "I will go and check if we're finished with her." He looked up at the clock on the wall. "Interview terminated at twenty-two hundred hours." He pushed the "Stop Record" button on the black box, which in turn emitted a long, loud beep.

So it had been almost four hours since Janis had called and asked me to pick her up on The Avenue. Four hours, first of terror, then of decision, determination and deed, and finally of euphoria at still being alive, followed by the boredom of having to explain everything to the police in minute detail.

True, I did also feel rather bashed and bruised, with a very sore neck and a persistent ache across my chest, where the seatbelt had been, so say nothing of the ongoing ache in my ankle.

But it was so much better to be hurting than to be dead.

* * *

DS Hamilton eventually came back into the interview room, and he brought Janis with him, and he seemed quite happy for a change. Our versions must have matched. And we had solved his murder case.

Janis rushed over to me, and I took her in my arms. She was clearly still distressed, and close to tears.

"Is the nightmare finally over?" she asked.

"Yes," I said. "It's finally over."

But I still wasn't confident of getting my job back.

"Can we go now?" I asked the detective sergeant.

"You certainly can," he said. "We may need to speak to you again, but you are both free to go home for tonight. I'll be outside when you're ready."

He left the room and took DC Clarry with him, leaving us alone.

I gave Janis a tight hug and a kiss, and so wished that I could take her home with me tonight, to my bed. But that would be for another day.

"Have you called you mother?" I asked. "She'll be desperate with worry."

"I had seven missed calls from her altogether, but I did finally speak to her when we first arrived here. She was very cross that I was still not at home, and that's an understatement. But I think I convinced her that everything was fine, and I was perfectly all right."

Janis had retrieved her phone from Geoff Pollard's coat pocket while we had been trying to resuscitate him. The missed calls list showed it had been her mother who had been trying to call her all those times it had been ringing.

"Did you tell her you were with me?"

She laughed. "Of course not. I'd told her earlier that I was working late, doing the accounts with Mr Pollard, and I'd catch a taxi home later. I just said it was taking longer than we had thought."

"On a Saturday evening? Did she believe you?"

"I don't think so, but I wasn't going to tell her the truth, now was I? That would have given her a complete panic attack, especially the bit about being in your car and colliding with a tree just outside RAF Lakenheath. She has a total phobia about that place."

"But it's been several hours since we arrived here. You'd better call her again."

"I will. In a minute." She hugged me tight. "I love you so much."

"But I love you more."

"That's all right then," she said, and snuggled closer into me.

* * *

DS Hamilton even offered us a lift in a police car, but we opted to go by taxi because a police car turning up outside the Thompson household may have caused a major inquisition, and Janis wasn't quite ready for that yet.

She had called her mother again before we left the investigation centre, and I could clearly hear the torment in Sarah's voice.

"It's okay, Mum," Janis had said over and over, trying to reassure her. "I'm fine. I'm just about to leave, and I'll be home soon."

"But you will have to tell her everything eventually," I said after she'd hung up. "She'll find out from the news, or someone will tell her, and that would be worse."

"I will tell her, slowly, tomorrow. And I'll also tell her how you saved my life."

"She might think that it was my fault you were put in danger in the first place. I'm sure David will."

And he'd be right: it definitely had been my fault.

* * *

I went with Janis in the taxi to Soham, and as expected, her mother was waiting impatiently on the front doorstep.

I asked the taxi driver to wait for me.

"Don't be long," he said. "I've got another job booked."

"Just a couple of minutes," I said, climbing out.

Janis and I walked up the path.

"What the hell are you doing here?" Mrs Thompson demanded loudly, even before I had a chance to say hello.

"I'm bringing Janis home," I said.

"Has she been with you all evening?" Her tone was accusatory, and the question was directed at me rather than at her daughter, as if it were all my fault.

"As a matter of fact, she has," I said.

She redirected her ire towards Janis. "You, young lady, should learn to do what your father tells you. I've been worried out of my mind."

"Mum, I'm no longer a child," Janis said in an assertive manner. "I'm twenty-eight years old. And that's quite old enough to decide who I spend my time with. And I don't need to check in with you every five minutes."

This uncharacteristic show of defiance seemed to shock her mother, who remained silent for several long seconds.

"Where have you been?" she asked finally, more quietly.

"It's a long story," Janis replied.

The taxi driver impatiently beeped his horn.

"Sorry," I said to Janis. "I must go. I'll call you when I get home."

Then I kissed her on the lips, just like that, right in front of her mother.

*   *   *

The taxi took me back to Newmarket and dropped me in the driveway behind Beaumont Court. For the first time in over a week, I walked unconcerned to my front door, without even bothering to glance into the shadows.

It was almost eleven o'clock, and there was no sign of Alex in the flat. The last train from Cambridge to Newmarket on a Saturday evening was the 22:47, getting in at 23:08.

I texted him, hopeful that he might be on it.

You okay?

His reply was almost immediate.

Having a fabulous time. Back later, or maybe tomorrow!!!!

I smiled. I was pleased for him. He clearly wasn't on the last train, but he could always get a taxi if he needed to get back tonight. He was old enough, and sensible enough, to look after himself.

So I went to bed.

When safely under the covers, I picked up my phone from the bedside table and sent a text to Janis.

Are you still awake?

It was delivered and she called back almost immediately.

"Oh my God. I thought she was going to kill me."

Hardly an appropriate choice of words, I thought, considering what had just occurred in Thetford Forest.

"When she couldn't get an answer from my phone, it seems she called the sales company switchboard number. She spoke to the caretaker and asked him to tell me to call home. But he told her that all the offices were empty. He'd just been over there and locked them all up."

"Awkward."

"She was so worried she even called the police and reported me missing."

"What did they say to her?"

"Nothing about what had happened in the forest, thank God." She laughed. "It seems that the man she spoke to tried to explain to her that a young woman in her twenties who was a couple of hours late getting home was not really classified as missing, especially when it was only eight o'clock on a Saturday evening. Apparently, Mum was absolutely furious with him."

She laughed.

"But when you left in the taxi, she demanded to know where I'd been, and she wouldn't let me in to the house until I told her."

"What did you say?"

"I told her the truth. Well, some bits of it. What else could I do?"

"How did she take it?" I asked.

"Remarkably well, I think. I made a big thing about being safely home, and I left out quite a lot, like being over at Lakenheath and everything about the bicycle pump and Mr Pollard trying to kill you."

"So you didn't actually tell her much."

"Not really. But I did tell her about the collision with the tree. I said it was an accident, and no one was hurt, but the police took ages to come because there was no phone signal where we were. That was also the reason I hadn't called her. I said the police took

us to Bury St Edmunds Police Station because your car was too
badly damaged to drive. I also told her that Mr Pollard was the one
who insisted on me being there, not you, and that I had no choice
in the matter."

"Did she buy that?"

"Maybe. She was very quiet throughout. Amazingly so, in
fact."

"Where is she now?"

"She's gone up to bed, thank God. I'm still in the kitchen."

"What did your dad and David say?"

"Nothing. They're both watching *Match of the Day* in the front
room. They couldn't have cared less about where I'd been, as long
as I arrived home safely. For them, soccer is much more important!"

"Does David know you've unblocked me from your phone?"

"I don't care. I unblocked you this morning and told David to
get lost when he tried to check at breakfast."

"Well done," I said, smiling in the dark.

That's my girl!

"So what are you going to do tomorrow?" she asked.

"I am definitely not coming to Sunday lunch with you," I said
with a laugh. *Was it really only a week since I'd been there?* "But can
you get away later in the afternoon? I could collect you in a taxi."

"Mum tried to tell me that I'm grounded, but I told her to
stuff that."

"Shall we get a flat together?" I asked suddenly, out of the blue.

"Sounds like a wonderful idea," she said, laughing. "Where?"

"Here in Newmarket. I could start looking tomorrow
morning."

"But you don't know if you'll still have a job in Newmarket
after Monday."

"Good point," I said. "Let's wait and see what happens."

Earlier, I had told her that the nightmare was over, and it was,
as far as risk to our lives was concerned, but now the fallout and
the recriminations would begin, and there was no saying what the
outcome of those would be.

34

I DID NOT SPEND Sunday morning looking for flats. Instead, I sat down at the kitchen table and went through the events of the last couple of weeks, first in my head, then by writing it all down on a notepad—every detail I could remember, in chronological order, starting with the sale of the three-million colt and finishing with the events of Saturday night.

Alex returned at eleven o'clock and was initially rather evasive about where he'd actually spent the night, and who with.

"Had a good time?" I asked him.

"Really good, thank you."

"Meet someone nice?"

He didn't reply verbally, but his broad smile gave me the answer anyway.

"What's his name?"

He said nothing.

"Come on," I urged. "I'll tell no one."

"Victor."

"And how old is he?"

"Twenty-six."

"And does he live in Cambridge?" I asked.

"He's actually from Wolverhampton, which is only fifteen miles from Stourbridge. He's doing a PhD in anthropology at King's College."

"That sounds absolutely perfect."

"It is." He threw his head back and laughed—a very happy laugh.

But once Alex had started talking, it was difficult to get him to stop.

"I went to the pub straight from the station. It was pretty empty, so I sat at the bar on my own. I was that nervous, I nearly jacked it in and came straight home again, but then a few more people came in. There was a group of five, all men, and Victor was one of them. He walked across to where I was sitting, and he asked me to join them. It was lovely."

I smiled at him. "And the rest, as they say, is history."

He smiled back, with just a touch of embarrassment.

"The other four left after a couple of drinks, but Victor and I stayed and had supper together, sitting side by side at one of the tables in the bar. After we had finished eating, he suddenly leaned over and kissed me. It was marvellous. Then he took me to another bar for a nightcap. It all felt so right, so obvious."

"So now you know."

"Yes," he said. "Now I do know. And for sure. Thank you."

"What for?"

"Because it was your idea to go to a bar in Cambridge in the first place. And I'm so glad I did."

"So now we just have to work out a way to tell your parents."

"Oh God!"

* * *

On Monday morning, at eight o'clock sharp, I walked into the sales company estate through the pedestrian gate on Queensberry Road, and I carried with me the notepad in which I had also written down everything I wanted to say at the disciplinary hearing.

I hadn't been given a specific time to be there, but I wanted to be early enough to ensure that nothing started before I arrived.

There was a week's break between the end of the October yearlings sales and the start of the horses-in-training sale, so the place was pretty much deserted other than by the company staff.

One of the security team saw me arrive, and he strode purposefully over towards me.

"I'm here at the invitation of the chairman," I said.

He spoke into his two-way radio and seemed reassured by the reply that he received through his earpiece.

"That's fine, Mr Jennings," he said. "The chairman says to go straight on up to his office."

I went through to the main office building and climbed the stairs, passed the infamous gents' restroom at the top, and walked along the corridor to the chairman's office.

I knocked loudly on his door.

"Come in," said a voice from the other side.

I went in, but things had clearly already moved on because the chairman was not alone. Detective Sergeant Hamilton was there ahead of me.

"Ah, there you are, Theo," said the chairman. "I've called you several times this morning, but you haven't answered any of them."

He had obviously been calling my old number, the one that was still recorded in my personnel file.

"I'm afraid the board meeting and your disciplinary hearing have had to be postponed. I hope you haven't made a wasted journey,"

"When have they been postponed until?" I asked.

"I'm not sure yet. We're having a bit of a crisis here at the moment. Geoff Pollard had been due to present the annual accounts to the board today, but this policeman, here, tells me he's had some sort of stroke, and he's in hospital."

I turned to the detective sergeant. "So he's still alive, then."

"Just about. And only thanks to you, it seems. We found the pump in the daylight yesterday. It was where you said it would be. The doctors reckon he missed his heart with it, and hit an artery instead. The air bubble went straight to his brain, causing a major cerebral embolism. It's similar to a stroke. They don't know yet whether he will survive or what state he will be in, even if he does. Oh yes, and one other thing. We've found your old phone, during our search of Mr Pollard's premises, with the three missed calls clearly showing on it from Elliot Mitchell's number."

"That's great," I said. "When can I have it back?"

"Just as soon as forensics are finished with it. They're still checking it for fingerprints and DNA."

The chairman had been listening to this exchange, and he was clearly confused. "I'm sorry," he said. "Do you two already know each other?"

"Indeed we do," said DS Hamilton. "I was hoping Mr Jennings was going to be here this morning. I have a forensic accountant coming up from London to go through your company accounts, and he will need to speak to Mr Jennings before he starts his work."

"Our company accounts?" repeated the chairman. "But they are private and confidential."

"I have a search warrant," said the DS, removing a folded sheet of paper from the inside pocket of his jacket.

"A search warrant? What *is* all this about?"

"We have reason to believe that a fraud has been committed on these premises, in addition to the murder we have also been investigating."

"A fraud? What sort of fraud?"

The policeman didn't answer, but turned to face him. "Peter Radway, you do not have to say anything, but if you do not mention, when questioned, something which you later rely on in court, it could damage your defence. Anything you do say may be used in evidence."

The chairman was totally shocked. "Court? Defence? Evidence?" he spluttered. "What is going on? Have I just been arrested?"

"No, sir, not at this time. But I have cautioned you so that anything you say may be recorded as evidence. My team will be expecting your full cooperation in our investigation, and that of all your company staff, and that includes Mr Jennings here."

"But I am not currently a member of the company staff," I pointed out. "I've been suspended."

The detective looked at the chairman in a questioning manner.

"I am sure your suspension can be lifted for today, Theo."

"Good," said DS Hamilton. "That's settled then. My forensic accountant will be here shortly. He will require full access to all your financial systems and records."

"We will also need Janis Thompson's help," I said. "She will know exactly where to look."

"Janis Thompson?" the chairman said. "What's she got to do with it?"

"She was the one who found it in the first place," I said.

"Found what?" The chairman looked from me to the policeman and back again. "Will one of you please tell me what the bloody hell is going on?"

*　*　*

While DS Hamilton went off to meet with his forensic accountant and sort out the rest of his investigation team, I sat across the desk from the chairman in his office and read out to him what I had originally prepared for the disciplinary hearing.

I started with the sale of the three-million-guinea colt and concluded with the events in Thetford Forest on Saturday evening—and I covered everything in between.

I told him all about my trip to Ireland, including my meetings with Patrick O'Connor and Grace Ryan; and how Elliot Mitchell had switched the X-rays of the colt's hocks; and that he had, in fact, already owned the colt he later "bought" for three million guineas in our sale ring, as an attempted insurance fraud.

And I described my visit to meet Eileen Murphy at number 64, Main Street in Cashel, the accommodation address for Starsign Bloodstock, and how she had positively identified Elliot Mitchell, from a photograph, as one of the two fellas who had come to collect the mail, to be sure.

I told him about meeting with Brian Kitman in his yard office, and replayed a few selected extracts from the recording of our conversation, in particular the bit about how Mitchell had killed the colt by injecting air into its jugular vein with a bicycle pump, and in a manner that Andrew Ingleby had been unable to detect.

I explained to him about the VAT swindle that Elliot Mitchell and Geoff Pollard had been carrying on for years using a false VAT registration number for Starsign Bloodstock, and how Geoff had killed Elliot because he was becoming too greedy, and also too careless, and was therefore in danger of exposing everything, including Geoff himself.

I then told him about how Geoff Pollard had forced me to drive to Thetford Forest, with the intention of killing both Janis and me, and how his plan had been foiled when I purposely crashed my car into a tree at high speed.

I described how my car had subsequently caught fire, how Geoff had tried to kill himself with the bicycle pump, how Janis and I had managed to drag him clear, and then how we had saved his life, using CPR for twenty minutes until the ambulance arrived.

The only thing I played down rather than up was Brian Kitman's role in the collusive bidding on the colt, making out, as best I could, that he had been more of a victim of Elliot Mitchell's threats, as opposed to a true villain himself. After all, without Brian Kitman, I would never have found out how Mitchell had killed the colt, or about the VAT swindle and Geoff Pollard's involvement in it. But depending on how the chairman reacted, Kitman would now have to take his chances with the Ethics Committee.

"And that," I said, leaning back in my seat, "is what the bloody hell has been going on."

The chairman had sat quietly all the way through my monologue, and even when I'd finished, he remained silent for several more minutes, sitting in his high-backed black leather executive chair, staring at me, as if in disbelief at what I had just told him.

Finally, he stood up.

"Theo," he said. "I owe you an apology. You were right and I was wrong. Your suspension is hereby revoked, and permanently. And there will be no need for any disciplinary hearing. Welcome back on board."

He took my company tie out of his top right-hand desk drawer, where he had previously put it, and handed it back to me. Then he stretched out his right hand. I stood up and shook it.

So I still had my job.

Maybe there was a God after all.

*　*　*

By mid-afternoon, the forensic accountant, with Janis's and my help, had made an extensive list of the horses sold in our sale ring over the past year, for which Starsign Bloodstock had been the first entity paid.

Our task had been greatly helped by the discovery of several stubs of chequebooks in the top right-hand drawer of Geoff Pollard's desk.

The drawer had been locked, and the key couldn't be found, but the lock had proved to be no match for a burly policeman with a crowbar.

The VAT swindle had netted Pollard and Mitchell rather more in the previous year than Geoff had told me in the car, at a fraction less than two hundred thousand pounds in total. As he had said, a useful sum for holidays in the Maldives, but a relatively small amount compared to the more than four-hundred-and-thirty-million-pound turnover of the sales company as a whole.

Janis and I left the accountant to delve deeper into the records, going back over previous years, while we went for a walk together through the estate.

I had already told her the good news about me still having a job in Newmarket, and that now resurrected my question about getting a flat together.

"But can we afford it?" she asked.

"With our two salaries, and also combining what we have each saved separately for a deposit, I think we should just about be able to manage, as long as we live on nothing else but packet soup and baked beans."

"I love packet soup and baked beans."

We laughed, then hugged and kissed.

We had come through something truly dreadful together, and if our relationship could survive that, I was confident that it could survive anything, even her mother.

35

THE FOLLOWING FRIDAY, Alex spent the night in Cambridge with Victor, and it seemed to have been another great success—him coming home at midday on Saturday with a smile on his face as big as that of the owner of Lucky Mike.

I had used the opportunity of Alex's absence to persuade Janis to come and spend the whole night in my bed.

"How did you get your mother to agree to you staying?" I asked her, as we snuggled together, naked, beneath the duvet.

"I simply told her that, if she wanted to see her grandchildren, she had better stop treating me as if I were still a little girl."

"Grandchildren!" I pulled away and looked at her. "Are you pregnant?"

"It's too early to tell," Janis said with a grin. "I doubt it. But would it worry you if I were?"

I was suddenly both overwhelmed and hugely excited by the prospect.

"It wouldn't worry me in the slightest," I said. "In fact, it's a great plan. Let's have another try right now."

So we did. And we tried again in the morning.

* * *

Janis left after breakfast, taking a taxi home in time to go to an event in Ely Cathedral with her gran.

Not having a car of my own was becoming a bore.

The insurance company had so far offered me barely enough to cover the cost of the petrol in the tank, which, despite the best efforts of the fire service, had spectacularly gone up in flames, along with the rest of the vehicle. And they also hadn't been much amused when they found out from the police that I had driven into the tree on purpose.

The forensic accountant had completed his analysis of the sales company's books on Friday afternoon, and he'd concluded that Geoff Pollard had been acting outside of his designated remit, and therefore the company was absolved of any criminal responsibility for the fraud itself.

Not that it got away completely scot-free.

The accountant was critical of the systems, or rather the lack of them, that had allowed one man to be able to manipulate the financial rules and regulations, specifically those concerned with money laundering.

He made a list of recommendations for changes that the chairman eagerly promised to implement—anything to try and keep himself and his company out of the courts.

* * *

On Sunday, Alex took me to Stourbridge to have lunch with his parents, with the intention of him telling them that he was gay.

"I could do with your support," he said desperately.

I could tell he was very nervous.

Stourbridge is a small market town lying about twelve miles west of Birmingham, in the Black Country, a name that stems from the first half of the nineteenth century, when the local heavy coal-fired industry of the time left the area covered in soot.

But there was not a speck of soot to be seen anywhere when Alex pulled the car into the driveway of a smart detached house in Norton, a leafy suburb a few miles south of the town centre.

"Oh God," he said, turning the engine off. "Can't we just go back to Newmarket now, rather than going in?"

"Come on," I said. "It won't be as bad as you think."

He gave me a look, which indicated that he thought it would probably be worse.

We had stopped briefly at a supermarket on the way, for Alex to pick up another bottle of single malt whisky for his father, while I had bought a bouquet of flowers for his mother.

"Peace offerings," Alex had called them.

"Come on in. Come on in." Martyn Cooper said, opening the front door to the two of us.

He looked younger than I had imagined, considering he was past sixty, still sporting a full head of thick, dark hair, and with a youthful sparkle in his eyes.

"It's so good to meet you at last, Martyn," I said, shaking his offered hand.

"And also you, Theo," he replied. "Alex tells me that all your employment problems have been sorted out. I'm so pleased."

"Thank you. And also thank you for all the VAT information. You were spot on. Fake the number, and then keep the VAT."

"I'm glad to have been of assistance. I'll be sending you my bill later."

I stood stock-still, looking at him, and then he laughed. "Nearly got you."

He led us through the hall into the kitchen, where Alex's mother was busy at the cooker, wearing an apron. The apron reminded me slightly of meeting Sarah Thompson two weeks previously, but that was where the similarity ended. This time there was no inspection of my clothing, and Mrs Cooper was upbeat and excited to see us, especially Alex, in comparison to Mrs Thompson's reticence at seeing anyone.

Alex gave his mother a kiss, and I gave her the flowers.

"You shouldn't have bothered," she said to me, but she was clearly pleased that I had.

"It's the least I could do, Mrs Cooper," I said. "Your husband has been very helpful to me."

"Georgina, please."

She lifted a cut-glass vase down from a high cupboard and placed the flowers in it with some water.

"There," she said, smiling. "They're lovely."

"So who would like a drink?" Martyn asked, clapping his hands together.

"Here, Dad, I brought this for you," Alex said, holding out the bottle of whisky towards him.

"Thank you, Alex," his father said, taking it from him. "Two bottles of single malt in two weeks. Theo will think I'm an alcoholic." He laughed. "So what would you like?"

"A gin and tonic for me, please," I said. "If you have it."

"Coming up. And for you, Alex?"

"I'll just have a Coke, thanks, Dad. I've got to drive later."

He went over to the fridge to find one.

"Theo," Martyn said, "come and help me, so I don't make your gin too strong."

I followed him out of the kitchen, across the hall, and into the dining room, where the table was already laid for four.

He opened the drinks cabinet in the corner and lifted out a bottle of gin.

"Ice and a slice?

"Yes, thank you."

"Now, tell me," he said, purposefully turning round to face me, "are you Alex's boyfriend?"

I was stunned. "I'm not sure I know what you mean."

"Are you romantically involved with my son?"

"No," I said. "I am not. I have a girlfriend."

He nodded. "It's always good to know where we stand."

He turned back to the drinks cabinet, put ice and some lemon in a tumbler, and began pouring gin over it.

"But you clearly do know that Alex is gay?" I said.

Martyn opened a small tin of tonic water and splashed some of it into the gin. "I have suspected it for a long time, and he all but confirmed it to me two weeks ago, on the morning of my birthday bash."

"Does it worry you?" I asked.

"Not particularly. As long as he's happy. But I think his mother won't be best pleased."

"Because she's desperate for grandchildren?"

"Exactly."

He turned round and handed me my drink.

"He's come here today to tell you both," I said. "I'm here as his moral support."

"Then you're a good friend to him, Theo." He put an arm round my shoulders, steering me back towards the hall. "I'll have a quiet word with Alex and tell him that I know, and that I will break it to his mother gently after you've gone."

*   *   *

"What the bloody hell did you say to my dad?"

We were back in Alex's car on the way back to Newmarket after an excellent lunch of roast lamb with masses of veg.

"He asked me straight out if I was your boyfriend."

"And what did you say?"

"I said I wasn't. But he clearly already knew you were gay."

"I know. He told me. He said he's known for ages. Probably even longer than I have." He paused. "He also said I shouldn't tell Mum. Not today anyway. He said he would tell her later, gently, after we'd gone. I suppose it made the lunch a bit easier, except for that time when she again asked me if I'd found a girlfriend." He laughed. "And I could hardly believe it when she even asked you to find one for me. Poor Mum—she's going to have a bit of a shock to her system later, but I'm sure she'll get over it."

He drove on for a while in silence, then I heard him quietly humming in contentment.

"Perhaps I'll take Victor with me to lunch there next Sunday."

"Good idea," I said.

*   *   *

On Monday morning I was up early, eager to get back to selling horses from the auctioneer's rostrum. For the occasion, I dressed in a white shirt, company tie, and my best suit, the invisible mender having weaved his magic on the trousers, such that it was almost impossible to see that they had been cut to ribbons with surgical scissors.

The horses-in-training sale itself started at nine thirty, but I was in my office well before eight, reading up on the pedigree and the previous race form of the horses I was due to sell.

Many were three- and four-year-olds that had not made the grade on the flat and were being offered for sale as possible future hurdlers or steeplechasers. Others might go point-to-pointing, and some into dressage or three-day eventing.

Flat racing is mainly a sport for young horses, mostly those aged two, three, and four, and it can be very unforgiving. If a horse fails to win, and win quickly, then it's shipped out to make room for the next year's crop, and its future can often be quite bleak.

Much effort is expended by many kindly people to look after retired racehorses, even those that retire when they are little more than babies, but racing is a hugely competitive business, and the major stables have no time to carry passengers. Every horse has to pull its weight and win its races, or it's out. And many of those that are surplus to requirements in such yards would be coming through the sale ring this week in the hope of finding a new owner and, with it, a new lease of life.

Nigel Stanhope arrived, as usual, at a quarter past eight.

"Well, hello," he said sarcastically as he came into the office. "And how is our cross between James Bond and Sherlock Holmes today?"

"Shut up, Nigel," I said, but I smiled at him, nevertheless.

News of what had really happened in Thetford Forest had begun to circulate amongst the staff, towards the end of the previous week, after a report had appeared on local television, and both Janis and I were being hailed as minor heroes.

Meanwhile, Geoff Pollard was still clinging to life.

I'd been told that there had been a few positive signs pointing towards some level of recovery. He was now able to breathe on his own, and there had been an increasing iris reaction to light shone into his eyes. But DS Hamilton had also quietly informed me that the doctors at Addenbrooke's Hospital had indicated to him that there was almost no chance of him ever being well enough to stand trial for Elliot Mitchell's murder.

Perhaps it might have been better for him if Janis and I had let him die in the forest. But how could we have ever done that?

*　*　*

There were six of us on the auctioneer's roster for the horses-in-training sale, as it would start early and finish late, with over fifteen hundred lots due to go under the hammer over the four days of the sale.

I was scheduled to be the third auctioneer on the rostrum, but I wandered through to the sale ring soon after proceedings started. I just found the whole theatre of the sales intoxicating, and I felt that I had missed out on the excitement during much of the October yearling sales.

However, on this occasion, the chairman, Peter Radway, who was first up, was struggling to engender much enthusiasm amongst the buyers for the first dozen or so lots of the day.

Where was Elliot Mitchell, I thought, when you needed him?

As the time moved towards ten o'clock, things slowly started to warm up, with more human arrivals into the seats and also down by the gate.

I took over at 10:35, relieving Liam Barton.

"I hear you went to Cashel," he said as I transferred the microphone from his company tie to mine.

"Yes," I replied. "But I've a top tip for you: don't ever stay in the B&B across the road from the cathedral."

"I know," he said, laughing. "That dreadfully noisy clock chimes all bloody night long."

I stepped up to the rostrum and switched on the microphone.

"Right," I said theatrically, looking round expectantly at the faces in front of me. "Next up is lot twenty-eight, Sameera, a four-year-old bay gelding by . . ."

I suddenly stopped talking, and a song started playing inside my head: *"It's a long way to Tipperary, It's a long way to go."*

Liam Barton, from Donegal, way up in the north—even farther north than Northern Ireland, and a long way from Tipperary—had told me at Newmarket races that he'd never been to Cashel, while Geoff Pollard had told me in the car that he'd never even been to Ireland.

And Geoff had clearly been the only one of the two telling the truth.

A fraction less than two hundred thousand pounds, split three ways, not two, was about sixty-five grand each, just as Geoff had said.

"Liam Barton," I said loudly, my voice reverberating through the public address system both inside the sale-ring building and outside, "I know who you are. You're Eileen Murphy's other fella."